PERFECT NIGHTMARE

Perfect Nightmare

THAMES RIVER PRESS
An imprint of Wimbledon Publishing Company Limited (WPC)
Another imprint of WPC is Anthem Press (www.anthempress.com)
First published in the United Kingdom in 2013 by
THAMES RIVER PRESS
75–76 Blackfriars Road
London SE1 8HA

www.thamesriverpress.com

All the characters and events described in this novel are imaginary
and any similarity with real people or events is purely coincidental.

A CIP record for this book is available from the British Library.

ISBN 978-0-85728-346-7

Cover design by Sylwia Palka

This title is also available as an eBook

PERFECT NIGHTMARE

Norman Stanton

THAMES RIVER PRESS

CHAPTER 1

'Very superstitious, writing's on the wall.
Very superstitious, ladder's 'bout to fall.'

The strains of Stevie Wonder's 'Superstition' blasted in Arnold's car. It was his favourite song and he loved to play it as loud as his ears could take. He particularly wanted to hear this song today. He was going into his office to complete the handover of his solicitors' practice. He didn't need to go in by car – it was only a five-minute walk from his house – but it seemed appropriate.

He drummed his fingers on the steering wheel as he passed the high street shops that were so familiar. Usually, he saw each shop as a legal transaction – he had acted for most of the shopkeepers. But today the high street had an air of unfamiliarity about it. He couldn't help noticing the new awning above Saeed Patel's shop. It was bright red, and the shiny plastic seemed to blazon out like a beacon. He turned into the small car park behind his office.

They were all there when he arrived. The whole thing seemed unreal for him. Lots of handshakes all round added to the pantomime. The truth was he had found it very difficult to settle back in, following the death of his wife three years ago. The practice was going reasonably well, but his heart was no longer in it and he had sold out to his partners. In fact, over the last few months he had hardly been in at all. One of the secretaries was dabbing her eyes with a tissue, and said: "It won't be the same without you."

"Pastures new and all that," said Arnold. "I'll be able to do all the things I wanted to do but never had the time for."

He left without regrets. Thinking about it, his whole working life up to now seemed trivial, unimportant and without passion. He couldn't remember the drive back to his house, except for Patel's awning that seemed so out of place.

§

Dee was bored. University was fun but the final year was interminable. She had a reasonable degree, but jobs were not falling into her lap. In the meantime, she was stuck in her Father's off-licence filling time.

It was a quiet time of day, and once all the bottles in the shop were neatly lined up with their labels in serried ranks, there was nothing for her to do but daydream out the window and watch the world go by. The high street looked smaller than when she was younger. The thought of spending the rest of her life looking out of the shop window filled her with horror.

Most of the people who passed by the shop were known to her; the dullness of the scene offended her senses. She did, however, notice one splash of colour: her father's solicitor's bright red jaguar. It was an old S-type and she remembered travelling in it once with her father. They had all gone to see a shop he was thinking of buying; Arnold had just bought the car and took them for a ride.

As Arnold drove past, Dee thought he had a pained expression on his face – maybe he was daydreaming too.

§

Arnold went to bed that night relaxed but unfocused – much the same as any other night. He woke up covered in perspiration. The dream – or was it a nightmare? – had been particularly vivid, and the images and smells were still reeling in his mind. He reached for the glass of water on his bedside table and took a few sips. Maybe yesterday's events had initiated the dream. Whatever the reason, the images refused to be shaken from his thoughts.

He wasn't someone who was prone to fanciful ideas. In fact, he fitted very well into the stereotype of the dull solicitor. He didn't mind. Dull, yes, but also solid, dependable and honest – perhaps with a streak of bloody-mindedness. Yet the dream still bothered him.

He dressed quickly and left the house. The mess didn't matter; Mrs M would come in later to clean. He bought a newspaper and settled himself in his usual place in the café near his office – his former office, now. He tried to concentrate on the newspaper while he drank the coffee in front of him, but the dream images kept passing in front of his eyes. He couldn't really put them together as a coherent whole. But wasn't that a characteristic of dream images: that they did not represent a unified narrative? One particular sequence dominated his introspection. It included, of all things, the daughter of one of his ex-clients, Saeed Patel, who ran the local off-licence. He remembered Saeed telling him that his daughter had just finished university and was working temporarily in the off-licence until she could find a permanent job. He had known the girl, Deepal – Dee to her family and friends – since the Patels had arrived in the town some ten years earlier. They were a hard-working family. Overcoming prejudice was not easy for them, and putting their daughter through university had been quite an achievement. He remembered having to have 'a few words' with their bank manager when they first arrived in the town. The manager had been unusually reluctant to sanction a loan, even though they had adequately qualified for one – at least according to Arnold.

He was about to pay the bill when Deepal Patel walked in. She spotted Arnold, strode over to his table, and sat down.

"I've been looking everywhere for you," she spluttered, her face flushed. "I went to your house first, and then your office. They told me you might be here."

Arnold paused for a moment before speaking. Some people thought it was a device to give his words more gravitas, but in fact he used it as a means of coping with a slight stammer, which he had had since childhood.

"Why were you looking for me, and what's your hurry?" he asked.

He asked this as his mind recoiled at the possibilities that were invading it. Her presence and demeanour suggested to him that somehow this was all mixed up with his dream. He couldn't remember the last time he had seen her – it had probably been several months earlier. It must be a coincidence: she must just be in some kind of trouble and need his help.

She looked at him quizzically. She had known Arnold since she was a child. He had, through his firm, acted on behalf of her father in a few legal matters and her father had always spoken highly of him. To be honest, she had not thought much about him, seeing him just as one of those minor background characters that collectively make up one's upbringing. That is until last night, until the dream.

"I've never known you to be dishonest," she said. "You had the same dream I did last night."

It was not a question.

She didn't suffer fools, and on many occasions her abruptness had lost her friends. At school, and even at university, she hadn't had any close friends. She was always restless, always in a hurry. The dream last night had really animated her.

She described some of the images from her dream to Arnold, and it was clear to her, as she continued her narrative, that he had witnessed the same images in his dream.

"You know, to the American Indians, dreams were an important part of life and culture," she said. "Especially shared dreams."

Arnold was still in a state of shock and disbelief, although he managed to regain some of his composure.

"Okay," he said, "so what if we had a shared dream? What follows? What are we supposed to do about it?"

"Do?" she exclaimed. "You saw those terrible images. It's not just a question of 'following your dream,' we have to help those people, we have to save the world."

This time he looked at her quizzically.

"I think you're being a bit melodramatic."

He paused, and then added, "Mind you, those images *were* pretty vivid."

He ordered Deepal a coffee, and they sat in silence for a few moments. The tables around them were beginning to fill up with people. The banal landscape around them seemed to take on an air of unreality. The images of their shared dream invaded the scene. After a while he said, "America! Some of the places in the dream were in the States."

"So they were," she said. "We'll have to go."

"Don't be silly," said Arnold. "You can't up sticks and leave just like that."

"What ties do you have here?" asked Dee.

Arnold hesitated. He had just sold his practice; he was now wealthy and had more time on his hands than he ever could have imagined.

"Okay, my only ties are the fact that I live here. I'm used to this town," he said. "But what about you? You have your family here."

"My parents are here and I'm on reasonably good terms with them," said Dee. "But I need to do something with my life. This dream has given me the impetus I needed."

She stood up and said in an abrupt voice, "You book the plane tickets. I've a few things to pick up. I'll meet you at your house in fifteen minutes."

She turned and, without waiting for a reply, walked out onto the street.

Arnold sat for a few moments. The scene around him had not changed, but he felt that somehow the world was now a different place. He paid the bill and hurried home deep in thought.

The house was the same as he had left it. There was an answerphone message from Mrs M. Apparently she was going to visit her sister, who was ill, and wouldn't be coming in to clean for a while. He looked around at the room. The house no longer seemed to mean anything to him. He didn't feel any attachments. Even the town seemed remote, unrecognizable. He telephoned the airline.

"Two tickets, one way to the USA," he said. "Where? Oh, Washington… Yes, DC"

It had been the first place in the States that had come into his head.

He phoned a local minicab firm and arranged for a car to the airport. He was halfway through putting a few clothes into a suitcase when there was a loud knocking at his door. It was Dee. She was wearing a different set of clothes and was carrying a kind of knapsack on her back, and had another one in her hand.

"I've brought a spare backpack for you. I thought you wouldn't have one. You can't save the world with a suitcase."

She helped him transfer his clothes to the backpack.

"Pick up your passport and let's go," she said. "The station's around the corner, we'll be at the airport within the hour."

"But I ordered a taxi," he said.

After he cancelled the car, they left the house. As they walked along the street, he scanned the buildings on the way to the station. He had walked this route countless times and yet, today, the road seemed quite different, almost alien. He didn't even remember buying the rail tickets. The people waiting on the platform didn't seem to take any notice of them. The train finally arrived and he found two seats in the corner of the carriage. As he sat down he realised that Dee hadn't asked him where exactly in America they were going.

§

As she sat on the train with Arnold, Dee's thoughts kept going back to the dream. She realised that the dream was not one incident that had occurred last night, but was a part of the whole sequence of her life up to this point. Her parents meant well and wanted the best for her, but life in this town was stifling her.

This feeling was more than simple teenage angst. She had always felt this way, as far back as she could remember. And, in any case, at twenty-two she was hardly a teenager any more. The reality was that she was waiting – had always been waiting – for the dream. The vividness of the dream, though, was odd. And the absolute certainty she had in her mind that Arnold had shared this dream with her was also odd. True, as it happens, but maybe that was the oddest part.

She turned to Arnold.

"By the way, where exactly are we going to in the States?" she asked.

"Washington," he replied. "DC, is that okay?"

"It's as good a place as any to start," she said.

"This dream we had," she began in a whisper. "You know that there were other people in it, not just us? I don't mean just background characters. I know that it was not just us that shared the experience."

The rhythm of the train merged into the background. A man wearing headphones in the seat in front of them started to move his fingers in time to music they could not hear.

"I must admit that that thought crossed my mind as well," he said. "There's nothing we can do about it, I suppose. We'll meet these people as and when we need to."

The answer seemed to satisfy her.

The man with the headphones seemed lost in his sonic world. He started to sway his head, and they could just hear the faint boom from his headphones. It was irritating.

Dee was pleased to leave this world behind her. She had told her parents that she was going on a trip with some university friends for a few weeks. They were not happy, but at twenty-two there wasn't much they could do about it. She knew what kind of life they had mapped out for her; a good marriage, kids… Maybe one day, but not now.

The train pulled into the airport station. Arnold went off to collect the tickets. They agreed to meet in the bookshop. Dee wandered along the shopping boulevard. The lights and garish notices screamed out from the various shops. Promises of a sophisticated world for the discerning traveller poured out from the shop windows, all with the exquisite delight of 'duty free.'

She finally found the bookshop tucked away at the end of the concourse. There were not many people browsing the shelves. The shop had two assistants; one was packing shelves and the other stood behind the counter wearing a bored expression. Dee picked up a book at random. The shop was full of other people's stories; she wouldn't find her own here.

Arnold appeared in front of her.

"We can walk through to the gate," he said.

They shuffled through security and performed the elaborate dance ritual that goes with embarkation. Finally, after being shoehorned into their seats and having witnessed the arm gyrations of the air hostess explaining the safety procedures, the plane took off.

Dee was sandwiched between Arnold – he had to have a window seat – and a rather large gentleman. Conversation was difficult, so she just lay back, closed her eyes and tried to snatch some sleep.

She woke with a start. She didn't know how long she had been asleep.

"I didn't want to wake you," said Arnold. "You've been asleep a few hours."

At that moment the loudspeaker was blaring out. Apparently there had been a small electrical fire at Dulles Airport, Washington, and the airport was closed. Their flight would be diverted to Roanoke. Dee had never heard of Roanoke. Arnold told her that it was in West Virginia, near the Shenandoah Valley. She was none the wiser. She closed her eyes and went back to sleep.

Dee looked out of the airplane window as they made their

approach. She couldn't see all that much because Arnold was in the way. What she did see was mostly trees, with mountains in the distance. It did look quite beautiful. As she stepped out of the aeroplane onto the stairs, she wasn't prepared for the heat, or the humidity. It hit her in the face, taking her breath away.

The airline was bussing them to a hotel in Roanoke, and then onto a coach to Washington the next morning. The bus went through the town and deposited them at their lodgings on the northern outskirts of Roanoke, next door to a mining company's office. It felt like they were in the middle of nowhere, but Dee didn't mind; she felt a strange familiarity with the place.

After they had checked in to the hotel, they went out for a walk looking for somewhere to eat. They found a diner just around the corner. It wasn't crowded and the two found a convenient table in the centre of the room. They ordered some food and a couple of coffees, and then sat back watching the people around them.

"You know, Dee, I was a bit reluctant to come on this trip at first," said Arnold. "I'm glad I did though; I needed someone to wake me up."

"Do you believe in fate?" asked Dee.

"I don't know," said Arnold. "But I do know that I couldn't face the idea of spending the rest of my life with nothing to do. The idea of filling my days with trips to the supermarket to buy groceries, just to pass the time, filled me with horror. Do you think we're fated to be here?"

"We can never know the answer to that," said Dee. "But even though I believe we have free will, I do believe that we are constrained by certain patterns of nature. Some people call that fate."

"I don't know about that," said Arnold. "All I know is that going to my local newsagent early every morning to buy a daily newspaper just as a means to get me up in the morning to an empty day, is not something I could spend the rest of my life doing."

At that point a group of scruffy-looking men came in, most probably from the mining office next to the hotel. One of the men turned around and stared at them. He was wearing faded jeans and a bright red shirt; his hair was tied back in a ponytail. Arnold and Dee returned the stare.

§

It had been a hard shift. Not so much because of the nature of the work – Amos was quite used to mining – but because he was troubled by the dream he had last night. He'd always had dreams – it was in his blood. Half Naskapi Indian, he remembered meeting his maternal grandfather when he had visited him and his mother as a child. To Amos his grandfather had seemed very old, and the journey from Labrador to Idaho had exhausted the old man. In spite of this, Amos remembered his piercing eyes, which had always seemed to look right through him.

"Your dreams are part of what makes you a human being," his grandfather had told him. "Your name is *Puwaamuun* – Dreamer."

He had never forgotten his Native Indian name.

His mother had met his father when she was quite young. He had been in the US Navy and was spending a holiday trekking with friends through eastern Canada; she had been living on a Native reserve in Labrador. They had married and moved to Idaho, where his father had been sent by the Navy.

It had been a wonderful place to live as a child. Amos would spend many days in the summertime with classmates around Lake Pend Oreille, not far from the Navy Training Base where his father worked. He hadn't really thought much about his Native Indian roots or about his dreams until his grandfather had come to visit just after the death of his father in a car accident.

His grandfather had told him that his dreams were a window into his inner being, and that one had to find their meaning and truth in order to be a complete person.

It had been a confusing time in his life. His mother had retreated into herself and Amos, who was never very inspired at school, had left Idaho and drifted around the US from job to job, mostly in the mining industry. Eventually he had ended up in West Virginia working for a mining company in Roanoke.

§

Amos walked over to Dee and Arnold's table and sat down rather hesitantly. Arnold was the first to speak.

"This situation is a bit surreal."

"You reckon?" Dee interjected. "You knew what was in store as soon as we left England; you've experienced the dreams."

Amos's brain started to kick in, and with it his voice and manner became more animated. "Amongst my people, shared dreams are not that uncommon."

"Who are you?" said Arnold.

"And who are your people?" added Dee.

Amos explained about his American father and his Canadian mother's Naskapi Indian heritage.

"When I say 'my people,' I mean my Naskapi Indian roots. I have been a 'dreamer' for as long as I can remember. My Naskapi name means Dreamer. Even my American name – Amos Talbot – is tied with dreaming; the biblical prophet Amos saw visions of an earthquake before it happened. I have always felt deeply in touch with my Naskapi origins."

Amos paused. He had never spoken in this way to anyone before, let alone to complete strangers.

"Well, I am Arnold and this is Dee," said Arnold. "And I don't know about you, but I'm starving."

At that point the waitress brought over Arnold and Dee's food, and Amos ordered a steak.

The hubbub in the background enveloped the three as they ate. A lot of miners frequented the diner and as people had left, others replaced them, so the noise continued. It wasn't just the noise of the people in the diner that impinged on them, however, it seemed that the collective noise of the whole world was present, giving the scene a sense of unreality.

Dee was the first to speak.

"What are we going to do? I've never really been able to make a decision my whole life, and yet now I seem to be taking charge – it's weird."

Arnold still felt confused. The images from his dream were still vivid in his mind and he couldn't come to terms with the events that had occurred since that night. He felt swept along by events, by the dream, by Dee.

"We all have our demons as well as our dreams," said Amos. "I've never been able to focus on any one thing. I've spent my whole life drifting around scared to think, scared to do anything."

He chuckled. "I'm like the lion in the Wizard of Oz – just a scaredy-cat."

"Look," said Arnold. "We've all had the same dream and we're all here together. There's a kind of familiarity about this place, about the whole town. Something bad is going to happen, and we're here to do something about it."

"Something to do with the mine," said Amos. "It has to be some kind of mine disaster. This town is used to mining disasters. Some of the mines are barely solvent; they cut safety down to a minimum to save money."

Amos, Arnold and Dee finished their meal and went back to the hotel where Arnold and Dee were staying.

They sat in the hotel bar and continued their discussion. It transpired that the dream they seemed to share had common parts, but was not exactly the same in all of them, nor was it clear or specific. Apart from the impressions and vivid imagery that each of them felt, there was an urge to do something. Not a compulsion exactly, but an impulse; an overriding need to act.

"Join with us," said Dee to Amos.

"Yes," said Arnold. "We've a lot of work to do, we're a team now. Stay here in the hotel and leave the mine, we've plenty of money."

It wasn't much of a decision for Amos to make. The place he was staying in was very basic accommodation provided by the mining company.

"Thanks, I'll go and retrieve my things and tell the mining company I'm not doing any more shifts."

When Amos returned, it was Dee who instigated a plan of action. She and Amos decided to go to the local newspaper offices to look up information on previous mining disasters, and Arnold volunteered to go to the town hall to see what records he could ferret out on the same subject. It was getting late, but the animation of the conversation and the events of the last few hours kept their adrenalin going.

The barman wanted to close up. He had just taken delivery of a large quantity of beer in preparation for a wedding party the next day. It was going to be a very late night for him the next day.

§

It wasn't a particularly auspicious start to the next day. The skies were grey and it looked as though it was just about to rain. They had all slept soundly – no dreams – and Dee was the first to get up.

There were a few people having breakfast in the dining room. The hall outside the restaurant was piled with crates of beer, and Dee had to squeeze past them to enter the room. Arnold and Amos joined her after a few minutes.

The room had seen better days. The walls were painted, but some of the paint had peeled off. After breakfast they walked out onto the street and agreed to meet back at the hotel in a couple of hours.

Arnold walked in the direction of the town hall, which Amos had told him was two streets away past the mining office. Dee and Amos started in the other direction towards the offices of the local newspaper.

The *Roanoke Times* was close by and Dee and Amos were greeted by a smiling woman behind a desk as they walked into the office. It wasn't quite what they expected; an open plan office with four desks neatly arranged around a water dispenser. They didn't receive many requests for archival material and the receptionist seemed genuinely interested.

"We've had plenty of mining disasters here," she said. "Even earthquakes."

After a few minutes she returned with a couple of boxes of files. She pointed to a desk that they could use and Arnold and Dee started to sift through all of the material. Going through the papers was quite boring at first, just one disaster after another. But slowly a pattern started to emerge.

It wasn't what Dee and Amos were expecting. Yes, the mining companies were not always as careful as they should be in training staff, maintaining plant equipment and following safety protocols to the letter, but on the other hand, the companies did their best and most of the disasters had been down to human error, poor communication or just plain bad luck. Even Amos grudgingly accepted that though they did try to cut costs as much as they could, the companies did tend to follow the safety regulations.

"Have a look at these."

An elderly man came up to their desk with another box full of clippings.

"These tell a different story."

He sat down on an empty chair and pulled out the first clipping.

"This was a nasty one last year; quite a few miners were killed. You think the mining companies are good on safety? Think again."

He pulled out a few more clippings and threw them onto the desk.

"They're lax on safety, which results in fines that they then appeal. It goes on for years. Whatever they can evade they evade, and whatever they can delay they delay."

"Well thanks for the information," said Amos. "I'm Amos and this is Dee."

"I'm Bill; I've been a reporter on this newspaper for yonks. What are you doing in town?"

Dee hesitated.

"We're here with Arnold, a friend, and we think that something terrible is going to happen soon, and we want to do something to stop it or help."

She didn't mention anything about the dreams.

"Well let me know if you need any help," said Bill. "It's about time somebody tried to do something."

On their way back to the hotel, Amos was deep in thought. Finally he said, "Well, are the mining companies at fault or are we misjudging them?"

"It doesn't really change anything," said Dee. "We're here for a reason. It's something to do with the mines and it doesn't matter who, if anyone, is to blame."

Amos agreed, but was still preoccupied.

"I'll catch you up at the hotel," he said. "I just have to go into the mining office to pick up my wages."

Arnold was sitting at the hotel bar when Dee arrived. She explained to him that even though there had been quite a few mining disasters over the years, the mining companies' present safety record seemed okay, except for what Bill, the journalist, had said.

"I searched through a mass of records at the town hall," said

Arnold. "You wouldn't believe the mass of safety regulations the mining companies have to follow, and the safety checks they have to undergo. How much of these checks they actually follow, I don't know, but I think that you're right, we have to be here for some reason and it must be some sort of mine disaster."

At that point Amos came in to the bar, agitated.

"I spoke to my mother in Idaho; she has had some problem with her widow's pension so I had to send her some money."

"Don't worry, we've enough money for us all," said Arnold. "The question is: what is our next step?"

They discussed things for quite some time, going round and round in circles. Arnold spotted the hotel owner, who was cursing as he navigated around the crates of beer in the hallway.

"Is everything OK?" asked Arnold.

"Cancelled," said the hotel owner. "They cancelled the wedding. What am I going to do with all this beer?"

"I've an idea," said Arnold. "Let's have a public meeting."

He turned to the hotel owner. "We'll give you cost price for the beer, if you let us have free use of your main room for a meeting."

The hotel owner beamed in surprise.

"Done, and I'll throw in a few packets of potato crisps as well."

"With free beer, we'll have a packed meeting," said Arnold. "We can invite everyone in the town for a meeting on mining safety."

The others agreed it was a good idea. At that moment Bill came into the hotel bar.

"I thought I'd find you here," he boomed. "So you must be Arnold."

He stretched out his arm and shook Arnold's hand.

"I'm Bill from the local newspaper. So, what's your story?"

Arnold leaned forward in his seat and addressed the room.

"We believe – no, we're convinced – there is going to be some terrible disaster in this town, and we want to do something to help stop it or at least to warn people."

Bill's expression didn't change, but his demeanour took on a focused aspect. His voice started quietly, but it didn't end quietly.

"But how did you three come to be together, and why Roanoke? What makes you so convinced that something is about to happen?"

There was an awkward silence. Arnold was about to say something but Bill interjected.

"I've been a newspaper man for long enough to smell a story. If you want my help you'll have to level with me, and in this town you'll need my help."

Bill's abrupt manner woke up Arnold and the others. Arnold smiled and said:

"You're not going to believe this."

"Oh, you just try me," said Bill, "I've heard a few wild stories in my time."

Bill and the others sat in silence while Arnold recited all the events of the last couple of days that had brought the three of them to this point.

"So this is all the result of a dream you three shared?" exclaimed Bill. "Wow! I don't know if I believe your story, but what's important is that you all believe it."

"What do you think about a town meeting?" asked Dee.

"It's a great idea," said Bill. "You must come to the newspaper office, and I'll run you off a few hundred handbills you can put around the town to advertise your meeting."

"We need to time the meeting right," said Amos. "We need to catch the mine day shift after they finish and the night shift before they start, so that all the miners have a chance to come. Let's say we have the meeting at six o'clock in the evening."

"We'll have the meeting tomorrow evening," said Arnold. "I don't think we can wait any longer."

The others agreed. Arnold's assertion brought a sombre mood to the room. He ordered some sandwiches for the group while they discussed strategy. It was Bill who raised the question of why they had had their shared dream and what, if anything, was behind the whole bizarre sequence of events? Things had moved too fast for Arnold and Dee to think much about what was really going on. Amos was different. The spiritual dimension to his life had always been important. In particular, dreams for him were a connection with nature – with the Earth.

"We've been chosen by nature," said Amos. "It's a sympathy or resonance between the Earth and a consciousness that we embody. This is what I believe. The Earth has a consciousness through the people who inhabit it, and we are representatives of the Earth."

"I suppose it's the lawyer in me talking," said Arnold. "But I interpret what you are saying as: the Earth is our client."

"Does that make us all solicitors?" said Dee.

They began to laugh and the hotel owner brought in their sandwiches.

"Buck here is my brother-in-law," said Bill shaking hands with the hotel owner. "It's a small town; everyone is related to each other."

Arnold grabbed a pen and paper and sketched out the wording for a handbill. Amos and Bill went to the newspaper offices to pick up the handbills that were being printed while Arnold and Dee went with Buck to the meeting room at the rear of the hotel.

It wasn't the largest of rooms but could comfortably seat a hundred people. There were some trestle tables down one side and they stacked the crates of beer on them.

"We need glasses as well," said Dee.

"I have some paper cups," said Buck. "Although, quite frankly, most people will drink their beer out of the bottles.

"Do you really think there will be a mining disaster here?" Buck continued, after a pause.

"It's why we are here. I can't describe the vividness of our dream or the feeling of certainty that the three of us share. Just take my word for it," said Dee.

"I have to prepare something to say at the meeting," said Arnold.

He sat down at the back of the room and became lost in thought as he covered a sheet of paper with his neat handwriting.

Amos and Bill arrived back at the newspaper office. Bill went straight to the print section of Arnold's leaflet design while Amos waited by the front desk.

The woman behind the desk smiled at Amos.

"Hi, I'm Arlene," she said. "I've never seen Bill so excited."

"We're trying to arrange a meeting," said Amos. "We think there's going to be some sort of mining disaster."

"Oh, that would be terrible," said Arlene. "There was one a year or so ago, and quite a few miners were killed."

"The meeting will be tomorrow night at our hotel nearby," said Amos. "We're trying to persuade as many people to come as possible, there's even going to be free beer."

"Now that'll draw a crowd," joked Arlene.

At that moment Bill appeared.

"They're running off a few hundred copies of your handbill. They should be ready in a few minutes."

"How much do we owe you for the printing?" asked Amos.

"Don't worry about that," said Bill. "I'm doing a story for tomorrow's edition, you can give me an interview instead of payment, and my story will advertise your meeting."

While they were waiting for the handbills to be printed, Bill and Amos talked. Arlene listened in rapt attention.

It was like a stone being dropped into a still pond, the ripples moving out in a circular wave until the whole pond is affected; Amos's early life, his dreams, and Arnold and Dee, all merging into an ever-expanding wave of cause and effect.

Amos left Bill writing his story and went back to the hotel, carrying the stack of handbills. When he arrived he went into the rear meeting room of the hotel and placed the pamphlets on one of the trestle tables. Arnold was in the corner busily scribbling away writing and Dee was setting out the chairs.

"How many have we here?" said Dee, thumbing through the handbills.

"I don't know," said Amos. "Around five hundred I think. And we don't have to pay for them."

"How come?" said Dee.

"Bill is writing a story on what we're doing," said Amos. "We don't have to pay for the handbills and we'll obtain free publicity for the meeting tomorrow; the article will be in tomorrow morning's edition."

"I heard that," Arnold looked up from his page. "We have to deliver as many handbills as possible. We need all the publicity we can drum up. We'll have to split up. Let's see how many shops, restaurants and other places we can persuade to put up our meeting notice."

It was quite hard work trudging round the town, and by the time they returned to the hotel that evening, they were all exhausted. They had had quite a mixed response. Half the time the shopkeepers wouldn't even read the pamphlet and would just indicate a noticeboard that their notice could share with the many advertisements for lost dogs and 'help wanted.' There were a few exceptions, such as the lady in the drug store around the corner who had known one of the miners killed in the mining accident last year. She placed their handbill in a prominent location on her window and promised to bring some of her friends to the meeting.

"Our main publicity for the meeting should be directed towards the miners themselves," Arnold told the others after they'd returned.

"First thing in the morning, we'll go to the mine," said Dee.

"I know the manager there," said Amos. "It won't be easy."

§

The three were up quite early the next morning. There had been no dreams during the night – much to everybody's relief – but there was definitely a feeling of expectation and apprehension in the air.

Arnold was the first down for breakfast. He picked at his food and was lost in thought when Dee and Amos entered the hotel restaurant.

"We've a busy day today," said Dee as she tucked into a plate of bacon, eggs, sausages and French toast from the breakfast buffet.

"I don't know how you can eat all that stuff," said Arnold.

Amos spread butter thickly onto his two rolls and shook his head at the pile of food on Dee's plate.

"It's going to be difficult convincing the mine manager," he said. "He'll be polite and pretend to listen to us but I'm not sure if we'll have any success."

"Don't worry," Arnold replied. "Just so long as we can persuade a few miners to come to the meeting. We'll see what happens."

The hotel manager came into the restaurant with a sheaf of newspapers under his arm.

"Fame at last," he said, beaming broadly. "The papers have just come out and you're all on the front page."

They all eagerly poured over the morning edition of the *Roanoke*

Times. It wasn't the lead story, but it was on the front page. About halfway down there was a small box with the headline 'Three Dreamers To Save Town.' The article, which continued on page eleven, detailed a summary of their story so far.

"Well," said Arnold. "At least he mentioned our meeting this evening."

After breakfast, and clutching a pile of handbills, they set off for the mine. It wasn't far, perhaps ten minutes to the edge of town and then another five, mostly uphill. They didn't talk much on the way, each lost in their own thoughts and trying to remember images from their dreams.

Neither Arnold nor Dee had ever been to a mine. All they had to go on were pictures they had seen on television – usually when there had been some sort of disaster.

As they approached, the most striking image they saw was the tower which operated the lift. Behind, there were various other structures and buildings placed seemingly at random in an open area surrounded by fencing. It was an eerie landscape, contrasting with the ordered layout of buildings in the town. There was a small gatehouse at the entrance to the compound, above its door was a sign reading 'Roanoke Mine.'

"Hi Amos," said a rather portly guard. "Who are your friends?"

Amos stepped forward and addressed the guard.

"We'd like to see the boss. We're having a meeting in the town hotel tonight on mining safety."

The guard flashed a knowing smile at the three.

"Good luck with that..." he said. "And sweet dreams."

The irony in his voice was unmistakeable.

They marched along the path to the mine office and were shepherded into a small ante room by the mine manager's assistant. The room was quite bare except for a few faded pictures on the wall and a stained coffee table with a copy of the morning's newspaper on it. The pictures on the wall were mostly group photographs of the serious faces of miners and officials at the opening ceremony of the mine in the early '60s.

Eventually the office door opened and a burly man in an ill-fitting suit appeared. Gruff in manner and with large hands – he was an ex-miner – he strode across the room and greeted Arnold and Dee. His voice was more piercing than deep and his face wore a forced smile, showing teeth that had seen better days.

"My name is Earl White, I'm the mine manager. How can I help you folks?"

Without waiting for a reply he turned to Amos.

"Back so soon? I hope you've told your friends good things about the mine. Sure was an interesting article about you all in the paper this morning."

The last sentence was tacked on as an aside, but it sounded more like a veiled threat. It was clear to them all that bad publicity for the mine would seriously not be welcome.

Arnold came straight to the point.

"We're concerned about the mine's safety," he said.

"Aren't we all?" interjected Earl.

Arnold continued. "As you may have read in the newspaper this morning, we've arranged a meeting in the town hotel at six o'clock tonight. Will you come?"

"Sounds great," said Earl, almost spitting out the words. He beckoned to his assistant.

"Arlene will show you around."

Then he disappeared back into his office before any of them could say anything.

Arlene stood somewhat uncomfortably in front of them. Her streaky blonde hair was tied back rather severely and, in spite of makeup, her complexion showed signs of premature aging.

"Come this way," she said, and she led them out across the compound.

It was a desolate expanse, surrounded by unkempt buildings. On the other side from the mine office stood the lift tower. Arlene peremptorily indicated the latrines, shower facilities and changing rooms. The mine, apparently, was nearing the end of its life; it had used to employ upwards of three hundred miners but was now down to only sixty, comprising two shifts of thirty miners each. The day shift was below ground at the moment. They were due up just after 5.30 that evening. The night shift started at 6.30, with the men assembling from about 6.15.

"May we put up some notices for our meeting tonight?" asked Dee.

Arlene shrugged.

"I don't see why not," she said.

While Dee was busy putting up the meeting advertisements, Amos went over to talk to a couple of miners that had wandered over to where they were. Arnold was left with Arlene.

"I can see a lot of safety notices all around," said Arnold.

He paused, and then continued.

"But we are concerned that something bad may happen here in the very near future."

"I don't know about any dreams," said Arlene, sarcastically. "All I know is that we do everything we are supposed to and follow every safety regulation."

Her voice became more animated.

"We even had a safety inspection last month."

Amos and Dee came back in time to hear Arlene's last comment.

"Well thank you for showing us round, Arlene," said Dee, trying to pacify the situation. "I hope we see you and Earl at our meeting tonight."

Arnold took a few pictures of the area with his camera phone as they walked out of the mine on their way back to town.

"I spoke to a couple of miners," said Amos. "They promised to pass on the details of our meeting tonight to the rest of the workers."

"That's not all," he continued. "There's a bit of a row brewing. The miners think that there may be a few layoffs, or that the owners might even close the mine."

"We have to keep focused," said Arnold. "We're here because we are convinced that something bad is going to happen and we must do everything we can to stop it. Or at least help people, if we can't stop it."

"The important thing is not to let our meeting tonight be hijacked. Either by miners worried about their jobs or by the mine manager telling us how wonderful everything is," Dee added.

"I think our next stop should be the mayor's office," said Arnold. "But first we need to go back to the hotel to make sure that everything is ready for our meeting tonight."

As they approached the hotel, they saw Bill standing outside with another man.

"I'm glad I caught you," said Bill. "How did you like my article?

I've brought Frank along to take some photographs; we need a few pictures for my follow-up piece tomorrow."

The three struck up a pose and pictures were duly taken.

Amos and Dee went inside.

The meeting room looked ready. Lines of beer bottles and plastic cups were arrayed on the trestle tables, together with a few bowls filled with potato chips – the hotel manager had been true to his word. There were about a hundred chairs in lines and a trestle table along the front of the room, which also had three seats facing the audience.

"What sort of crowd do you think will come?" said Dee.

"We should fill the room," said Amos. "But I wouldn't be surprised if the mine manager was plotting something."

"What do you mean?" asked Dee.

"Well we might have a few hecklers, or even some kind of disruption."

Dee grimaced.

"We'll be ready," she said.

Outside the hotel, Arnold was talking to Bill.

"Thanks for your help, Bill," said Arnold. "I don't think anyone would have taken us seriously if it wasn't for the publicity your article gave us."

"You still have an uphill climb," responded Bill.

"We thought of going to see the mayor next," said Arnold,

"Now there's a wily fox. I know him well. He's up for re-election soon."

Then Bill's voice took on a sing-song quality, clearly mimicking an advertising jingle.

"*If there are votes in it, Sam Schanks is your man*. I'll come with you, if you want."

Amos and Dee came out of the hotel.

"Everything seems to be in order for the meeting," said Dee.

"Bill has offered to come with us to see the mayor," said Arnold.

"That's kind of you," said Dee.

"If I tell the mayor our photographer will be at the meeting, he'll come for sure. Any excuse to get his ugly mug in the newspaper. He is desperate for publicity at the moment, what with the upcoming election."

They walked towards the mayor's office.

"My impression, Bill, is that you don't much like the mayor," said Arnold.

Bill smiled.

"Now don't misquote me," he said. "I have to be non-partisan in my job, and for me that means I hate all politicians the same. To be fair, Sam is no worse than many others. Hell, he was in my class at school. But I know what makes him tick: it's Sam Schanks first, and Roanoke second."

"How did he come to be mayor?" asked Arnold.

"After college he went into the Navy. He was always good at politics – making alliances, schmoozing with the right people. He was a natural candidate."

As they walked along Amos and Dee stopped at various shops and public places trying to persuade owners to put up their adverts for the meeting that night. The library was next door to the town hall and it had a civic notice board outside. Dee emerged from the library with a thumbs-up sign.

"They're putting our advert on their notice board," she said.

They all went into the town hall and Bill went over to speak to the receptionist. She was clearly someone that Bill knew quite well.

"As I thought," said Bill. "The mayor's quite happy to see us, provided that there's a photo opportunity."

After a minute or two the receptionist beckoned to Bill, indicating that they should go up the staircase.

They all marched up the stairs, past a row of photographs of former mayors of Roanoke that lined either side. The last picture showed a figure sitting uncomfortably on a horse, wearing a beaming smile and waving at the camera. It was Mayor Sam Schanks.

They all trooped into the mayor's office. He was sitting behind a desk and bore an uncanny resemblance to his photograph on the stairs – albeit without the horse. The walls of his office were lined with as many pictures as the stairway; most of them showing the mayor in naval uniform meeting various dignitaries. Arnold thought he recognized a former US president in one of the photographs.

"Good to see you, Bill," said the mayor. "And you all must be the dreamers who've come to save our town."

There was a copy of the *Roanoke Times* on his desk.

He shook hands with everyone, and indicated a sofa and some easy chairs for them to sit down in. The three introduced themselves in turn. Mayor Schanks' beaming smile never left his face.

"We've had our problems in the past, but now we're all really hot on mine safety in this town."

"We don't doubt that for a moment, Mr Mayor," said Arnold, with his fingers crossed behind him. "I've seen all of the regulation and safety notices, but what we're concerned about is the gap between theory and practice."

"Please, call me Sam," said the mayor. "I'll give you a fair hearing. Any ideas you have to improve safety will be welcomed and seriously considered. Can't say fairer than that."

It was the mayor's turn to (mentally) cross his fingers.

He looked at Frank, the photographer, and then Bill. As if on cue, he stood behind the sofa on which Amos, Dee and Arnold were sitting and struck a pose. The camera flashed, and then again for a second picture.

On the pavement outside the town hall Dee turned to Bill.

"He's such an arsehole," she said.

"Yes, but he's our arsehole," Bill laughed. "I'd better check back at the newspaper, we'll see you at the meeting tonight," he added, and left with Frank.

Amos, Arnold and Dee stopped off for some lunch at a nearby diner. Arnold was quiet and seemed thoughtful. While they were waiting for their food, Dee asked him what was wrong.

"It's all very well," said Arnold. "But these dreams and what we're doing here; do they bear any relationship to reality? I don't know what to say at this meeting tonight. I have this terrible feeling that we are just making fools of ourselves."

"It's natural that you think that way," said Amos. "But you know that my whole cultural upbringing has been to take dreams seriously, and we all shared the same dream."

Dee gripped Arnold's arm.

"If we are here to represent the Earth or whatever, then there must be a reason that there are three of us," she said. "We have to help each other. We each bring something special to what we're doing. I don't know what that something special is, but we're all here for a reason. I'm absolutely convinced of that."

"We're like Moses, Aaron and Miriam," said Amos. "I remember learning in Bible class as a kid that Moses was reluctant to meet the Pharaoh – I think he even complained to God that he had a stammer."

"Well, I don't think we're about to lead the miners of Roanoke to the Promised Land," said Arnold, causing them to laugh.

"But I take your point," he added.

The exchange cleared the air and they walked back to the hotel in good spirits.

§

There was still a lot of work to be done to prepare for the meeting. Dee found an old roll of lined wallpaper in the hotel storeroom and she proceeded to staple it to the front trestle table to serve as a banner. She wrote on it in huge ornate letters: 'THINK MINING SAFETY.'

Amos and Arnold were trying to work out an agenda for the meeting. Arnold was still agonising about what to say and Buck, the hotel manager, was skipping around adjusting chair positions and putting up notices on the walls. He had found a newspaper that had pictures from the mining disaster the previous year, and was busy cutting out the articles and pinning them onto the wall.

All this activity was in full swing when Bill and Frank, the photographer, arrived. Frank took a few pictures while Bill sat down next to Amos and Arnold.

"We want to start the meeting with a few introductory remarks from Amos and then I'll come in with a longer piece on mine safety," said Arnold.

"We'll then open the meeting to questions," added Amos.

"Sounds sensible," said Bill thoughtfully. "I'd keep the remarks short though. Most of the miners will have to leave just after six to start their night shift."

As five-thirty came and went, the atmosphere in the room started to hot up. Buck brought round some sandwiches and coffee for everyone – he'd become part of the team now.

Amos, Arnold and Dee took up their positions at the front trestle table facing the assembled chairs. Buck had placed a jug of water as well as some fresh coffee in front of them – a nice touch. Buck, Bill and Frank took up their positions in the second row of seats – they wanted to leave the front row for the mayor and his entourage.

People started to arrive soon afterwards, with a sudden rush as the day shift miners came in en bloc. There was quite a large crowd and the stock of free beer on offer was almost depleted. Bill leaned across and said in a loud whisper to the three:

"I think you should start the meeting now, otherwise when the beer runs out they'll all go."

"Okay," said Arnold.

The room was now jam-packed – there were even people standing outside. Amos stood up and tapped the water jug loudly with a spoon that was lying on the table. As he did so the mayor and a few others with him came in and sat themselves down in the front row. The mayor looked around at the audience, waving and nodding to people he knew – his broad smile still plastered onto his face.

"Welcome everybody," Amos started.

The hubbub barely died down, and so he repeated himself at full volume.

"Welcome everybody," he bellowed.

The room finally settled down. He continued.

"My name is Amos; many of you miners know me. I've worked at Roanoke mine for some months now and my two friends here, Dee and Arnold, as well as myself, have been increasingly concerned that something bad is going to happen pretty soon in this town. To explain further, I will hand you over to my friend Arnold."

He sat down and Arnold stood up, nervously clearing his throat.

Arnold began his address.

"A few days ago I was a solicitor in England – that's equivalent to a lawyer, here. Dee, here on my left, was working temporarily in a liquor store, having just graduated from college. As you may have read in the newspaper this morning, the three of us all had a shared dream."

"Two men and one woman in a dream, it must have been some dream," someone shouted out from the back of the room.

Bill turned to Frank and said, "I know that man; he's one of Earl White's men."

The meeting was not going well, and Arnold was becoming even more nervous, but he continued.

"As I was saying, we believe – no, we are convinced – that something bad is going to happen—"

"Yes, the beer is going to run out!"

This interruption was from a second heckler. Both were part of a group standing at the back of the room.

Arnold tried to continue, his fists beginning to clench in a new wave of exasperation and determination that began to overwhelm him.

"Shouting at me is not going to save the mine, or the town, from impending disaster…"

Other hecklers from the same group at the rear of the room began lobbing insults, and the meeting was now in danger of falling apart. The mayor and his group at the front started to leave – they didn't want to be around if a fistfight was to break out.

Arnold straightened himself up and pounded his fist three times on the table as hard as he could.

"This meeting," – one, "will come," – two, "to order!" – three.

At the third pound of his fist the room shuddered. It was not a metaphorical shudder – the room actually moved. Some pictures on the walls fell down and a number of people in the audience fell off their chairs.

There was an immediate hushed silence, more a pause of breath, in the room. Then the main shock of the earthquake hit. It only lasted for a few seconds, maybe ten or twenty seconds at most. There was an unbearable noise, mixed in with screams of panic. Those people outside the room were already on the street outside the hotel. The room quickly emptied as people staggered over the moving floor to the exit.

Arnold was stunned at first, staring in disbelief at his hand that was still clenched as a fist. Amos was the first to move and he and Dee managed to bundle Arnold onto the pavement outside the hotel.

Surprisingly, there was little sign of devastation outside. Yes, a few chimney pots were lying in the road – one had fallen onto a car –

and a few lampposts were standing at odd angles, but the buildings were all relatively intact.

Fortunately, nobody seemed to be injured apart from a few minor cuts and bruises, and one woman who had twisted her ankle. They could hear sirens in the distance.

Then someone in the crowd shouted: "The mine!"

They all turned in the direction of the mine. They couldn't really see anything as there was a certain amount of obscuring dust in the air, so the group started to walk in the direction of the mine. As they came to the edge of town it was clear that there was something peculiarly wrong at the mine. It wasn't what they saw, but rather what they didn't see. They couldn't see the lift tower and other tall buildings that were normally visible.

As they came up the road to the mine, Earl, the mine manager was staggering towards them. He was covered in dust and obviously in a state of shock. He kept repeating:

"I can't believe it."

As they approached the gatehouse, the guard was sitting outside with Arlene, Earl's assistant. They were both covered in dust but otherwise uninjured. Arlene had her head in her hands and was weeping.

Amos, Arnold and Dee, together with Bill and Frank and a few others, went through the gatehouse to the mine compound. Frank was busily taking pictures.

A strange scene confronted them. The mine office, instead of being in front of the compound, was now perched on the edge of a precipice. To be exact, it wasn't really a precipice, but the edge of a crater. The pit extended right across what had been the mine compound. The lift tower and all associated buildings were stretched out like broken matchsticks at the bottom of the crater, which must have been at least twenty metres deep. The whole mine seemed to have fallen in on itself, anyone underground would have been instantly killed. By a miracle, no one had been in the mine when the earthquake struck – they had all been at the meeting.

The sirens of emergency vehicles grew louder. When they arrived, the paramedics attended to Earl, Arlene and the guard, who had only sustained superficial injuries.

On the way back to the hotel, someone played a radio news broadcast from a mobile phone. The local station had lost transmission when the earthquake hit, but was now back on air with reports from all over the state and beyond. According to reports the earthquake, which had reached 7.3 on the Richter scale, had struck at six p.m. Its epicentre was located just outside Roanoke, at the precise location of the mine. The source of the earthquake was several miles below the surface and the mine had sat right on top of it. Only minor injuries had been reported, but there were many people with shock as well and the hospitals were slowly filling up.

"You were wrong about mine safety," said Bill. "But, by golly, you saved the lives of all those miners."

"We should've realised it was an earthquake that was coming," said Dee.

"We knew it was something, and we knew it was bad," said Amos.

"It's incredible," said Arnold. "Twenty minutes either way and dozens of miners would have met their deaths. It can't be a coincidence."

"It was your fist," said Bill.

They laughed nervously. It was a welcome relief from the scene they had just witnessed.

"A fist can't cause an earthquake," said Arnold.

"I don't exactly mean that," said Bill thoughtfully.

He continued.

"Clearly the earthquake was going to happen, and it was going to happen at that time and place. But, and this is just a speculative thought, suppose the Earth or whatever could slightly delay the exact moment the earthquake was going to hit? Suppose it was waiting for a cue from you, Arnold? Maybe that's what it means when you say you are acting on behalf of the Earth."

They arrived back at the hotel. There was a whole scrum of people there. The mayor was outside on the pavement being interviewed by a TV station, which had already set up camp on the other side of the road from the hotel. He saw Arnold and the others approaching and sprinted over to them with the camera crew in tow.

He beamed at Arnold, Dee and Amos.

"Our heroes, our saviours," he said in a stentorian voice. "Thanks to you, hundreds of lives have been saved."

He was not one to stint on hyperbole. He ushered the TV crew to point their cameras at the three and he, of course, placed himself in the middle of the picture.

The group managed to extricate themselves from the mayor's embraces and get inside the hotel, leaving Bill and Frank outside with the press pack. They were all pretty exhausted – the events of the last few hours had taken their toll – and agreed to meet up for a quiet meal later on. But first they needed to clean up, rest and think.

They had a lot to think about. In particular, what were they going to do now? Even though the shared dream that they had all experienced was confusing and disorderly, it was clear to them that the events in Roanoke represented only a small part of a whole. There were many images and events in their dream that included other places and involved people whom they had not yet met.

Things had quietened down a lot by the time the three met up in the hotel bar. Most of the debris from the earthquake had been cleared up.

Arnold was the first to speak.

"I'm not sure what exactly happened before," he said. "I've been thinking about what Bill said. Is it possible that anyone can control or even slightly delay when an earthquake is going to strike?"

"Why not?" said Dee.

"It can't be that simple," said Arnold.

"Maybe it is that simple," said Amos. "For me, the idea that I have a close link with nature is not at all strange. It's part of my makeup, my whole being. To take this idea one step further, there are some people who have a strong empathy and understanding of the natural world. It is not that fanciful to imagine. We are, after all, part of nature, we are part of the Earth; we're the animate, living part. We are the means by which the Earth thinks."

"Wow. That is profound. I never thought about things in that way," said Dee.

"So where do we go now?" said Arnold.

Amos thought for a second.

"Well, the two of you were on your way to Washington, when you were diverted to Roanoke. Why not complete the trip? The images in my dream were just as vague and confused as yours, but I'm sure I saw images of the White House and the Capitol in Washington. Maybe that is where we should go now."

Arnold and Dee agreed.

Just at that point Bill came into the bar.

"I thought I'd find you all here," he said. "You won't believe what's been happening since the quake. I've written an article that is coming out in the morning. It's been picked up by the nationals and syndicated and so has Frank's pictures of the mine."

"We're all pleased for you, Bill," said Arnold.

"So what are you three going to do now?" said Bill.

"We were just discussing that," said Dee. "We're going to Washington, DC"

"It's part of our dream," said Amos. "We saw images of the main sights of the city, so we're going tomorrow."

"Have you anywhere to stay there?" said Bill.

They all shook their heads.

"You must stay with my cousin, Charlotte," said Bill. "Her husband died ten years ago, and now she runs a bed and breakfast at Dupont Circle. She's full of energy, always running around, you'll like her. I'll call her and tell her to expect you."

Bill rushed outside to phone his cousin as there wasn't any signal on his mobile in the hotel. Buck came over with a handful of leaflets.

"You're going to Washington? I've a load of maps and leaflets here. You can go straight there by Greyhound bus, it takes about six hours. I've a timetable, somewhere."

He foraged around and pulled out a timetable.

"Here we are, the bus leaves Roanoke at 1.45 p.m. tomorrow".

Bill came back into the bar.

"Charlotte is delighted you're coming. I told her all about you. Here is her address in DC"

He gave Dee a piece of paper.

"She'll be expecting you tomorrow evening."

"They're going by bus to Washington," said Buck.

"I'll stop by in the morning and drive you to the bus stop," offered Bill.

"It's kind of you Bill, but you don't have to," said Arnold.

"What? After all you've done, it's the least I can do," said Bill. "I'll see you in the morning."

Bill left and the three poured over the leaflets that Buck had given them. Arnold and Dee had never been to Washington, and Amos had only briefly passed through the city many years ago. It was quite late before they eventually all fell into bed.

§

The next morning at breakfast Buck came into the dining room with the early edition of the town newspaper, together with a sheaf of national newspapers.

The *Roanoke Times* had a picture of the crater that the mine had become, and underneath was a photograph of the smiling Sam Schanks with his arms around Arnold, Dee and Amos, together with the headline: 'HEROES SAVE MINERS.'

The national papers had picked up the story, though it was not on the front page. Frank's crater picture was reproduced in all of the papers.

There were also more reported details of the earthquake – apparently it had been felt as far away as Washington, DC and throughout the eastern United States. There were no reported deaths but a fair amount of injuries, and a few were quite serious. At a magnitude of 7.3 it was an average strength earthquake, although it would have been expected more in California than Virginia.

Bill came in with Frank. They helped themselves to coffee and waffles, which were always available in plentiful supply at breakfast, and the three congratulated Bill on his article and Frank on his photograph.

"The mayor asked me to come to the Greyhound bus stop early," said Bill.

"He wants to give you a personal send-off," said Frank.

Both he and Bill collapsed into laughter.

The three said their goodbyes to Buck.

"We'll miss your breakfasts," said Arnold as he grabbed an extra waffle to eat in the car.

Then they all piled into Bill's Jeep and departed for the bus.

As they approached the bus stop they couldn't believe their eyes at the sight that greeted them. A smiling Sam Schanks was in the middle of a mêlée consisting of dozens of miners, what looked like the whole town council, and a brass band.

As Bill's car approached the scene the mayor signalled to the band, who immediately struck up 'Colonel Bogie.' It was a redoubtable performance, considering that the mayor had corralled them from a practice session earlier that morning at the Naval academy.

Bill and Frank, who could hardly contain themselves with laughter, retired to a safe position behind Bill's Jeep.

Sam Schanks addressed the three. Even though they were only a few feet away, his voice was at full volume. He hailed the three as the town's heroes and the miners' saviours. At the end of his speech, he announced that they had been unanimously voted Honorary Citizens of Roanoke, and presented them with certificates. Arnold, on behalf of the three of them, thanked the mayor and town council.

Just before the three made their way to the waiting bus, the mayor leaned forward and spoke to them in almost a whisper. The ubiquitous smile was strangely absent and his voice, though calm and quiet, was determined.

"I know that your opinion of politicians is probably quite low, but I want you to know that I, Sam Schanks, owe you folks big time. One of the miners that would have been killed but for you three was a relative of mine. I spoke to the mining company..."

At this point his face broke into a conspiratorial smile. He continued.

"They want me to give you this as a thank you."

He handed Arnold an envelope.

"We can't accept anything—" Arnold started to say, but Sam held up his hand.

"We won't take 'no' for an answer. Don't open the envelope until you're on the bus. And remember, Sam Schanks never forgets his friends. Anytime you need my help, just phone me – and I mean that."

Without waiting for any response from the three, Sam turned to the crowd and, with his full beaming smile firmly back in place, waved goodbye to the three as they were shepherded onto the bus. They didn't have a chance to say goodbye to Bill and Frank. They just waved at them from inside the bus. Bill held up both his hands and gave them a double thumbs-up sign.

As soon as they were on board, the engine started. The band struck up The Beatles' 'Yellow Submarine,' and the bus pulled out of Roanoke.

"That was some exit," said Dee.

Arnold opened the envelope that Sam had given him. It contained a cashier's cheque for $10,000 and one of the mayor's cards.

"That Sam Schanks is some operator," said Amos.

"Yes, but things are not always black and white," said Arnold. "Those last, almost whispered, comments he made to us showed us his soul. Whatever shady things he is involved in as a politician, deep down there's a good person trying to break out."

Arnold smiled, and added, "Anyway, that money will set us up nicely in Washington."

They settled back in their seats. It was a long journey ahead and they would have to change buses in Charlottesville.

CHAPTER 2

The Virginia scenery was conducive to thought and Dee, Arnold and Amos had a lot to think about as the bus sped along on its way to Washington. They needed to define, or redefine, who they were and what they were going to do.

"It's not just the dream we all had," said Amos. "We work together well, even though I only met you two a few days ago."

"It's a kind of complementary chemistry," said Dee. "We each bring different characteristics to the mix. Maybe that's why we were chosen?"

"Chosen, by whom?" said Arnold.

They couldn't really answer that question. The bus trundled along a few more miles.

"For me, I see this in terms of clients and representatives," said Arnold. "I think maybe that's because I'm a lawyer, and that's the way I think. We are representatives who act for our client: the Earth, for want of a better description."

"Well, if we represent the Earth, then why not say so?" said Dee.

"What do you mean by that?" said Amos.

"When we reach Washington let's set up the Earth Office," said Dee.

"That's a brilliant idea," said Arnold.

"The Earth Office it is," said Amos.

After a few hours the bus stopped at Charlottesville and the three had a chance to stretch their legs and get some coffee. The next leg of the journey would take them to the capital. Having agreed on the name of their organisation, they were feeling quite refreshed and reanimated when they stepped onto the bus for the last part of their journey.

"We'll set up our office and invite people to contact us with problems and information to do with matters that concern us," said Amos.

"We'll have to be careful," said Arnold. "Otherwise every weirdo in Washington will be driving us mad."

"Good point," said Amos.

"We'll need to write out a manifesto and mission statement," said Arnold. "We don't want to be confused with organisations that want to 'save the planet' from global warming or reduce carbon emissions; there are plenty of those kind of groups tackling green issues. What we're about are issues where the Earth itself, through us, can be involved in saving lives."

"It sounds a tall order when you put it like that," said Dee.

"But it's important to each of us that we do this work," said Amos, adding as an afterthought, "I think we should write something down on paper before we arrive in Washington."

They were almost oblivious to the passing scenery as they argued back and forth over the right wording for their declaration. Even as the bus pulled into the bus station in central Washington they were still putting the final touches to their work.

The bus finally came to a stop and its weary occupants spilled out into the bus station. Arnold went over to the ticket office to ask for directions to Dupont Circle, the address that Bill had given them for his cousin Charlotte's bed and breakfast.

"I've bought the tickets," said Arnold on his return. "We have to walk a short distance to pick up a local bus that will take us to the 20th and O Street intersection, which is only about 300 metres from Dupont Circle."

Dee said, "O Street is a funny name for a road."

"It's alphabetical," said Amos. "Lettered streets go east to west and numbered streets north to south."

They walked to the bus stop and, after a few minutes wait, a bus arrived.

"This is it," said Arnold. "The D3 bus is what we want."

The three clambered aboard.

The route didn't take them past any of the main sights of the town, although Amos did point out various imposing buildings which they passed on the way, including a bell tower. They alighted from the bus in a smart area of town.

"There are a lot of foreign embassies in this area," said Amos.

After a brief hunt they found the building corresponding to the address that Bill had given them. It was part of a terrace of different properties in Connecticut Avenue, just off Dupont Circle. There were five steps up to the front door, which were protected by a canopy, and some steps led down to a sub-basement from the street. The sub-basement was empty, but it had clearly been a real estate office. Shops and restaurants nearby included a second-hand bookshop and a tattoo parlour. Dee rang the bell on the front door.

After a few seconds it opened.

"You've arrived!" A large woman wearing an apron greeted them.

"I'm Charlotte," she said in a sing-song southern accent. "You must be Arnold, Amos and Dee; Bill has told me about all of you. You must be exhausted and hungry, come in, come in."

She ushered the three into a front dining room. Before they could hardly speak, food suddenly appeared on a table and the three were consuming large amounts of spaghetti, pizzas and salads. They hadn't realised until now how hungry they were after their journey from Roanoke.

"We can talk tomorrow," said Charlotte. "Right now Ellie here will take you to your rooms, you need to rest."

§

By the next morning the three had recovered from their journey from Roanoke and were keen to plan their strategy.

At breakfast Arnold said to Charlotte, "I noticed that your basement office is empty, would you let us use it?"

"Absolutely, honey," said Charlotte. "It's been empty for a while. The realtors who had it before went bust. They left some furniture and stuff, which you can use. I just haven't gotten around to re-letting it yet. It just needs a coat of paint and cleaning up, I won't charge you much extra rent for it. What kind of business are you thinking of starting?"

"We're going to set up an organisation called the Earth Office," said Arnold.

He showed Charlotte the notes he had made on their manifesto. He added:

"We need to have this printed up, together with some cards."

"Round the corner is a printers, they'll do it for you. Just mention 'Charlotte' and they'll give you a discount," said Charlotte.

They all thanked Charlotte and went downstairs to their new office.

"We can tart this up in no time," said Amos. "We just need to buy some paint and stuff."

"Well, you and Dee can start the ball rolling on decoration while I go to the printers and the bank," said Arnold.

By the afternoon the office had already been transformed out of all recognition. Dee had done one of her banners, which they hung in the window. It proclaimed in large ornate lettering: 'The Earth Office.'

Over the next few days the office was a hive of activity. Arnold had their manifesto printed up and framed. It was on the wall together with the framed certificate of their honorary citizenship of Roanoke, Frank's 'crater' photograph and Bill's articles from the *Roanoke Times*.

Arnold had placed an advert in a local paper, consisting of a short summary of their manifesto and an invitation for readers to contact them. The advert was due to come out at the end of the week.

The three used the remaining time before then to familiarise themselves with the city. Their work was important to them, but they didn't think the Earth would mind if they were just simple tourists for a couple of days.

Washington was a beautifully laid out city, with wide boulevards and majestic buildings. They gawked at the White House along with all the other sightseers and they toured around the domed Capitol building, which housed a copy of the United States Constitution. Their heads reeled with all the museums and other sights they visited.

But beyond them all, the sights that had the most significance for them were the Holocaust Museum and the Vietnam Memorial: the former because of the incredible cruelty of the death camps and the latter because of the total negation of life that is war.

The tears sprang to Dee's eyes when she looked at the small, inconsequential items that families of the dead had left under the names of their loved ones, which were carved into the black stone wall of the Vietnam memorial: a pair of shoes, a toy train, a teddy bear. The banality of the objects intensified the sheer horror and sadness of what the wall represented. 'Death is inevitable, but life still has to be fought for,' she thought.

This, at root, was their mission, and the three were even more determined to follow their dream and fight against the forces of chaos that threatened their world.

The morning that their advert came out saw the three ensconced in their new office. The office was clean and bright, in delicate shades of magnolia and grey – presumably colours that were on special offer from the local do-it-yourself store.

The first telephone call they received was from someone trying to sell them insurance, and the first person to walk in was a sweet elderly lady who had lost her cat.

"I really felt sorry for her," said Dee, having sent the lady on her way with promises to call her if they happened to find her cat. "When I was young my cat went missing for a whole week, and I was jolly upset."

About mid-morning a man in his mid-twenties came into their office. His clothes were fairly non-descript and his manner was distinctly nervous. He had just graduated with a degree in chemical engineering and was hoping to obtain a job in the chemical industry. His name was Richard Whewell, known to his friends as Dick.

"I don't know if you can help, or if it's up your street," said Dick.

He paused, and then after some encouragement continued.

"As part of my degree, I did a summer placement in a chemical works in Delaware. I don't know if you know that Delaware is the chemical capital of the USA, probably of the world?"

"No, I didn't know that," said Dee.

Amos and Arnold shook their heads in agreement.

Dick continued, in a more confident voice.

"The chemical works were on the Atlantic Coast, around eighty to ninety miles from DC. The plants are quite old and need money spent on them to bring them up to scratch – a lot of money. The security is lax. There are all sorts of safety regulations but, on the ground, a lot of them are ignored. A broken fence and a 'Keep Out' sign are not going to deter an RPG."

"Sorry, what's an RPG?" said Arnold.

"What planet have you been living on, Arnold? It stands for rocket-propelled grenade," said Dee.

"A bit like a bazooka?" asked Arnold.

"Yes, but much more powerful, more compact and easily transportable. You can put one in the trunk of a car," said Dick.

"Well, first off we'll have to do some research," said Arnold.

"I've brought a whole load of documents, mostly from the Internet. Your welcome to go through them," offered Dick.

"We'll phone you in a day or so then, and maybe we can go and have a look at the chemical plant you're worried about," said Arnold.

After Dick left Amos turned to the others, "Sounds like just the sort of thing for us."

He picked up the sheaf of papers and had just started thumbing through them when they heard a commotion at the door. It was Charlotte, and she was very excited.

"You won't believe the surprise that I have for you," she said.

Just at that moment Bill and Frank appeared.

"Wow! Look at these swanky offices, Frank," said Bill

"You've done yourselves proud here."

They all greeted each other warmly.

"How long are you staying for?" asked Amos.

"Forever," said Bill.

Frank pointed to the pictures on the wall. "My crater picture and Bill's article were syndicated all over the world, not just in the States."

"The *Washington Post* contacted us and here we are," Bill said, "I started as a rookie reporter in Washington, before I ended up in Roanoke, so I know the city pretty well – I've retained my contacts."

He turned and whispered to Amos and Arnold out of earshot of Frank, who was in animated conversation with Dee on the other side of the room, "Frank didn't need any persuading to come to Washington. I think he's taken a shine to Dee."

Amos and Arnold smiled.

"It's good to see you both," said Arnold.

Over sandwiches and coffee, which Charlotte and Ellie managed to conjure up, Bill and Frank brought the three up to date with news from Roanoke.

"Sam Schanks was re-elected mayor, and he goes round now like a dog with two tails," said Frank.

They all laughed.

"So, what's the next project?" asked Bill.

"Well, it's funny you should ask," said Arnold.

The three told Bill and Frank all about Dick and his concerns over the chemical works in Delaware.

"There have been a string of problems over the years with safety and security in the chemical industry, and a huge amount of it is located there. I've brought my jeep, I could take you all out for a picnic on the coast of Delaware," said Bill.

They phoned Dick and arranged the outing to Delaware for the next day. There was a lot to do that afternoon preparing for the trip. Arnold and Amos went through all the documents that Dick had left, and Dee helped Frank organise the cameras and photographic equipment.

§

Bill and Frank came over early the next morning.

"The drive should take a couple of hours. The chemical works are on the coast just outside a town called Dover," said Bill.

"That's a nice English place name," said Dee.

"Oh, you and Arnold should be right at home there; nearly all the places in Delaware are named after English towns and counties," Frank added.

They loaded up the car. Charlotte and Ellie had prepared an enormous picnic basket of food and, with Frank's photographic equipment, the car was fully laden.

"You'd think we were going on an expedition across the Sahara," said Amos, surveying the amount of stuff they had packed into the trunk of the car.

Dick arrived and the three introduced him to Bill and Frank.

"I phoned a guy I used to know, last night," said Bill.

He continued only after a pause to get everybody's attention.

"I met him when I was a reporter in Washington many years ago. His name is Larry Perez and he had just joined the FBI. He's now in Homeland Security and runs their office in, guess where?"

There were shrugs all round. Bill continued.

"Dover, Delaware."

"Well that's a useful contact," said Arnold.

"We can stop off at his office on the way to the coast, he's expecting us," said Bill.

It took an interminable time to finish loading up the car. Eventually, to waves from Charlotte and Ellie from the side of the road, the wagon rolled on its way.

The journey took them through the heart of the city, past the Washington Memorial and then through Maryland, over the Chesapeake Bay Bridge and onto Delaware and the coast.

They were all in good spirits, although Amos was still troubled about his mother's pension problem.

"Perhaps we can help?" said Arnold.

Amos told them what he knew so far. Since his father's death his mother had received a widow's pension from the Department of Veterans Affairs, as his father had been in the Navy at the time of his death. But last month they suddenly stopped paying her pension, and the letter of explanation she received didn't make any sense.

"I've been into the Veterans Affairs Office here in Washington, but they don't seem to know anything," said Amos.

"Did they give any reason at all for stopping the payments?" said Bill.

"They just say it's down to the local office in Boise, Idaho," said Amos. "I haven't seen my mother for a year or more now, so I think I'll visit her and try to sort out the mix-up as well."

"Bureaucratic inefficiency is rampant these days. I'm sure that's all it is," said Bill.

"I hope so," replied Amos thoughtfully.

In spite of the traffic in Washington, after a couple of hours they reached the outskirts of Dover. The first thing they saw as they approached the city was a large sign on a wall proclaiming: 'The City of Dover: Capital of the First State.' Underneath the sign was what was presumably the city's insignia.

"What does it mean by 'the first state?'" asked Dee.

"Delaware was the first state to accept the US Constitution," Amos answered.

"This state may be small in size – I think only Rhode Island is smaller – but there's a lot of history here; it goes right back to the late seventeenth century," said Bill.

Bill pulled up the Jeep in front of a large, bland office complex.

"This is where Larry's office is situated," said Bill.

They all trooped into a large foyer and were ushered into an escalator and up to the third floor. They had to pass through airport-type security. Finally parked in a corridor waiting area, they found themselves outside a door marked 'Larry Perez: Director of Homeland Security.'

Larry came out to greet them. He and Bill shook hands warmly and Bill introduced him to everyone. His office was plain though smartly decorated, and there was a framed photograph on the wall of Larry standing next to President Bush, Sr. Apart from a keyboard and computer screen, his desk was completely clear. He was friendly to everybody, but his eyes showed a keen and incisive mind.

After initial pleasantries Dick explained who he was and why he was concerned about the security and safety of the chemical works just outside town.

Larry turned to Bill and said, "You hit a nerve when you telephoned me, Bill. We've been concerned about that chemical works for some time. I phoned the plant manager earlier and told him to prepare for an inspection."

The drive to the chemical plant took about half an hour and the last few miles driving along a winding road afforded them numerous views of the ocean.

The guard at the gate waved them through as soon as he saw Larry, and they pulled up outside a single-storey building. The manager's office was the complete opposite of Larry's. Piles of papers were everywhere – clearly the manager was a man under pressure.

The manager said, "We've implemented nearly all your recommendations on safety and security. Short of having a permanent garrison of troops here, I don't know what else we can do."

"Well, right now, I just want you to show my friends here around the plant," replied Larry.

The manager gave them a twenty-minute tour. Dick didn't know the plant manager as he had worked under his predecessor. The plant had seen better days, and the upkeep was even shabbier than when Dick worked there. They walked past three gigantic chlorine tanks which, they were told, were partly underground. Other chemicals were also made and stored at the facility in smaller tanks.

After they left the plant they drove up the narrow coastal road behind and above the chemical works. The weather was pleasant and Larry was happy to join everybody in the sumptuous picnic that Charlotte and Ellie had provided.

They drove off the road and followed for a few hundred yards a track that opened out into a clearing. The view out to sea was majestic, in spite of the chemical works in the foreground.

"I have my job to do, but I can't help feeling some sympathy for the guy that runs the chemical works," said Larry.

"It's not him, he's doing his best," Dick replied. "It's those at the top of the chemical corporations that starve the plant of the cash and resources needed to carry out their security and safety checks properly."

"At the moment it's unclear what our role is," said Dee.

"This place, this whole area of the coast, has a certain familiarity about it; I think we're somehow on the right track. We just have to be patient, things will become clear in time," said Arnold.

"These turkey sandwiches are fantastic," said Bill.

They all laughed and for the moment the problem of the chemical works receded and they just enjoyed the picnic.

"Before we go, I'm just going to take a few pictures of the chemical plant from up here," said Frank.

"I'll join you. I need a bit of exercise after that meal," Arnold added.

The two walked parallel to the coastline through a grove of trees, as Frank tried to achieve the best vantage point for his camera. As they approached another clearing they saw two men in dark suits standing with their backs to a limousine, looking through binoculars at the chemical plant just below them.

Their manner was suspicious and Arnold held back quietly while Frank surreptitiously took photographs of the men and their car. After a minute the car sped off. The men clearly had not noticed the pair watching them.

"I don't know who they were or what they were up to, but I have a bad feeling about them," Arnold stated.

"I agree. Let's return to the others and see what Larry makes of what we saw,"

They hurried back to the picnic site and told everybody what they had witnessed.

"Seems mighty suspicious to me; we'll go back to my office and I'll run a check on the licence plate," said Larry.

They hurried back to Larry's office and gave the memory card from Frank's camera to one of the agents, who took it away to their laboratory. After a couple of minutes the agent came back with a sheaf of photographs, which she laid out on Larry's desk.

"All I have to do is put the licence plate of the car into the system and it will give me the name and address of the person it's registered to," said Larry.

He typed rapidly on his keyboard and waited for the screen to respond.

After a few seconds he exclaimed, "Well I'll be damned. The car is registered in the name of the Syrian Embassy in Washington, DC. I can pull up all the names and faces of the embassy staff and match them to the two men in the photographs. It should only take a few seconds."

He furiously tapped the keyboard.

"One of the men is a middle-ranking attaché. He's been at the embassy for a few years and is probably Syrian Intelligence – they all are. The second man is interesting."

He continued tapping vigorously on the keyboard while he was talking.

"Now this other fellow is down as a chauffeur. He only arrived at the embassy a few weeks ago, but he's red flagged; I'll have to go into another screen."

He tapped the keyboard a few more times.

"Here we are," he said triumphantly. "He's not Syrian but Lebanese. He's been red flagged in a report by the Israelis: they think he's Hezbollah. I think we likely have here a full-blown terrorist, or at least someone who organises terrorists."

He looked up from the screen and said:

"I want to thank you folks. We've a major lead here and we may be able to avert some terrible catastrophe."

"What happens now?" said Arnold.

"This is in our hands now," said Larry. "I'll contact Washington and they'll mount surveillance on these people. We'll find out what they're up to and put a stop to it."

Larry turned to Bill and Frank and said, "Needless to say, you can't publish any of this yet. But I'll give you the heads up and you'll be the first to know when the story breaks."

On their way back to Washington the three were in pensive mood.

"I suppose our part in this is over now. We have to leave things up to Larry and the other agencies he'll bring in," said Dee.

"We're not the police," added Arnold.

"You can't interfere in the investigation. Larry will keep me informed on what's going on and I'll pass on the information to all of you," said Bill.

"I'm not so sure, I still have the feeling that our role in this is not over," said Amos.

The next day was stormy in Washington. The summer days were moving towards fall, and more unstable weather patterns were the order of the day. Even though it was hurricane season, by the time they reached the Washington area most cyclones that started out in the Caribbean ended up as tropical storms by the time they reached that far north. Even so, blustery conditions and driving rain were not pleasant.

"We need a proper website for the Earth Office," Dee announced.

"It's a good idea, but I'm not good with computers," said Arnold.

"Me neither," said Amos, shaking his head.

"Looks like it's down to you, Dee. Maybe you could get Frank to help you?" said Arnold playfully.

"Maybe I will," replied Dee.

"Talk of the devil."

At that moment Frank and Bill came into the office. Bill had a serious expression on his face and said, "I just spoke to Larry, and it's not encouraging."

"What's the problem?" asked Amos.

"When Larry contacted Washington, they told him that the Syrians had been under intense surveillance for some time. They were surprised that the two men from the embassy we saw at the chemical works had slipped the net. In addition, they had no idea that the Syrians or whoever were even interested in the chemical works. The problem is that because of diplomatic privilege, they can't enter the embassy and they can't arrest or question anybody without risking a diplomatic incident. Without definite evidence, their hands are tied. All they can do is watch and wait – it's frustrating."

"I think we need to sit down and work out what's happening here and what we are going to do. You may be right, Amos, we may still have a part to play here," said Arnold.

He turned to Dee. "Phone Dick to come right away, I think we are going to need his input."

Dick arrived after a few minutes and they brought him up to date on the situation.

"There are three questions, to my mind," said Bill, pacing up and down the room as he talked. "What are they going to do? When are they going to do it? And how are we going to stop them?"

"Only three questions? Don't you think Larry and his colleagues haven't already made this analysis? And they are much better equipped to deal with situations like this; after all, we're just amateurs," said Dick.

"Maybe so, but we have something they don't have," Arnold replied.

Dick's brow furrowed into a questioning look.

"Isn't it why you came to us?" said Dee.

At that moment Charlotte appeared with Ellie in tow. The sandwiches and coffee were welcomed by everybody and helped to defuse the tension.

"Let's take the first question," Arnold started, turning to Dick, who sat down and drummed his fingers on the table.

After a few seconds Dick said, "Look, they can do anything. But if it was me and I wanted to destroy the chemical works, I would either plant explosives all round at strategic points, timed to go off together, or…"

His words trailed off.

"Or what?" encouraged Arnold.

"If I couldn't easily infiltrate the plant, then the only other way is with a missile – preferably several – fired into the works from outside."

"The RPG that you mentioned before?" said Arnold.

"Yes, but to what end?" asked Dick.

"Isn't that what terrorists do? Blow up things, cause death and destruction?" said Amos.

"No, it's not as simple as that," Dick paused. "Yes, there are a lot of nasty things produced at the chemical works – the chlorine, in particular, would form a lethal cloud that could kill or severely disable a huge number of people – but the problem, from their twisted point of view, is that the plant is on the coast."

"Why is that a problem for them?" asked Arnold.

"Because if the wind is blowing out to sea, then the only harm done by a cloud of toxic chlorine would be to the seagulls out in the Atlantic."

"Dick has a point," said Bill.

"You know, I've been thinking," Amos began. "The coast at Delaware is too close for Washington not to be somehow involved".

"You're right, there must be some connection to the DC area, but what?" said Frank.

They kicked around ideas for the next hour or so, without reaching any conclusions. Dick went through a pile of papers that he had brought, and Dee and Frank searched the internet for any clues.

Meanwhile, outside the skies became greyer and more threatening.

"We're in for a storm tonight," prophesised Amos.

"In England we never know what the weather is going to do," said Arnold.

"Normally that's true here as well. But in this case we know that there is going to be a storm," said Amos.

"How come?" said Dee.

"It's the remnant of the hurricane that hit Florida last week. Generally hurricanes move north and when they reach here usually turn into a tropical storm. That's how we know what's coming," said Amos.

"So what's the weather between Delaware and Washington going to be?" asked Arnold.

"The same – stormy,"

"That's it!" said Arnold. He stood up and became quite animated. "An approaching tropical storm from the south means a strong easterly wind towards the coast from Delaware all the way to DC. We have to tell Larry."

"We can phone him," said Dick.

"No, we have to convince him, and we need to be there ourselves," said Arnold.

Arnold raced towards the door and they all followed him out to Bill's car. Egged on by Arnold, they all piled in and sped off.

Arnold used his mobile to phone ahead to Larry. He didn't explain anything but said that they needed to see him urgently and would be there in a couple of hours. Dee looked puzzled and whispered to Frank, "I don't understand. How do we know that there's going to be a strong easterly wind between here and the coast?"

Frank put his arm around Dee as they sat huddled together in the back of the Jeep. He explained:

"The way it works is like this. Tropical storms and hurricanes are cyclones. That means that in the Northern Hemisphere they rotate counter-clockwise. And that means that if you are due north of a storm, the winds are from the east—"

"It's the answer to my second question," interjected Bill. "The trouble is that although we think we've worked out what they're going to do and when they're going to do it, we still haven't worked out how we're going to stop them."

"They can't fight the Earth," said Arnold.

Bill started to say something, but decided there was no answer to that, or if there was, he couldn't think of one.

The car ate up the miles and, in spite of the worsening weather conditions, they made good time. They arrived at Dover refreshed – most of them had slept a little during the journey.

In Larry's office Arnold set out his arguments to Larry. Larry politely listened and then addressed the group.

"Look, Arnold, on your point about the use of RPGs, I'm with you on that. Our analysis is the same as yours. In fact, the most difficult thing about the use of RPGs is obtaining them. But this is easy for an unfriendly foreign power; they can import them into the USA in parts through their diplomatic bag, and we would be none the wiser. The other point you make I'm not so sure about. Yes, a cloud of toxic chlorine gas on its way to Washington would be devastating. We would have to evacuate the city, which would be impossible, and hundreds, maybe even thousands, would die. But so far our surveillance has drawn a blank. There doesn't appear to be any additional activity at the Syrian embassy. There's no evidence of anything impending. I don't know what we can do."

"Warn them at the chemical works; let's go there now," said Arnold abruptly.

"I don't like chasing wild geese, but as it's you – what the hell," said Larry.

He phoned through to the chemical works and told the manager to secrete himself and his staff into their safe room. That was at least one safety measure that they were able to implement. They all then followed Larry out into the general office.

Larry called to the only person in the room, a young girl sitting behind a desk.

"Where is everybody?" said Larry.

"They're all out because of problems with the storm. I'm the only one here," she said rather forlornly.

"Remind me, what's your name?" asked Larry.

"Trainee agent Mary De Santis," she replied.

"Well, you're with us, Mary. Follow me," said Larry.

Larry strode out the room waving everybody to follow him.

"We'll go in my SUV, which I just took delivery of this week. It's big enough to take us all, and it's armour plated with lots of extras."

By now the skies had grown dark and the rain started spattering the windscreen of the SUV as they sped along the road towards the chemical works.

They finally stopped by the road on the cliff overlooking the chemical works. The wind and driving rain from the sea took their breath away.

"It's going to be a real stinker of a storm when it arrives. It may even still be classed as a hurricane," said Larry. He shrugged his shoulders. "Well, we're here and I don't see anything."

"Maybe we should look around," said Amos.

As he spoke there was an almighty bang. A streak of fire emanated from a point no more than fifty yards from where the group was standing and a missile careered off in the direction of the plant.

Larry and Mary with guns poised rushed towards the source of fire. The missile had scored a direct hit on one of the huge chlorine tanks and in the flash of light they could see two men crouched on the edge of the cliff next to what looked like an RPG launcher.

Larry called out to the men a warning and Mary approached them from the side. One of the men stood up with his arms raised in surrender, but the other fired a second missile. Mary, who was nearest, rushed forward and kicked the RPG away, managing to wrestle the man to the ground and handcuff him.

The rest of the group reached the spot just as the second missile turned another chlorine tank into a fireball. The east wind was fierce now, and it seared into their faces as Larry and Mary secured the two prisoners. One of the terrorists turned to the group and said, "We are not afraid of death. We have succeeded in our mission. You will all die."

The group could see the giant cloud of toxic gas from the chemical plant rising in the air and coming towards them. The chlorine would not only kill all of them, but also result in death and destruction over a vast area.

"I know you are not afraid of death," said Arnold. "But you are afraid of failure. You have not succeeded – you will fail."

His voice was calm and resolute. He turned his back on the terrorists and faced the ocean. Amos and Dee stood next to Arnold also facing the ocean.

"You will fail," shouted Arnold as he stamped his foot on the ground.

Amos and Dee picked up the rhythm.

"You will fail," they intoned in unison, and then a third time.

"You will fail!" they yelled, coupled with stamping their feet on the ground.

Everyone watched in amazement. Even the terrorists were half surprised and half amused at the performance. The three then turned around and in silence faced everybody.

"These Americans are crazy," said one of the terrorists.

"You can't beat the Earth," said Arnold. The chlorine in the air was beginning to sting his eyes.

Dick was the first to see it. He raised his arm and pointed inland. "What the hell is that?" he said.

They all turned to look in the direction he was pointing. A colossal and terrifying black column was on the horizon, rapidly approaching their position. It was accompanied by a howling noise.

"I think it might be a good idea to take cover," said Arnold.

There was a brick bunker nearby, half buried in a mound of earth. It was a gun emplacement from World War II and part of the gun turrets could still be seen at the front. Larry forced open the door and they all piled in. As it was half underground it would offer reasonable protection, and they could see out through the front in spite of dense vegetation that was covering the structure. Frank had his camera out and was franticly taking pictures.

"What is that coming towards us?" asked Dee.

"It's a twister, or what you in England would call a tornado," said Larry. "We have them now and again."

The howl turned to a shriek and then to a roar. Then they saw Larry's car. His brand new SUV was about fifty feet in the air, hanging vertically in the slipstream of the whirlwind. It then swung round and followed the twister in the direction of the chemical works.

They watched as the twister settled on the chemical works. It sucked up everything in its path in a swirl of mountainous debris. Then it moved out to sea, taking everything with it: chlorine cloud, tanks, buildings, Larry's SUV, and everything else.

When the twister made contact with the ocean, water shot up into the maelstrom, transforming the twister into a waterspout. They watched dumbstruck as it disappeared towards the horizon.

The storm began to abate after the passage of the twister, and Arnold put his face close up to one of the terrorists. "I told you that you would fail. You can't beat the Earth."

"Reinforcements will be here shortly," said Larry. "I contacted base and they're sending out a crew to take us back and secure the prisoners."

"If I didn't see it with my own eyes, I wouldn't have believed it," said Bill. "Hell, I did see it with my own eyes, and I still don't believe it."

"Don't ask questions, Bill. Just be thankful that Amos, Arnold and Dee are on our side," said Larry.

"How did you enjoy your first experience in the field, Mary?" asked Dick.

"Not quite what I expected," she replied.

"You did great," said Larry. "And you're not a trainee agent anymore; I promote you to Agent De Santis."

The sirens pierced the wind and rain as the reinforcements arrived, bringing with them hot drinks and blankets. The group hadn't realised that they were all soaked through. Back at Larry's headquarters, they all were able to change into dry clothes.

"I just heard from the manager of the chemical plant," said Larry. "They were all safe and sound in the secure room when the twister hit."

"Look at this, Larry," called Frank.

He showed him a picture of his SUV hanging in mid-air over the cliff.

"I'm going to frame that and hang it on the wall behind my desk," Larry laughed. "Mind you, the paperwork to get a new car is going to be horrendous. I'll have to include your picture as evidence of what happened to the vehicle. 'Sucked up by a twister': it's a great line."

Larry turned to Dick.

"You know, we have you to thank you for bringing the problem to the Earth Office in the first place."

"Thanks Larry," he replied, sheepishly.

"I know a few people in the chemical industry here in Delaware – if you're looking for a job I could ask around," said Larry.

"I would appreciate that very much, thank you," Dick smiled.

The next day was hectic. The story hit the news organisations straight away, and the involvement of the Earth Office in the arrest of terrorists put them centre stage. The 'coincidence' of the twister appearing at just the right time and removing the danger of a toxic cloud was put forward as a lucky freak of nature – no one would believe anything else, according to Bill's editor at the *Post*.

After such an advertisement a steady stream of callers began to show up at the office. Most of the problems people came in with were not relevant to what the three could do, but all were dealt with politely. Even the woman who had reported her lost cat on their first day was satisfied; Dee found the cat sitting by their front door the next morning. The woman was so delighted to retrieve her feline she gave a donation of one hundred dollars, and wouldn't be persuaded otherwise.

Amos continued to be troubled by his mother's problems.

"I think I'm going to have to visit her and sort this out," he said one morning. "Though I feel bad about leaving you both to cope on your own."

"No problem," said Dee. "I want to work on setting up our website. Go and see your mother. In fact, why don't you take Arnold with you? He needs a break. Frank will help set up the website and Charlotte can look after things at the office."

"You have it all worked out, Dee," replied Arnold.

"I'd be delighted if you came with me. Lake Pend Oreille is magnificent at this time of year," beamed Amos.

"Okay, you book the tickets for us, Dee. But you must keep in touch and let us know what's going on," said Arnold.

CHAPTER 3

If truth be told, Dee was happy to be on her own for a few days. Or perhaps not entirely on her own; she was hoping that Frank would keep her company. She did want to organise the Earth Office website and the office needed sorting out, but she also needed some thinking time.

Since the day of 'the dream' things had been manic. The earthquake in Roanoke had been scary enough, but on the cliff above the chemical works, all of them had faced certain death. She didn't know what had made her more scared: the chlorine cloud, the tornado, or the terrorists.

It wasn't that she was having second thoughts about the Earth Office, but the gung-ho attitude she tried to project of herself masked the fears and uncertainty that she was really feeling underneath. It didn't help that she'd received a nasty, threatening letter in the post that morning. It was to be expected, of course, there are always a few cranks around, but it still unsettled her.

She managed to bundle Amos and Arnold off to the airport. They had a long journey ahead of them: DC to Spokane via Denver, Colorado, and finally a rental car to Lake Pend Oreille. The place names didn't mean anything to her; they were just points on a map of the US, which she had pinned to the wall of the office.

Frank came round in the afternoon and noticed her mood. After a few questions he managed to elicit out of her that she had received a threatening letter.

"We must pass these on to the authorities, when we receive them," said Frank. "They're mostly just oddballs who send this type of letter, but with the terrorist connection you can't be too careful."

Frank telephoned Larry, and within twenty minutes an FBI agent arrived at the office.

She introduced herself as Special Agent Helen Chandler. She was black, in her late twenties and spoke with a southern accent. Dee warmed to her immediately; Helen had a quiet confidence that put her at ease.

"We deal with these pathetic individuals all the time. They have nothing better to do than send out nasty letters," said Helen.

"Thanks for coming to see me so quickly," said Dee.

She handed Helen the letter.

"My boss used to work for Larry Perez when he was in the FBI. As soon as Larry phoned, I was ordered here post-haste," said Helen. "I'll give this letter in to the lab at headquarters, they'll try to match its handwriting to our database. We just might strike lucky and nab this guy."

"What's happened about the terrorists that were caught?" Frank asked.

"Interesting," said Helen, who paused for a moment. "Now, this is off the record, right?"

Frank nodded in agreement. Helen continued.

"The two that fired the RPG were both Lebanese. They had no links that we could find to the Syrian embassy who, as you would expect, denied all knowledge or connection with the incident. The RPG was recovered but was untraceable and the two men you saw earlier from the embassy were 'merely sightseeing' according to the Syrians. With no direct proof of involvement, there is not much we can do – it's a politically sensitive time at the moment in the Middle East, our state department doesn't want to make a fuss. I've only been a special agent in DC for one year and I'm still learning about the politics involved when dealing with foreign embassies – they don't teach you that in law school."

"Where were you in law school?" asked Dee.

"I'm from Louisiana, originally. I wanted to be a journalist, so I went to the state university. Then I had an opportunity to study law at Loyola Law School in New Orleans," said Helen.

"And then you joined the FBI?" said Dee.

"No, then I was a TV news reporter. I didn't join the FBI until much later. I've been with the Bureau three years now, one year here in Washington."

She gave Dee her card.

"Here is my mobile number; you can reach me day or night. I don't want you to worry about any threatening mail or phone calls, just pass anything along to me and I will deal with it. I'll also liaise with Director Perez in Delaware; I'm a great believer in interagency cooperation."

With a wave to Frank, she breezed out of the office. Dee's spirits were lifted, not only because of the presence of Frank, but also because she had never met anyone like Helen. Her self-assurance was encouraging and empowered Dee's feelings of self-worth.

§

Amos sat quietly in the cab as they left the office on their way to the airport.

"I'm sure we'll sort out your mother's pension," said Arnold reassuringly. "Unless… there's something else bothering you?"

"I don't know," replied Amos. "I asked her if there were any other problems, but she said there weren't."

"So what's the problem?" asked Arnold.

"My mother is not one to complain. She tries to shield me from everything. I just caught something in the tone of her voice. I think there is something else, that's why I want to see her in person. Then she won't be able to hide it from me."

"Don't worry Amos. We'll find out what is really going on and the two of us will sort it out," said Arnold.

Amos smiled. "Thanks, you're a good friend Arnold. And you will love the lake near where I was brought up."

"Tell me about it," said Arnold.

"Idaho is in the Pacific Northwest, just beyond the Rockies. It runs from Nevada and Utah in the south right up to the Canadian border in the north. But, there is a panhandle in the northern part of the State – that's where Lake Pend Oreille is situated. The lake nestles between Washington State to the west and Montana and the Rockies to the east. In fact, the width of the state narrows down to only forty-five miles at the Canadian border."

"What's the lake like?" asked Arnold.

"Exquisitely beautiful; rugged, surrounded by forests, you feel so close to nature," said Amos. "And we have a monster."

"What, like Loch Ness in Scotland?"

"Yes. You have Nessie, we have Paddler."

"Have you ever seen it?" asked Arnold mockingly.

"Many times, although everybody really knows that 'sightings' of the monster are really just of Navy underwater craft – they used to do all kinds of experimental testing here in the lake. But to me and my friends, they were the monster."

The cab pulled up to the airport terminal. The pair wandered around the shops while they were waiting to board their flight. Arnold didn't mind flying, but he disliked airports. The first leg of their flight was just under four hours flying to Denver. Then after a forty-minute stopover it was another two and a half hours to Spokane.

Arnold managed to encourage Amos to open up and talk about his childhood.

"Arnold, don't think I don't love Idaho and its people, but if you ask many Americans, they would associate Northern Idaho with racism and white supremacists. We do have our fair share of them but I, personally, found negligible prejudice against me or my mother."

"Where did you go to school?" asked Arnold.

"When my folks first moved to Idaho they lived near my father's navy base, but after my father died my mother and I moved to the northeast of the lake, near a place called Clark Fork. We had a small holding of a few acres near the Clark Fork River just a few miles from the Montana border, and I went to school in the town of Clark Fork. I was the only Native American in the school, but my father had been in the military and people just accepted us as we were – I have only happy memories."

They arrived at Spokane mid-afternoon local time. The flight was not too onerous and they were both eager to start their drive to the lake. The journey on to Amos' mother's house took about two hours. Arnold drove first. He liked driving in the States, it was relaxing; the roads were wide and often dual carriageway, and even though the cars were 'gas guzzlers,' fuel was much cheaper than in England. The rental company upgraded their car and so with the air-conditioning turned up they breezed along in quiet luxury.

They had to take Interstate 90 east to Coeur d'Alene and then the 95 north to Sandpoint, which was at the northwest point of the lake. The start of the drive, though, was disappointing. The first leg to Coeur d'Alene was just a straight road, flat and monotonous. As they approached Coeur d'Alene, Arnold's stomach caught up with the fact that they hadn't eaten much since they left Washington.

"I'm starving. Shall we stop somewhere?" he said.

"There's a place up ahead just after we turn onto the 95," said Amos.

They entered the town and made a left turn to go north.

"It's just here on the right," said Amos. "They call this crossroads 'Donut Intersection.'"

They pulled off the road and drove a short way up to a restaurant which had a large sign outside advertising 'Muffins & Donuts.'

"This place is famous," said Amos in a hushed tone.

Arnold couldn't see why a doughnut restaurant should be famous. He sat down at a table and after a few moments Amos brought over some coffee and doughnuts.

"We're in luck, they had some huckleberry doughnuts left," said Amos.

"So why is this place famous?" asked Arnold.

"Well first off because of the doughnuts – especially the huckleberry ones, as huckleberries are the official Idaho State fruit," said Amos.

Arnold took a bite of his doughnut and nodded in agreement.

"Second," continued Amos, "when I was growing up here they had a bulletin board on display which made fun of local politicians and dignitaries. There's a new owner now and the messages are much friendlier, but this place is still trading on much of its past glory."

"I don't know about the politics, but I like the doughnuts," said Arnold as he wolfed down the rest of his doughnut.

"This is just to keep us going until we reach my mother's place – she'll have a meal ready for us when we arrive," said Amos.

A trucker on the next table asked where the pair was headed. Arnold wasn't used to such friendliness. In England people didn't really chat to each other in restaurants. Before they could reply, he continued, "Seattle to Boston, I travel the whole length of Interstate 90 and I always stop here – the best doughnuts in the world."

Arnold wasn't sure how many countries outside the US the trucker had visited, but he recognised his passion on the subject of doughnuts.

After they left the restaurant, Amos drove the car, and they ate up the miles as they approached the lake.

"The lake is east of us but too far away to see," said Amos. "We hit the lake at the northwest end and cross the Priest River estuary to Sandpoint. We then pick up Highway 200 which will take us around the northern edge of the lake to Clark Fork."

Amos became much more animated as they approached territory that he was familiar with. 'There is something about going back to one's roots where childhood memories transport an individual in time back to their youth,' thought Arnold. He could see that change envelop Amos.

It was a small bridge that they encountered at the crossing point to Sandpoint, but Arnold didn't really notice it as the breathtaking view of the lake had filled his field of vision. It wasn't so much the background mountains and forests which impinged on his senses, after all you could see similar sights in the Lake District in England or the alpine lakes of Switzerland or Italy that he had visited on holiday. No, what was different was the stillness of the water; Arnold had never witnessed such calm. The lake was huge and the forces of nature had conspired to produce perfect tranquillity of epic proportion. He knew the power and forces that nature could unleash – had unleashed – to form the lake and surrounding topography. Yet here and now a timeless stillness had been created.

Amos spoke, which disturbed Arnold's reverie.

"Amazing isn't it? Once you've seen the lake, the image never leaves you."

They crossed the bridge and entered Sandpoint, the largest town on the lake.

"This town is built on tourism," said Amos. "Fishing in the summer and skiing in the winter."

They picked up Highway 200 and made their way easterly towards Clark Fork. They stopped a couple of times to enjoy panoramic views of the lake.

They finally reached Clark Fork, and Amos pointed out his old school as they drove past.

"What's that?" asked Arnold, pointing to a stone block with a drawing of a strange creature on it outside the school.

"Ah, that's our school mascot, the Wampus Cat," said Amos.

"I don't think I've ever seen an animal that looked like that," said Arnold.

Amos laughed.

"I hope that you never do. It's a legend from the Native Americans who once lived here. It's like a large cougar, but with a spiked ball on the end of its tail which it uses to club its victims."

"First a lake monster – Paddler – now a fearsome mythical feline. Is there anything else I need to know?" Arnold joked, joining in the merriment.

They turned off the main road and crossed a bridge, which ran over the Clark Fork River that fed the lake. After a few hundred yards they turned into a farm, set back from the river. As they approached the main house, Amos's mother came out to greet them.

She was a tall, statuesque woman. Her grey hair was tied in plaits and her face, though lined with age, was testament to a dignified beauty. She embraced Amos and greeted Arnold.

"I'm Monique, please come in."

She led them into the house. It was larger than Arnold had expected: a two-storey wooden construction typical of houses in the US. The main room was neat to perfection with photographs and knick-knacks lining the shelves.

Most of the photographs were of Amos, either on his own or with one or both of his parents. One particular photograph of Amos's father was particularly poignant. It was the only photograph in a black frame and showed Amos's father in naval uniform.

The other items on the shelves were an assortment of minerals, rocks and gemstones.

"Idaho is famous for its gems," said Amos, noticing Arnold looking at them.

He held up a polished red gemstone.

"This is a six-ray star garnet. If you look at it in the sunlight, you can see the 'stars' just below the surface of the stone – it's our official state gem. The only other place in the world outside Idaho that you'll find these is in India."

"Amos is very proud of his rock collection," said Monique. "Most of these specimens come from this area of the lake. Amos and his friends used to go rock collecting in the Clark Fork

River all the way to the Montana border, which is only a few miles from here."

"But I'm so remiss," said Monique suddenly. "You must be starving."

She led them into the dining room. The table had enough food on it to feed ten people, rather than three. Luckily the doughnuts Arnold had eaten earlier were a distant memory.

"It must be something to do with the lake air; I seem to be hungry all the time," said Arnold plaintively.

Monique served them with fried chicken, sweet corn and a whole host of foods she had prepared. This was rounded off with huckleberry pie – fast becoming one of Arnold's favourite dishes.

Amos brought up the subject of the problem Monique was having with the Veterans Office.

"We can talk about that tomorrow," said Monique dismissively. "Right now tell me about what you've been doing and what this 'Earth Office' thing is that you were telling me about."

Amos and Arnold spoke for more than an hour about their adventures with Dee and how they had decided to set up the Earth Office. Monique was particularly interested in the shared dream that had initiated everything.

"Amos takes after my father," said Monique. "They were both 'dreamers' – it's a tradition of the Naskapi Indians."

Monique stood up and left the room. After a few moments she returned holding a highly patterned leather coat.

"This was your grandfather's coat," she said to Amos. "It was his father's before him. I want you to have it. It's the only thing I have of my father's things. It's made of Caribou skin and, though the colours have faded, you can still see the red, blue and yellow pigments on the intricate design."

Amos smiled and took the coat, tears filling his eyes.

"You've both had a long day. I think it's time for sleep now," said Monique.

§

Arnold was woken by the smell of cooking food. As he walked into the kitchen, Amos and his mother were already tucking into French toast, sausages and beans.

"Come on, Ma," said Amos as he held her hand in his. "What's going on with the Veterans Office? Why have they stopped your pension?"

A veil of worry descended over Monique's face.

"I don't know Amos," she said. "I received a computerised letter and they just stopped my monthly payments. I tried to telephone them in Boise, where the main office for Idaho is, but all they would say was that they would look into the matter and get back to me. They never did, and I don't know what to do."

"I'm here now," said Amos. "We'll go to Boise, if necessary, and sort it out."

When Monique went out of the room, Amos turned to Arnold and said, "I know the Veterans Office is often inefficient and mix-ups are not uncommon, but there's something about this which seems odd."

When Monique came back in to the room Arnold spoke to her.

"Has anything else happened in the last few weeks, anything unusual?"

"I don't think so," she said, but there was a slight hesitation in her voice, which Amos picked up.

"Ma, what's happened?"

"Well it's nothing really. Do you remember Harlan Tyler, Amos?"

Amos visibly stiffened at the mention of the name.

"He was in the year above me at school. He bullied me terribly, him and his friends. Yes I remember Harlan Tyler."

"He runs the fish hatchery by the Cabinet Gorge Dam in the Clark Fork River, just a few miles from here. He's done well for himself," said Monique. "About six months ago he completely refurbished his house. I don't use my barn much nowadays, so I rented it out to him. He stored his furniture there, while the works were being done."

"I hope he paid the rent okay," said Amos.

"Oh yes, he didn't give me any trouble. In fact he was back and forth quite a lot during that period."

Monique continued.

"Then a few weeks ago he came to see me. He said he wanted to build a tourist fishing lodge on my land and would I sell him my property. I was a bit taken aback. I told him I had no intention of selling and thought nothing more about it. He has pestered me a couple of times since then, but I just kept telling him that he was wasting his time and that he should build his lodge somewhere else. I can't see that this has any relevance to my problem with the Veterans Office."

"You're probably right, Ma, but I think we'll go and see Harlan anyway," said Amos.

The dam which spanned the river a few miles upstream on the Idaho side of the boundary with Montana wasn't too far from the farm. It was a hydroelectric dam built in the 1950s which supplied electricity to North Idaho and Spokane. Beyond the dam – across the border in Montana – was a huge reservoir.

"After they'd finished building the dam, the fish population in the lake diminished rapidly," explained Amos as they crossed the river and picked up Highway 200 to the dam.

"As a result, they opened a fish hatchery at the bottom of the dam. They raise rainbow trout and various salmon species, although the main one is the Kokanee salmon – it's a lake species of the Pacific Sockeye."

"So you and this Harlan Tyler have issues between you?" said Arnold.

"Not all my memories are happy ones. Harlan and his friends gave me a hard time. I don't know what he's like now; it was a long time ago."

"So why did you leave the lake area?" asked Arnold. "And how did you end up in Roanoke?"

"I do have happy memories," said Amos, "but there are dark ones as well. I had a difficult time after my father died and we moved to the north side of the lake. I suppose I hung around with the wrong crowd and drank a bit too much. In the end I had to get away. And then I just drifted from job to job..."

His voice trailed off.

After a few miles they turned off the road towards the dam. They could see the dam in front of them with the hatchery tanks below.

As they drove into the car park Amos gave Arnold some background information on the dam and hatchery.

"This dam is part of a number on the river, which start in the Rocky Mountains. The river drains into the lake and then, on the other side of the lake, the Pend Oreille River joins the Columbia River and eventually empties into the Pacific. The hatchery is vital to the lake. Without it the fly fishing industry would collapse, and along with it the economies of all the towns around the lake that depend on fly fishing tourism."

As they parked the car a voice shouted at them, "Is it you, Amos?"

A burly man approached them. He was balding and had a beer belly, but was surprisingly light on his feet as he came bounding over.

"My old friend Amos," he said, and vigorously shook Amos' hand.

"Arnold, meet Harlan Tyler," said Amos in a decidedly flat tone.

"Call me Harlan. And what brings you two to my neck of the woods?"

He led them into a small office block behind the hatchery. Harlan's office was quite bare. One or two photographs in frames adorned a window ledge, but there was nothing else in the room apart from a desk and some chairs. The photographs were of Harlan holding a fish. By the size of the fish and Harlan's gleeful expression, it was presumably a prize catch of some sort. Looking at the pictures Arnold noticed between them, on the ledge, some irregular dust-free shapes indicating that a number of objects had been recently removed.

Seeing Arnold inspecting the photographs Harlan said, "That was my prize Chinook Salmon I caught two years ago in the lake."

Harlan hardly paused for breath.

"So Amos, what did you do after you left school?"

Without waiting for a reply he continued, "I and a few friends signed up for the Navy. We had a great time. I made a lot of contacts and, with a bit of help, landed this job as fisheries manager after I left."

Amos broke into Harlan's monologue.

"Why are you harassing my mother to sell her house, Harlan?"

Harlan's tone changed.

"It was a genuine offer, Amos – and it's still open. I want to build a fishing lodge on the river and make lots of money from tourists who come for the fly fishing. But, what the hell, if your ma doesn't want to sell then I'll have to build it somewhere else."

"How big a lodge did you want to build?" asked Arnold.

"I don't know exactly," said Harlan, taken unawares by the question. "Maybe a dozen rooms or so."

"Do you have architect's plans, a feasibility study or information on permissions required?" Arnold enquired in his lawyer-voice.

"Oh, I haven't figured out that kind of stuff yet," said Harlan, visibly confused.

"I think we'll go now," said Amos. He turned to Harlan. "Stay away from my mother; she's not selling her land to you or to anybody."

When they were in the car heading back, Arnold said to Amos, "When I was a lawyer in England I dealt with hotels and other kinds of developments all the time. Take it from me, he's about as much chance of building a fishing lodge as I have flying to the moon – he's completely clueless. Something else must be going on that we don't know about."

"I'm inclined to agree with you, Arnold," said Amos. "I don't remember him as being particularly bright, and it's clear the fishing lodge is just a ruse of some kind."

"I just realised," said Arnold, scratching his chin. "There were things missing from the shelf in his office. I can't be sure what they were, but I wonder if he has a mineral collection like you have, and had removed them from the shelf?"

"We all collected rocks and minerals when we were kids," said Amos. "We all thought we were going to find gold and become millionaires."

"As soon as we arrive back at your ma's house I'm going to telephone Sam Schanks," said Arnold.

"The mayor of Roanoke? Why?" said Amos.

"Well Harlan has a lot of buddies in the Navy. I wouldn't put it past him to organise a problem for your mother at the Veterans Office to put pressure on her to sell. Sam Schanks was also in the Navy and he offered his help to us if ever we needed it. Perhaps he might be able to find out something to help us. It's worth a try."

When they returned, Monique was in the kitchen preparing food for lunch. Amos told her about the meeting with Harlan.

"What did Harlan do here when he was renting your barn?" asked Amos.

"Well it was just after the river flooded. The house was not affected, it was far enough away from the river, but there was a lot of soil erosion from the land around the barn. The barn had dried out and Harlan said he wanted to rent it for a couple of months. He was here quite a lot, but as I said, he was polite and well behaved and he paid his rent on time without any fuss."

"I've just spoken to Sam," said Arnold as he came in to the room. "He was very helpful. He said he knew a few people in the Veterans Office in DC, and would come back to me if he had anything."

§

About an hour after FBI Special Agent Helen Chandler left, Dee received a call from Larry Perez. He was just checking up to see if the FBI had sent someone over to speak to Dee about the threatening letter. Dee assured him that she felt much better after Helen's visit and that she was keen to knuckle down to work. With Amos and Arnold out of the office for a few days, she wanted to make sure the website for the Earth Office was up and running.

Larry told her that the two Lebanese terrorists were securely under lock and key in maximum security at the Delaware Correctional Centre at Smyrna, just north of Dover. He said that she might have to give evidence at their trial, but that that wouldn't be for a few months yet.

Frank had gone back to work and was coming back later to take her out for a meal. In the meantime, Charlotte had brought in coffee and cupcakes and, for the first time in quite a while, Dee was able to relax.

She forgot the time and was immersed in website design when the telephone rang. The caller was a woman who introduced herself as Christine Nystrom. She worked for a charity and wanted to meet with someone from the Earth Office. It wasn't clear what she wanted, but Dee asked her to come in to the office.

About an hour later a tall blonde woman in her fifties came in to the office.

"I'm Christine Nystrom, we spoke earlier on the telephone," she said.

Dee beckoned her to sit down and offered her tea or coffee.

"I'm not sure if you can help me," she said. "In fact, it was my mother who suggested I come to see you."

"Your mother?" questioned Dee.

"Yes, apparently you found her lost cat," said Christine.

"I remember," said Dee. "A sweet elderly lady. I found her cat by accident; it came in to the office."

"She's a bit doolally sometimes, my mother, but she mentioned your organisation and I read something about you in the *Washington Post*, so here I am."

"How can we help?" asked Dee. "No more lost cats I hope?"

"No," smiled Christine. "I work for a small international charity based here in Washington. We try to promote pre-emptive planning for disaster emergencies. We lobby governments to mitigate the effects of natural disasters on the population by adopting pre-emptive planning strategies."

"Sounds a good idea," said Dee. "But don't governments do that already?"

"You're quite right," said Christine. "But most disaster planning by governments is about what to do after a disaster has happened. This is, of course, important. We can't stop disasters happening, and you have to plan to have hospitals and other emergency services ready when they are needed. My organisation Pre-Disaster Planning, PDP for short, tries to get governments to organise and plan things so that when disaster does strike it has less effect on the population."

"And where does the Earth Office fit in to this?" said Dee.

"Well there's a United Nations General Assembly Meeting coming up in a few weeks in New York – they have them every year. PDP wants to lobby as many governments as we can. The only trouble is that we have very little money and are extremely short staffed. I was talking to my mother about this problem and she suggested I contact you. Would you be able to help?"

"Well it sounds fascinating," said Dee. "My two colleagues are away at the moment and I would have to discuss it with them. Leave me some material on your organisation and I'll contact you in a few days."

Christine put a pile of documents on Dee's desk, and as she left said, "It would be great if you could help us at the UN lobby. I look forward to hearing from you."

Dee put the website design to one side and started to leaf through the papers that Christine had left her. She was still reading through them when Frank came in to the office.

"I've booked an Italian restaurant nearby," said Frank. "It's such a lovely evening and I managed to book an outside table. We'll be dining alfresco."

They strolled down 19th Street to the restaurant, which was just a few blocks away from Dupont Circle. On the way Dee told Frank about Christine.

"A lot of these charities do good work," said Frank, "especially in Third World countries. They're all starved of funds. It might be worthwhile for the Earth Office to look into it. Did she really come to you because you found her mother's cat?"

"Apparently so," Dee laughed.

As they approached the restaurant she paused. She had the odd feeling that someone was watching her. Dee looked around, but nothing seemed out of the ordinary.

"Is everything all right?" asked Frank.

"Yes, I'm fine," replied Dee, smiling.

The meal was perfect, and for Dee, the company was perfect as well. But she still couldn't shake the feeling of being watched.

§

Dee was up early the next morning. Over breakfast she asked Charlotte if she knew any good gyms in the area, and Charlotte recommended one on 19th Street, very close to the restaurant where she had been the night before.

"I think I'll go and join," said Dee.

"Good idea, but be careful!" warned Charlotte.

"Why, what's wrong?"

"Well, there's a bakery next door and they sell the most amazing cupcakes."

Dee walked to the gym. On the way she passed the Italian restaurant in which she'd dined with Frank. Just past L Street she crossed the road and went into the gym, making sure that she avoided the bakery next door. Charlotte was right to warn her. Fancy having a gym next door to a bakery!

She signed up for a three-month trial membership and vowed to herself that she would go to the gym once a day if she could.

On the way back to the office, she again had the feeling that she was being followed. She didn't care. It had been the visit from Helen Chandler, the FBI agent, which had somehow been a catalyst to a change in her way of thinking. That, and the events of the recent past few weeks. She was more confident now; the group she was part of would protect her. Maybe she was being overconfident, but whatever was going to happen… 'Bring it on!' she thought.

§

"While we're here I'm going to introduce you to fly fishing," said Amos.

"The last time I went fishing it was with a net for tiddlers in my local stream," said Arnold.

"You can't come to Lake Pend Oreille and not fly fish," insisted Amos. "It's a great sport. I'll arrange a boat and we'll go out on the lake."

Arnold became thoughtful.

"You know, Amos," he said. "I've been thinking about Harlan Tyler's missing rock collection. Let's go over to your mother's barn and see if we find anything."

They walked towards the river in the direction of the barn.

"It's changed a lot since I was here last," said Amos. "There are deep channels where the flood has eroded the topsoil and lots of places where bare rock has been exposed."

They reached the barn and went inside. Marks on the walls clearly showed the water level at the height of the flood. They were about three feet above the present ground level. There wasn't much to see in the barn itself as Harlan had removed all of his effects.

They both walked around the barn and covered the area down to the water's edge. Arnold was aimlessly scraping soil away from a large rock with his shoe when he all of a sudden he bent down and picked up a small irregular rock. What had caught his eye was a slight glint in the sun as one side of the rock had a yellowish sheen. Amos came over and inspected the specimen.

"I don't know," he said. "It could be gold, we would need to have it analysed by a laboratory to know for sure. Let's see if we can find any other unusual minerals."

They both dug around in the soil and ended up with five rocks. Arnold's mobile telephone rang and Sam Schanks' name flashed on across screen.

"I've struck gold."

Sam's crackly voice was just about audible – the signal strength was not very good.

"A friend of mine, who owes me a big favour, works in the Veterans Office in DC. He says we should speak to an old shipmate of his in Boise called Will Ortega. He works for the Veterans Office there and will be expecting your visit. He'll sort things out for you."

"Thanks Sam," said Arnold.

"You know me, Arnold. I never forget my friends."

The line cut off abruptly as the signal failed.

"We should go to Boise tomorrow," said Arnold, "Sam has given us someone to talk to at the Veterans Office."

"While we're in Boise, we can have these rock samples analysed," said Amos. "I know someone in the university there. I'll find out if he can do the analysis for us and then arrange us some transport."

They went back to the house. While Amos was busy arranging flights and telephoning old friends, Arnold rang through to Dee to find out what was happening in DC. They exchanged news, but Dee omitted to mention that she felt under surveillance.

"We'd better have an early night tonight," said Amos. "My pal, Manny, will give us a lift to Boise, but he's leaving at eight a.m. from Sandpoint."

§

The next day they were up at what seemed like the crack of dawn to Arnold. Amos was bright and cheerful, but Arnold, who was never very good early in the morning, walked around in a daze.

"We should be back in plenty of time to go fishing," said Amos. "I've booked a boat on the lake and arranged all the fishing tackle and supplies we'll need."

"Can't wait," murmured Arnold, almost inaudibly.

On the way to the airport Arnold began to wake up.

"My old school friend Manuel runs an air taxi and charter service out of Sandpoint Airport. He's taking someone to Boise today and we can go along as well; he'll bring us back when we're done," said Amos.

Arnold couldn't see any signs for the airport but they suddenly turned off the main road and found themselves outside an aircraft hangar. A man came out and greeted Amos, who, after the embrace, introduced Arnold to his friend Manuel.

"That sounds like a Spanish name," said Arnold.

"No, my family are Basque," said Manuel. "There are a lot of us in Idaho. I'm taking two men to Boise this morning. They have just finished a fishing trip. You are both welcome to come along."

Behind the hangar was an aeroplane. Arnold, who was not particularly good travelling on planes, went pale.

"Isn't she beautiful?" said Manuel. "She can take five passengers."

"But she's got a propeller," said Arnold.

Amos and Manuel both laughed.

"You'll be all right, Arnold. Manny's a good pilot," said Amos, reassuringly.

It took several minutes to load up the plane. The two men had just finished a week's fishing on the lake, and they had several suitcases and kitbags full of fishing gear. Arnold and Amos climbed on board together with their bags.

With five men and their luggage on board, Arnold was concerned about the amount of weight the plane was carrying.

"Do you think we'll be able to take off with all this weight on board?" Arnold whispered to Amos, who just smiled.

The engine started up and Arnold was deafened by the noise.

"It's a lot louder than a normal aircraft," he bellowed, trying to make himself heard above the noise.

"Don't worry," said Amos. "You'll acclimatise yourself to the noise."

The plane shot along the runway and climbed steeply into the air. It slowly levelled off and Arnold was able to look out through his window, which offered a magnificent view of the lake and the rising sun.

"It's quite fun," he said. "You really feel like you're actually flying; it's not like it is in a large aeroplane."

The noise was still deafening, but it seemed to disappear into a background hum. After a while Arnold ceased to notice it. The majesty of the lake and the rugged slopes that descended straight into the water filled his field of view.

The flight to Boise passed quickly and they arrived in under an hour and a half. The landing was as short and sharp as the take-off. One minute they were over the airfield and the next, Manny dropped the aircraft and parked it in a convenient bay.

They deplaned and walked towards the terminal building.

"I really enjoyed that," said Arnold. "I never knew flying could be such fun."

"I'll take you for a few flying lessons if you want to learn." offered Manny.

Arnold didn't know if he was serious or not; he didn't like flying *that* much.

"My car is parked here. I can give you a lift into town if you want?"

"Thanks, Manny," said Amos. "Could you drop us at the university, please?"

Boise State University was a sprawling collection of modern buildings on the south side of the Boise River, which snaked its way through the state capital. As the airport was also on the south side of the river it was only a few minutes before the car pulled up at the university entrance.

"We want the Department of Geosciences," said Amos.

They walked across the road and turned left.

"The building in front is the main administrative block, and I think Geosciences is next door. The department is in the same building as Mathematics," said Amos.

They walked in to the building next door and Amos spoke to someone behind a desk in the entrance foyer.

"My friend is on the second floor. He's an old school friend and he said we could drop the rock samples in for a quick analysis."

The person behind the desk gave them directions, and they walked to the lift. After exiting the lift they walked along a long corridor looking at the names on all of the doors. Eventually Amos said, "Here we are."

They knocked on the door and entered the room.

"Hi John," said Amos. "This is my friend Arnold I told you about."

The two shook hands.

"Amos and I used to go to the same school in Clark Fork," said John, "So where are these samples you want me to look at?"

Amos produced the five samples from his bag and lined them up on the table in front of John, who proceeded to inspect them carefully.

"You're thinking gold, I presume? Where did the samples come from?"

"They're from my mother's property. She lives by the Clark Fork River as it enters into Lake Pend Oreille. There was a flood a while back and a lot of the topsoil was eroded by the flood waters. These samples come from the rock and soil that was exposed."

"Leave them with me. We'll roast them first and then use Aqua Regia. That's a mixture of nitric and hydrochloric acid – it'll dissolve the gold, if there is any – and we can measure the concentration. It won't take long, you can come back in an hour or so and I'll have an answer for you."

They left the university building and crossed over the Boise River into the town.

"John Lee was a good friend of mine when I was at school," said Amos. "Not like some of the others. He was always top of the class. He went to college and ended up a professor of Geosciences here in Boise."

As they walked through the town Arnold could see a magnificent building in the distance along the street.

"That's the Capitol building. The Veterans Office is on the other side," said Amos.

They walked round the domed building, which was set in a park.

"A few trees in this park were planted by former presidents of the United States," said Amos. "I'll point them out as we go past."

Behind the Capitol building they found themselves on a wide boulevard. A little set back from the road was a sign that read 'Department of Veterans Affairs Medical Center.' Next to the sign was a small rock plinth with a US flag, onto which had been carved 'The price of freedom is visible here.'

"All veteran hospitals have that message at their entrance," said Amos. "The Boise regional office is here as well."

They walked across the manicured lawn to a modern two-storey building. It was light and airy inside, and Amos spoke to the two men at the reception desk.

"Will Ortega is expecting us," he said. Amos turned to Arnold and added, "I didn't realise he's the director. Sam Schanks certainly came up trumps here."

A secretary ushered them into the director's office. Will Ortega was seated behind a large old-fashioned desk with two computer screens in front of him. He was friendly but started off somewhat guarded.

"What can I do for you folks?" he said.

Amos explained the situation and handed Will the letter his mother had received. He didn't mention anything about Harlan Tyler. Will tapped the keys on his keyboard and stared intently at one of the screens on his desk.

"Well this seems odd," he said, his face carrying a puzzled expression. "According to the computer your father is still alive, hence the reason your mother's widows pension has been stopped. Don't worry, I can sort this out."

He pressed the button on his intercom and called in his secretary.

"We became fully computerised a few years ago but we still have paper records from before that time."

He asked his secretary to fetch in the file on Amos's mother.

"She'll only take a few moments," he said.

He tapped the computer keys while speaking to Amos and Arnold.

"You know, the only way a date of death record can be changed is if someone did it deliberately. It would have to be one of our employees keying in the information from his or her own terminal."

He picked up his telephone and said to a voice on the other end, "Charlie, can you come in here?"

There was a knock on the door. A tall man in his late twenties entered the room.

"This is Special Agent Charlie Boyd. Please meet Amos and Arnold; they're from Washington, DC."

Will continued, "We've been having problems here with money going missing for a while. I called in the Veterans Affairs Office Police and Charlie and his team have been investigating possible embezzlement of funds."

At that moment Will's secretary brought in a file, which she deposited on his desk. He leafed through it.

"As I thought," he said. "Here is a copy of Amos' late father's death certificate. There is absolutely no reason why Amos's mother's pension should have been stopped. What do you think, Charlie?"

Charlie took the file and turned to Amos and Arnold.

"When Will called us in to investigate possible theft of funds, the first thing I did was to modify the computer system so that we could trace every key stroke from any computer terminal in the building."

He leaned across Will's desk and started tapping keys on the computer.

"Every employee has their own personal password. I can determine whose password and which terminal was used to change Amos's mother's computer file, and hence to stop her pension payments."

After a few moments he paused.

"Well, well, well," he said. "The culprit is Robert Quinn."

"What will you do?" asked Arnold.

"Robert Quinn is one of the people on our shortlist of suspects for theft. We're going to have to have a serious talk with him. If you'll all excuse me."

He nodded to Will and hurriedly left the room.

"This is a nasty business," said Will. "I know we're not regarded as the most efficient government organisation, but we try our best. It's rotten apples like Quinn that give us a bad name."

He went back to his computer screen.

"Okay, I've reinstated your mother's pension, Amos. I have also paid all the arrears to date directly into her bank account, together with a bit extra in compensation for all the trouble she's had. She'll receive an official letter of apology. The least I can do for you two is to treat you to a coffee in our cafeteria."

Will led them out of his office and along the corridor to a large common room. He ordered coffee and doughnuts.

At the mention of doughnuts Arnold's ears pricked up.

"You haven't any huckleberry doughnuts, by any chance?" he inquired.

Amos and Will laughed.

"We do have some huckleberry doughnuts, but I'm afraid we can't match the ones you had at Coeur d'Alene," said Will.

After refreshments they were led around the facility. Even though it was a regional office, it was responsible for millions of payments to their members and the families of those who had served in the military.

They ended the tour back at Will's office. The telephone rang and Will said to others, "Charlie has some news for us."

Charlie popped his head round the door.

"It's better than we could have hoped for."

He walked into the office and plonked himself down in a chair.

"It was the falsification of Amos' mother's computer file that was the catalyst," he said, placing his file on the desk.

"As soon as we confronted Quinn with the evidence he cracked. Apparently he had run up massive gambling debts and owed money to the wrong people. When we were called in to investigate, he immediately stopped embezzling money, and that's why our investigation has not been bearing fruit. But his mistake was falsifying the computer file for Amos' mother's pension."

"But why did he change her computer record? How could he benefit?" asked Will.

"Motive is easy. It was a straight bribe. One of his old Navy buddies paid him two hundred dollars to alter the computer file and stop Amos' mother's pension."

"Who was it?" said Amos.

"The scumbag's name is Harlan Tyler. He lives near your mother at Clark Fork. Do you know him?"

"Yes, I'm sorry, I should've mentioned it when we spoke earlier, but Arnold and I only had our suspicions, we didn't know for sure. Tyler has been trying to pressure my mother into selling her house to him. What will you do now, Charlie?"

"Already done," said Charlie. "I spoke to Sheriff Johnson at Sandpoint. He's going to interview this Harlan Tyler. In due course he'll be arrested and charged."

"What will happen to him?" said Amos.

"He'll probably face two charges: conspiracy to commit computer fraud and bribing a government official. On conviction, he would definitely face a custodial sentence. But why did he want your mother's property so badly?"

"We're not one hundred per cent sure, but we think it's because of valuable mineral deposits on my mother's property. We've brought some samples for analysis at the university here in Boise. I want to thank you both; this is a great load off my mind. My mother was upset and worried about the whole thing, especially because she's an independent woman. She'll be pleased it's all sorted out."

"Amos, it's us who should be thanking you and Arnold," said Will.

"Absolutely," agreed Charlie. "My investigation was going nowhere."

"There was some talk of an official investigation if we didn't catch the criminal or criminals quickly. My job was on the line; I can't thank you both enough," said Will.

"Well, that creep Harlan Tyler will have to face what's coming to him," said Arnold.

"I know Sheriff Cal Johnson," added Amos. "He's a good man and will deal with Tyler promptly and firmly. In the meantime, I think Arnold and I should be leaving. There's some fish waiting for us in Lake Pend Oreille."

"I wish I could join you. Let me order you both a cab," said Will.

Arnold and Amos said their goodbyes. They had to promise to contact Will the next time they planned a fishing trip to the lake so that he could join them.

The taxi ride back to the university took them past the Capitol building and downtown Boise. When they arrived back at the Geosciences department, John came over to them looking very excited.

"We've just completed the analysis of your rock samples. One of them was just iron pyrites – fool's gold – but the others all contained real gold. One, in particular, had quite a high concentration."

"What does that mean, exactly?" asked Arnold.

"You described the site to me: a couple of acres not far from where the river goes into the lake, on ground that was recently eroded by floods. We would, of course, have to do a detailed site survey. But my guess is that at today's gold price you have between a half and one million dollars of recoverable gold on the property. You would have to file a patented mineral claim."

"My mother would never agree to mining on her land, and neither would I," said Amos. "The effects would be to pollute the river and the lake. But it explains why Harlan Tyler wanted the land. He would have had no compunction in strip mining the river bank, and hang the consequences."

At that moment Amos's mobile rang. It was Manny. He was waiting for them back at the airport and could take them back home at any time.

They hurriedly left John with more promises to contact him next time they went fishing – John was also a keen fly fisherman.

"Everybody seems so excited about the idea of fishing," said Arnold as the cab took them to the airport.

"Now that we can relax, I will introduce you to the wonders of fly fishing, when we return to the lake," said Amos.

Manny was sunning himself in a deckchair by his plane when they arrived back at the airfield. This time Arnold eagerly clambered into the plane without any fear. The flight was quick, with Arnold happily gazing out of his window as they passed by the lake. He had an affinity with the vast deep waters and could never tire of the panorama.

Amos' mother greeted them warmly when they arrived back. She couldn't believe the depths Harlan Tyler had stooped to in order to gain her land and the riches beneath it.

Amos was correct about her attitude to the possibility of mining the gold on her land. She had witnessed the terrible damage that strip mining had inflicted on the lake and she would never allow that on her own land.

"Now that you've sorted out my pension monies, I've no need for extra money anyway," she said. "Whatever happens to that evil man, Harlan Tyler, is well deserved."

"And now to serious business," said Amos. "The lake fish are waiting for us."

Amos's mother had prepared some food for them, which she packed in a hamper. Arnold realised that this was not the first time she had prepared such a hamper for Amos and his friends to take on a fishing expedition. Amos loaded up the car with all the fishing gear – 'Their car needs a larger trunk,' thought Arnold.

On the way to the boatyard Arnold couldn't resist opening the food hamper. Amos's mother had conveniently placed two cheese sandwiches separately on the top.

When they arrived at the boatyard, Amos introduced his friend

Oscar to Arnold. Oscar ran a fleet of fishing boats for fly fisherman out of Sandpoint. There was also a 'game and fish' shop by the jetty, supplying everything an aspiring angler would need.

"Would you mind sharing your boat with another person?" said Oscar.

"Of course not," said Amos.

"Sheriff Johnson wanted to go fishing this afternoon. He forgot to book and I don't have a spare boat. I'll throw in some free flies for you."

"We're happy to share the boat with Cal Johnson. As you know I make my own flies, but Arnold here could do with some good ones – it's his first time fishing."

Arnold went into the shop with Oscar.

"Why can't we use real flies?" he asked.

"What?" exclaimed Oscar. "First of all, it's against the rules; second, it would take all the fun out of the sport. It's a battle of wits between you and the fish. A lot of the skill is luring the fish with the right bait. Take this one for example."

He handed Arnold what looked to him like two small tufts of tied up thread.

"These are both size twelve. One is a 'Parachute Adams' and the other is called a 'Green Drake.' At this time of year these two flies are the most popular."

Arnold carried his precious lures out onto the jetty to show Amos. He found him talking to a large man who was dressed up in full fishing gear and carrying two rods.

"Let me introduce you to Cal," said Amos. "Cal has just come from seeing Harlan Tyler."

"Hi Arnold," said Cal. "That Harlan Tyler is a real nasty character. He and his gang are always in trouble. Usually it's for drunk and disorderly behaviour. But this time we've really nabbed him for something serious. Your mother, Amos, is such a lovely woman and to try to stop her pension monies and defraud her... I'm telling you, the judge is going to throw the book at him. Anyway, let's go fishing."

"What flies has Oscar given you?" asked Amos.

Arnold showed Amos and Cal the two flies.

"They look like a 'Green Drake' and a 'Parachute Adams,'" said Cal.

"How did you know that?" said Arnold, surprised.

They both roared with laughter.

The three loaded all the paraphernalia in the boat and cast off away from the shore.

"The lake is very deep," said Amos, as he unfurled his fishing rod. "It can go several hundred feet down just a short distance from the lake's edge in many places."

Amos and Cal showed Arnold how to cast his rod into the water. They then saw to their own rods and sat back in the boat and relaxed while they waited for the fish to bite.

"Talking of fish biting, I wouldn't mind a bite myself," said Arnold as he rummaged in the food hamper Monique had prepared.

There was plenty of food for all three of them to share. After eating they all sat back again, waiting for the fish.

If he was being honest, Arnold wasn't really interested in catching any fish. He just loved looking at the lake. The stillness of the water had a hypnotic effect on him and he closed his eyes to revel in the silence.

He must have drifted off to sleep, as suddenly he was awoken with a jolt. His line was being pulled from below.

"I think you've bagged one," said Cal as he brought over the fishing net.

"Just relax," Amos told him. "Ease it in gently."

It was all Arnold could do just to keep hold of the rod. Eventually a fish jumped out of the water hanging on to Arnold's line. He reeled it in and Cal caught it in the net.

"It's enormous," cried Arnold. "I've never seen a fish as big as that."

Amos and Cal tried not to laugh. The sheriff weighed the fish on some scales that he had brought along.

"Well that's a mighty seven pounds," said Cal. "Good for a first time catch."

"What kind of fish is it?" asked Arnold.

"What you have here is a Kamloops trout. That will make a nice dinner for us tonight. You're invited as well Cal," said Amos.

"Is it a record?" beamed Arnold.

"You're a long way from a record, Arnold. The heaviest Kamloops caught was thirty-seven pounds!" said Cal.

"To be fair to Arnold, most Kamloops are between two to eight pounds, so this one is a good size. You'll always remember your first fish, Arnold." Amos slapped him on the back.

They resumed their fishing. Cal was next to catch a fish but it was a bull trout. These were protected and had to be carefully thrown back into the water.

They had scarcely started to fish again when Cal noticed a small boat in the distance, coming towards them.

"He's going to disturb the fish if he comes too close to us," said Cal.

The figure in the boat was holding a rifle, not a fishing rod, and was shouting obscenities in their direction.

"I don't believe it, it's Harlan Tyler," shouted Cal, as he indicated to Arnold to start the motor.

A shot rang out.

"Everybody down! The idiot is firing at us and I don't have my side arm," Cal cried.

Arnold lay flat and tried to start the motor, which was proving to be obstinate. Amos, on the other hand, knelt down on one leg and hit the water with his hand. He then stood up and faced Harlan. Arnold understood the gesture but to Cal it seemed an odd thing to do.

Harlan tried to fire another shot at them but either because he was drunk or his boat had swayed in the current, he tottered on his feet and the shot went wildly off in another direction.

At last the engine fired and Arnold turned the boat to head back to shore. Amos was still standing, unmoved and facing Harlan, who was still shouting abuse and trying to fire at them from a crouching position in his boat.

And then Cal noticed that Harlan's boat was caught in an eddy of some sort. In fact, the whole part of the lake, with Harlan's boat at the centre, seemed to be in motion. Harlan, himself, was oblivious to the water; he was too intent on pouring forth his verbal venom towards Amos, who stood impassively watching him as he swirled round.

As their boat reached the shore close to the jetty, a small crowd had gathered, responding initially to the rifle shots but now witnessing the whirlpool. Harlan's boat was at the centre of a maelstrom of water, which was rotating so fast that the centre was several feet below the normal level of lake water.

Harlan's boat was sitting on the water not horizontally, but at an angle that was approaching vertical. Suddenly, like the flush of a toilet pan, Harlan, together with his boat, dropped like a stone into the dark abyss of the lake.

Almost immediately after Harlan disappeared, the lake waters began to regain their composure. A minute or two later the crowd of onlookers on the pier could hardly believe that the lake had been anything other than the calm and tranquil water that they now saw.

"What was that?" Cal said to Amos.

Amos didn't answer him, but just shrugged his shoulders.

Cal repeated the question to Arnold. Arnold raised his hands and eyes in a gesture of incomprehension and said, "Maybe it was the lake monster; maybe it was Paddler?"

Oscar helped them unload the boat.

"Look at this," he said, as he pointed to a rifle shell casing embedded in the side of the boat. "That was a close one!"

"That damned fool Harlan Tyler shooting at us! I'll have to write a report," said Cal.

He then turned to Oscar, "I'll send over one of my officers to remove the shell casing from the boat, we'll need it as evidence. I'll also arrange a team to search for the body"

"Harlan chose his fate by his own evil actions," said Amos, who was now becoming more relaxed.

"At least he didn't completely spoil the fishing," said Arnold holding up his trout.

They drove back to Monique's house. She was delighted with Arnold's catch.

"I know just the recipe for a Kamloops trout," she said.

They told her what had happened on the lake. She was much more concerned over the danger they may have been in than Harlan Tyler's eventual doom.

The story, like the size of Arnold's Kamloops, was already growing in stature as they repeated it over dinner. The legend of 'Tyler's Doom' would be part of the lake folklore for many years to come.

While Amos and Cal were regaling Monique with fishing stories, which she was listening to attentively – she had heard them all before

– Arnold went outside and called Dee on his mobile.

He told her everything that had happened that day; she was relieved to hear that no harm had come to them. Her day had been quiet. She had been with Frank most of the time, but had managed to finish the Earth Office website.

There was something about her voice that alerted Arnold to something amiss. After much pressing from him and declarations from Dee that "it was nothing," she finally admitted to having the sense that she was being followed. He didn't make too much of it, but told her that he and Amos would be returning to DC tomorrow.

Arnold returned to the dining room and recounted his conversation with Dee. Amos agreed that they needed to return to Washington, DC as soon as possible.

Arnold telephoned the airport and managed to book him and Amos on an early flight out of Seattle. It was only a short hop from Spokane to Seattle, but they would have to leave around four a.m., taking into account time zone differences.

Cal thanked Monique for a delicious meal and left, but not before extracting promises from Amos and Arnold to let him know the next time they went fishing – hopefully without the appearance of a homicidal maniac trying to kill them. After all their tribulations that day they were able to laugh together.

Amos and Arnold managed a few hours' sleep before they left – they could always snatch more sleep on the plane journey.

§

While Amos was busy packing up the car the next morning, Monique took Arnold to one side.

"It was wonderful seeing you and Amos," she said clutching Arnold's arm. "You're a good friend to Amos and it's a shame I couldn't meet Dee – you are all doing good work."

She paused a moment but did not let go of Arnold's arm.

"You, Amos and Dee are not the only ones who have dreams. My whole life I have had them as well – it's a family trait. Don't worry about me and please don't worry Amos, but we shall not see each other again, at least this side of the dream."

Arnold was startled by her declaration, but before he could speak Monique continued.

"It's okay, I am content. Remember that there are no goodbyes, only hellos."

Before Arnold could say anything, Amos came into the room. They said goodbye to Monique and set off for Spokane airport.

A few minutes after they left, Amos turned to Arnold and said:

"My mother spoke to you didn't she?"

Arnold started to reply but Amos stopped him.

"It's okay, you don't have to say anything – in my family we communicate more through our dreams than we do by normal conversation."

They stopped for doughnuts at Coeur d'Alene.

"I'm taking a bag of huckleberry doughnuts back for Dee and the others," said Arnold.

The journey from Spokane to Seattle was only half an hour. Arnold had a window seat on the left side of the aircraft. The strains of the early start to the day and the events of the day before began to catch up with him and he soon fell fast asleep.

Arnold woke up suddenly, refreshed. He looked around and found Amos asleep in the seat next to him. He consulted his watch: he had only been asleep for fifteen minutes or so. The first fingers of dawn sunlight were just beginning to creep over the landscape as he gazed out the window. And then, in the distance, the sun blazing its white head, he saw it fast approaching. The sun's rays then lit up the rest of its body and the terrifying, majestic spectacle of the mountain was revealed.

Amos had also woken up and was staring with steely eyes at the sight out of the window.

"It's just like in the dream," he said.

"What mountain is it?" asked Arnold.

As if in answer to Arnold's question, they heard a voice over the loudspeaker.

"We are now approaching Seattle; the view on the left side is of Mt Rainier, one of the few active volcanic mountains in mainland United States."

The voice then droned on with the usual safety notices and the consequences for anyone caught smoking.

"When we land in Seattle, I'll text Dee to do some research on the mountain – I think we're going to be back here soon," said Arnold.

In fact, owing to the time zone difference between Seattle and DC, Arnold was able to speak to Dee. He told her about the mountain. It was early morning in Washington and Dee was about to go to the gym. Frank was coming over mid-morning and she was looking forward to seeing them both that afternoon.

Amos and Arnold boarded their plane to DC. They were pleased to be returning to the place they now regarded as home.

§

Dee called out to Charlotte, "Arnold just telephoned, they'll be back this afternoon. Frank is coming over about eleven and I'm just off to the gym. I'll see you in about an hour."

Charlotte watched Dee from the second floor window as she walked off, gym bag in hand. She took her usual route down 19th Street. As she approached the junction with L Street, a white van pulled in front of her and parked on the pavement. There was a large space on the pavement and it was convenient for vans to park there to deliver goods to the shops and restaurants in the street.

Two men climbed out of the driver's cab and walked round to the back of the vehicle, in order to open its back doors.

Dee noted their dark complexion and presumed that they were of Middle Eastern origin. When they opened the rear doors of the van, Dee could see inside and realised that the van was empty. In a flash they jumped on Dee and bundled her into the rear of the van. She did not struggle; it was almost as if this was something that she was expecting. One man got in the rear of the van with her and the other rushed around to the front and drove the van at great speed down L Street.

There were some early morning coffee drinkers in the cafeteria on the other side of the road where Dee was abducted. They saw the whole thing and immediately called the police. One of them noticed that Dee's bag had been dropped on the ground, and gave it to the police when they arrived. The dropped bag gave the police Dee's name and address, and her gym clothes and towel told them her intended destination.

While the police interviewed the witnesses, the details of the crime flashed through the police and FBI systems. Helen Chandler had just picked up the police report when her director put his head round her office door.

"Deepal Patel, isn't that one of your cases?" he said.

She was out of her office in a flash. She picked up the rest of her team on the way to her car.

"And don't forget to bring all the telephone equipment," she reminded them.

Screaming sirens allowed the team to speed past the mid-morning traffic towards Dupont Circle.

Charlotte was starting to become anxious. Dee had not come back from the gym. She was looking out of the window to see if she could see Dee's approach, when she heard the sirens and saw the FBI van pull up. She started to panic and ran downstairs, straight into the arms of Helen Chandler. Charlotte began sobbing.

"It's Dee, isn't it?" she said.

Helen tried to calm her down. Her professional tone and reassuring manner belied what she was truly feeling, but it was needed in this situation.

"Dee's been abducted," she said. "But as far as we know she's all right. We will do everything possible to bring her back safely."

"What will happen?" said Charlotte.

"We have to wait. The abductors will likely telephone us with their demands and then we will deal with the situation."

Helen directed her squad into Dee's office so that they could set up all of their electronic equipment.

Frank arrived and was crestfallen at the news of Dee's abduction.

"Dee told me she felt like she was being watched." Blood drained from his face. "I tried to be with her as much as possible."

"Don't blame yourself," said Helen, comforting him by placing her hand on his arm. "It was well planned; they waited until you were out of the picture before they struck."

"We're all set up now," said one of Helen's team. "Any incoming calls will be recorded and traced, although we need to keep them talking for at least a minute to have a successful trace."

"Now we have no choice but to wait," said Helen.

The news also made it to Larry Perez in Delaware. He went ballistic and immediately telephoned Helen Chandler's boss, the FBI director in DC.

"Don't worry, Larry, Helen Chandler is the best there is," said the director.

"It says in the report that the two men were Middle Eastern in appearance. You know what that could mean," said Larry.

"Helen is waiting for the call from the kidnappers. They'll probably want your two terrorists released in exchange," said the director.

"You can rely on my help," replied Larry. "Whatever it takes, just say the word."

Back at the Earth Office, which had turned temporarily into Helen Chandler's headquarters, reports were coming in. The white van used for the abduction had been stolen the night before from North Washington and some CCTV cameras had picked it up going down L Street, but as yet there were no other sightings. Helen got hold of the FBI department that dealt with foreign embassies and, although there had been a reported increase in the amount of 'chatter' at the Syrian Embassy, there had been nothing specific detected relating to the abduction itself.

A few telephone calls came through to the office. They were mostly harmless inquiries and a couple of marketing calls. Each one caused a near panic as the phone rang.

Finally, the call came. It was brief. Clearly the abductors knew that the call could be traced and they didn't want to spend too much time on the line. The caller was male with a strongly accented voice – almost certainly Middle Eastern. There were a couple of words from Dee, demonstrating that she was alive. The remainder of the message was that the kidnappers wanted to swap Dee for their two brothers who had been arrested in Delaware. They said that they would telephone back in an hour to make arrangements. The conversation then cut off.

Helen was cool and controlled when the call came. She tried her best to engage the caller in further conversation, but to no avail.

They simply said what they wanted to say and then ended the call. Still, a recording of the call was sent to the FBI laboratory for analysis on the off chance that they were able to come up with something.

One can't keep up a hysterical state for any length of time. As the day wore on Charlotte filled her time making coffee for all the agents. Bill came over and sat with Frank, who had gone very quiet.

At last a cab drew up to the office. It was Arnold and Amos back from Idaho. As soon as they saw the FBI cars they knew that something bad had happened. Charlotte was the first to reach them and poured out the whole story of the morning's events. They then walked into the building and Bill introduced Arnold and Amos to Helen and the team.

"Dee told me all about you both and how the Earth Office was started," said Helen. "Dee and I really hit it off; I want to assure you we will do whatever it takes to make sure that she comes back safely."

"I spoke to Dee," said Arnold, as he sat down behind a desk. "She spoke very highly of you, and I know that you'll do your best."

"We know that Dee will be all right," said Amos, not looking directly at Helen, but fiddling with a pencil on the desk. "It's not that we are unreasonably optimistic, but Dee, Arnold and I are connected with each other and with the Earth in such a way that means we are protected."

At that moment a call came through Helen's mobile. It was Larry Perez from Delaware; the FBI director had evidently given him Helen's mobile number.

"This is Larry Perez, Homeland Security Director here. Is that Special Agent Helen Chandler?"

"Yes, Director, what can I do for you?" Helen's voice was, not surprisingly, a little stiff.

"I'm not trying to muscle in on your operation. I used to be in the Bureau, and I know what it's like. I just want to know, are Arnold and Amos back yet?"

"Yes, Director, they just arrived."

"Thank goodness for that. Listen, you are in charge of this operation and I know you and your team will do everything possible, but..." Larry paused, trying to find the right words. "Whatever Amos and Arnold want you to do, do it. The whole thing about the Earth Office may seem a bit strange to you, it's strange to me too. But they seem to know things or be able to do things that just defy sense. What I'm trying to say is that you can trust them, really trust them."

When Helen came off the telephone, Arnold was standing in the middle of the room. He turned to Helen, but was addressing the whole room.

"Listen, everybody. Dee is going to contact us in some way and let us know where she is being held captive. I don't know how she is going to do it, but she will do it. We all need to be alert to anything which may be a signal."

Arnold turned to Charlotte.

"Do you have a television we can use?"

"Yes, upstairs," she said. "I'll need someone to help me bring it down."

Frank went upstairs with Charlotte and they brought down and set up the television in the corner of the office.

"We need to set it on one of the local DC news stations," said Arnold.

Arnold sat himself down on a couch in front of the TV and told Helen, "You and your team need to be alert for anything unusual that happens in the DC area that comes through in your police reports. Amos and I will likewise follow the local news."

Helen wasn't sure what Arnold was talking about, but it was a harmless action and she decided to bear in mind the advice that Larry Perez had given her. She also noticed that the whole tempo of things had changed since Amos and Arnold had returned. She couldn't put her finger on it, but everybody in the room, even her own team, had become more animated. There was an air of optimism that hadn't been there before. Even Charlotte had a visibly grown in confidence. She didn't know if it would be good or bad in the long term, but for now it certainly appeared to be helping, so she was content to go with the flow.

§

Even though Dee had been half expecting something to happen, the abduction still caught her by surprise when it did. She knew it was pointless to struggle and was interested to see how events transpired. She didn't feel in the slightest danger – she could handle these two men at any time. It wasn't arrogance, or as some would say, stupidity, on her part. No, it was a kind of stoic inevitability. A state of mind that she could encompass what she wanted at will, where she felt she could take control of events with the merest of touches. But for the moment she was content to see what would happen.

She was handcuffed and gagged but otherwise unruffled in the back of the van. The man with her just sat there nervously, looking out of a small window, as they careened off down L Street. The greatest danger she was in, she mused, was the erratic driving of the other man, who was clearly unused to manoeuvring large vehicles.

Dee tried to work out where they were headed, but it was difficult with all the changes of direction, presumably, she thought, to avoid traffic cameras. These men appeared not to be complete amateurs and they had obviously planned well.

Eventually the van slowed right down, almost to a stop, and began to head down a slope. Outside seemed to suddenly go quiet and Dee assumed that they had entered an underground garage of some sort. The vehicle then came to rest and the rear doors opened. They didn't bother to blindfold her, but she couldn't really see anything anyway. They led her through a door and pressed the button for a lift, which was just inside a small vestibule. Not a word was spoken. When the lift arrived they indicated for her to get in first, and the three of them travelled up to the top floor of the building. The lift opened up into a small corridor. At one end was a door, which one of the men opened with a key and they all filed inside.

It was a vast loft apartment, similar to those that had become popular in Washington in recent years. The windows had all been taped up, so she could not see outside, although she guessed she was somewhere downtown. The men led her over to a chair and table next to a window and sat her down. They removed her gag and handcuffed one wrist to a radiator pipe next to the chair. There was a glass of water and some indifferent looking biscuits on the table. The two men ignored her and went to the other end of the room, where there was a large table and chairs. Each was speaking on his mobile in what Dee thought sounded like Arabic, but she couldn't make out what they were saying.

She knew everybody would be worried about her, and she was particularly upset that Frank would be in a state, but there was nothing she could do about that now. At least, she thought, Amos and Arnold would be back soon – things would work out for the best in time.

She took the opportunity to scan her place of captivity. The walls were freshly painted in a bland cream colour – her abductors had probably just rented the apartment for a short time. She could hear the steady noise of the street traffic below and in the distance she made out the solitary chime of a bell, indicating that it was one o'clock. She vaguely remembered seeing a bell tower on her wanderings around the city. If it was where she thought she was, she had been correct in her assumption that she was somewhere in downtown Washington. There was a small kitchen off the large room and also a bathroom. Her captors were quite relaxed about her using the bathroom facilities, although being handcuffed to a bathroom pipe was quite awkward. Even the windows in the bathroom had been covered up, but it did not really matter as she had a fairly good idea of where she was.

Her captors asked her if she was okay. She thought it rather a silly question for captors to ask their prisoner, but as soon as she replied that she was, she realised that they had taped her answer onto a recording machine. Presumably they would use that when they contacted the Earth Office with their demands. In her mind's eye she could see Helen Chandler taking the call.

She tried to engage her captors in conversation, but loquacity was not one of their strong points. In spite of this, she managed to elicit out of them that they wanted a prisoner exchange – her for the two terrorists that had been captured in Delaware – or 'brothers,' as they described them. She would not allow things to reach that stage, she thought.

There was a knock at the door. The two men leapt up and stood on each side of the door. A voice called in Arabic from the other side, and they let in a third man. He was quite tall but his face was completely covered in a headscarf. He spoke to the two men and then left as soon as he'd come in. Dee thought it odd that her two captors didn't mind if she saw their faces, but the third man had taken great pains to ensure that he could not be identified.

The men made a telephone call and played the tape of Dee's voice. She surmised that it was probably an initial call to set out their demands for the prisoner exchange. The afternoon wore on. They offered her more food, but she wasn't feeling hungry. Amos and Arnold would have arrived back in Washington by now, and she began to contemplate how she could signal them to where she was being held.

The bell tower in the distance again rang out the hour. Dee stood up and faced towards the sound of the bells. Firmly and methodically she stamped her foot on the ground in time to the bell ringing the hour: Ding, ding, ding…

She then abruptly turned and sat down again in her chair, resuming her nonchalant posture. But the bells did not cease their toll. The relentless knell continued. After about the fifteenth ring her two captors went over to the windows of the apartment. One of the windows opened onto a parapet, protected by a guardrail, which enabled the windows to be cleaned from the outside. They slid open the window and looked outside. The noise of the traffic increased and the bell tower could easily be seen, sticking out over the top of the building across the road. Apart from the incessant ringing, there was nothing untoward outside. They shrugged their shoulders, closed the window and went back to their table.

It must have been something about the shape and size of the room and its location, with respect to the bell tower, but the peal of the bell seemed to reverberate in a manner that was intensely grating on the nerves. Dee didn't seem at all bothered, but her two captors began to feel affected, even nauseated, by the relentless searing cacophony.

§

Helen Chandler was receiving information in a constant dribble. The stolen white van used by the kidnappers had been spotted the evening before on a CCTV camera coming into Washington from where it had been stolen. There were two figures in the front of the vehicle, but it was impossible to make any kind of identification as to who they were.

Arnold, Amos and the others continued to watch the local news TV station. Arnold, particularly, seemed transfixed by the run of inconsequential local news stories that filled the airtime. The hourly news had just finished and there had been nothing in it of any significance.

Then, an unusual item appeared.

"We are just receiving reports of a set of bells that have gone haywire. The Old Post Office bell tower on 12th and Pennsylvania Avenue won't stop ringing the hour. Here is our correspondent on the spot."

The scene then shifted to the Old Post Office, and the staccato sound of the bell could be heard ringing in the background.

"The Bells of Congress, as they are called, are a replica of those at Westminster Abbey in London, England. Usually they ring out the hour here in Washington, but at five o'clock this evening, instead of ringing five times, they have so far clocked up more than a hundred rings and there is no sign of them stopping, as you can hear. The engineer who deals with the bells will be here in about an hour. We'll keep you posted on the bell that can't stop ringing."

Arnold jumped up from the couch.

"It's the signal: the bells, the bells!"

He was like some demented Quasimodo. He turned to Helen and said, "Follow me."

Arnold rushed out the room, followed closely by Amos, Bill and Frank. Helen, not wanting to be left out of whatever was going on, shouted to one of the other agents.

"With me, now!"

Helen had an athletic build and was quite fit, but she had difficulty in catching up with Arnold. Outside she directed her assistant to drive the backup car, and she and the others piled into the lead car.

"Where to?" she asked Arnold.

"The Old Post Office tower on 12th and Pennsylvania Avenue," he said." But no sirens or flashing lights, and we need to park discreetly. We don't want to spook the kidnappers."

She radioed these instructions to her assistant, who was travelling close behind.

They reached the bell tower and parked in a side street well out of view of the main road. There was a lot of activity around the bell tower, with a crowd of about a hundred people behind a police cordon and a TV crew in front of the tower.

Bill went over to the TV reporter who was standing outside the broadcast trailer, parked by the side of the road. He beckoned Arnold, Amos and everyone else to come over.

"I know the reporter and she's agreed not to broadcast anything until it's all over: I've promised her an exclusive. That way, if the kidnappers are watching TV they won't see anything that may alarm them."

They went inside the trailer and the reporter showed them the TV screens corresponding to the cameras they had on the street.

"We need to look around for anything unusual," said Arnold, scanning the screens.

"The nearest street is 11th and it's probably likeliest she's there somewhere."

The technician altered the camera angles to scan both sides of 11th Street.

"We can zoom in to anything we see for a close-up," he said.

They were there about half an hour when one of the cameras showed a man climbing out of a window, on to a balcony or parapet, outside a top floor window. The building was on the corner of 11th and E Street and the apartment was about ten floors up.

The technician zoomed in on the man and his dark appearance filled the screens. It was unclear whether he was Middle Eastern, but what was obvious was that he was not standing there normally. It didn't appear as if he was going to jump, but his demeanour was wooden, almost zombie-like; his eyes were open and staring. This certainly counted as something unusual.

"Let's go," said Arnold.

This time Helen made sure she was in front. They sped along 11th Street and stopped just short of the junction with E Street so that the man on the roof wouldn't spot them. Helen indicated that they should make for the entrance to a car park underneath the building in question. They crossed the junction separately, so as not to alert anyone watching, and entered the garage.

There were no lights and it was difficult to see anything, but Helen led them to the back of the car park to a door. On the other side was a lift and stairs.

"Best to use the stairs," said Helen, indicating that she and her assistant would lead the way. "Stay well back," she said. "I mean that, there may be shooting."

Nobody argued with her.

They all climbed up the stairs to the top of the building. This time Helen was well in the lead, with Arnold in the rear.

"I must go to the gym more," he thought.

They arrived at the top floor corridor and Helen and her assistant stood each side of the door to the corner apartment. Helen indicated that she would kick the door in and that she and her assistant would go in first.

An almighty crack shook the entire building, as Helen kicked in the door and fell into the apartment. Dee was handcuffed and sitting in a chair, one man was standing motionless on the parapet and the second man was on the floor to Helen's left. He was in semi-foetal position with his eyes closed and hands over his ears. The sound of the chiming bell from the bell tower was echoing through the room.

They handcuffed the two men, who were pliant: their eyes were glazed over and they didn't seem to know what was happening. Dee stood up and shook the hand that was manacled to a pipe. The handcuff fell off.

"I think I could have done that at any time," she said.

Arnold, Amos, Bill and Frank all rushed into the room. Frank was the first to embrace Dee, tears of joy springing into his eyes. The others followed suit.

"Thanks for rescuing me," said Dee.

"I'm not sure you needed our help," replied Helen. "But I'm glad to see you are okay, you gave us all quite a turn."

"Hold on one second," said Dee.

She turned towards the window and stamped her foot once on the ground. As if by a miracle, the chiming bell suddenly stopped and all was quiet.

The rest of Helen's team arrived and they led out the abductors, who were now beginning to emerge from their reverie. As they passed by Dee, she asked them:

"Who was the man who visited you while I was being held prisoner?"

They ignored her question, saying nothing.

"We'll debrief back at the office," said Helen.

She directed her team to investigate and secure the apartment. Before they left, Arnold turned to see Helen standing over the spot where Dee had been when the bell stopped ringing. She stamped her foot a couple of times and looked expectedly out of the window, but nothing happened. She shrugged and then caught up with Arnold and the others for the trip back to Dupont Circle.

On the way Arnold telephoned Charlotte and then Larry Perez to let them know that everything was all right.

"Tell Helen Chandler that she did a good job," said Larry. "And tell her to let her boss know that he can send any convicted terrorists over to us; we know how to deal with murderers here in Delaware – we have the death penalty."

Arnold was taken aback at the mention of capital punishment, but realised that Larry was joking – or at least half joking.

Back at the office it was all celebration for Dee's safe return. The local TV station achieved their scoop and they watched the abductors being led away on the TV set Arnold had set up. Messages were coming in from all over. Even Sam Schanks in Roanoke had picked up the news item and telephoned in. Arnold had the opportunity to thank him again for his help in Boise.

"Oh, I forgot something," said Arnold. He rummaged in his bag and held up a large packet. "I brought back some huckleberry doughnuts for you, Dee."

Dee suddenly realised that she hadn't eaten much that day and started eating one of the doughnuts voraciously.

"Now this is divine," she said.

That evening it was difficult to wind down from the events of the day. Everybody left except the Earth Office crew, which included Bill and Frank as co-opted members. Helen was going to make enquiries about the third man that had visited Dee's captors, although it was going to be difficult even if they found the suspect, as Dee was not going to be able to make a positive identification.

They discussed Amos and Arnold's trip to Idaho and Dee showed everybody the result of her labours on the Earth Office website. They also discussed Mount Rainier. Dee was unable to do any research that morning, but it was something she intended to look into over the next few days. She also remembered something from her dream, and Amos and Arnold's description of the mountain tallied with what she recalled.

The main item for discussion, however, was the request from Christine Nystrom to help her organisation lobby the UN General Assembly meeting in New York.

"I think we need to meet with her," said Arnold.

They all agreed that her idea sounded intriguing, and something that the Earth Office could be involved in.

CHAPTER 4

The next day Dee put the finishing touches to the Earth Office website. It was important for them to have a window to the world as, despite being based in North America, they all agreed that Earth Office needed a world perspective. After all, there was a lot of the Earth outside of where they were located.

Dee had designed a homepage that set out their manifesto alongside links that would enable anyone to contact them, and Arnold had organised cards to be printed which they could hand out. It was all part of a move to put the office fully onto a professional footing. They were all serious about what they were doing, and realised that even though they may have 'resources' not available to others, they were not bungling amateurs.

Dee arranged a meeting with Christine Nystrom. They were all keen to explore her ideas and saw her connections as a way to internationalise their efforts by engaging with embassies in Washington and UN delegates in New York. Besides, Dee and Arnold had never been to New York and were keen to spend some time there. Christine had heard the report of Dee's kidnapping on the radio and said that she was relieved that she was okay.

They received a lot of mail and telephone calls that morning and the TV news had mentioned the Earth Office, though not Dee, by name. However frightening it was having one of your people abducted, it made for great publicity in any organisation.

In the afternoon Amos, Arnold and Dee went over to Christine's mother's house, from where her organisation, PDP, was run. Christine's father, who had died some years ago, had been a Swedish ambassador to the United States. He had married Christine's mother when he first came to America as a junior officer in the Swedish embassy. Christine's mother's name was Mary and she was from Boston.

The house was located near Embassy Row, not far from Dupont Circle. It was one of the many majestic houses that peppered the area. Christine lived there with her mother and they had converted a couple of rooms into an office. Christine introduced the three to her mother and to Grace Jacklin, the second-in-command at the organisation. It transpired that PDP consisted of only Christine and Grace, hence the staff shortage.

Mary was delighted to meet them and remembered that Dee had found her lost cat. The peripatetic feline also came to meet them, but then wandered off as there was no food to be had. They were directed into a large colonial-style room which was covered in a floral motif, testament to what had been fashionable at least twenty years before. But the rooms – like walking into some time capsule, Arnold thought – had a certain charm. The charm was in the faded glory of the embassy parties which must have reverberated within its walls.

Christine's mother and father were well connected in diplomatic circles, and when she had started her organisation, Christine had been able to mix with and lobby a wide range of diplomats from all over the world. The focus of the organisation, she told them, was to promote strategies in order to mitigate the effects of disasters when they struck.

"What exactly do you mean? Can you give an example?" asked Arnold.

"Yes, I'll give you one where we had some success," said Christine, thumbing through a few papers which she had to hand. "There's a town in India with a hill on one side, which is subject to mud slides. They don't occur often, but when they do they have a devastating effect on the people who live on the hill. Needless to say, only the poorest people in the town live on the hill, because land values are cheapest there. We tried lobbying the local government there to make available some land, which was in a safer place, and to relocate the hill population."

"How successful were you?" asked Amos.

"Well our biggest problem was not the cost of relocation, or even a shortage of land available, but apathy. No one was interested. Wealthier people in the town didn't have a problem. Politicians only responded to what the majority of people wanted – if at all – and the poor had no voice, nobody that would speak up for them. It took a lot of effort on our part, but eventually some land was made available. Even then, only about half of the people relocated. The rest didn't want to move."

Christine looked up at the three sitting on the settee opposite her.

"It's like that in this business. A lot of hard work with a small amount of success gained one painful step at a time."

"What kind of system do you have?" asked Dee.

"Grace can best answer that," Christine replied, turning to Grace.

"We research the different ideas we want to suggest or promote. Some we find ourselves, others come in from people who contact us. We have an irregular newsletter, which we send out all over the world. Each project is typed out on an A4 sheet and copied, and then we use them to lobby and inform people about what we want to achieve. We have dozens of these projects, but there are only two of us – we can only do so much."

Grace picked up a sheaf of papers that were on a table in front of her and handed them out to the three.

"How does the UN fit into all this?" asked Arnold.

"Every year the UN holds a General Assembly in New York. Delegates come from all over the world and it's a great opportunity to lobby important diplomats and civil servants who would otherwise not come to the States. I've managed to register PDP as a non-governmental organisation – NGO for short – and we get passes to go into the UN building and lobby delegates."

"These projects look really interesting," said Dee, leafing through the papers and handing some of them to Amos and Arnold.

"I think," said Arnold nodding to Amos and Dee, "that we would very much like to help you. What you are doing is very worthwhile and fits in with our manifesto perfectly. Our organisation – the Earth Office – is more Earth oriented, if I can put it that way. But at its heart it is about people and how they are affected by the Earth. I'm sure that we can work together."

At that moment Mary came in with a tray.

"Who would like some tea?" she asked.

"My parents were at the London embassy for a few years and my mother became used to the idea of serving tea every day," said Christine.

"Very good idea," said Arnold, helping himself to some biscuits.

"We've some spare space at the office, you can come and set up things there and we can work together to prepare for the UN meeting if you want?" offered Dee.

The next few days were very busy. Christine and Grace found some desk space at Dupont Circle, and brought over the files on their previous lobbying of the UN. Christine arranged passes so that everyone could enter the UN building, and booked them into a small hotel a few blocks away which she and Grace had used on previous occasions.

Bill and Frank were also drafted into the enterprise. The *Post* always covered the annual UN General Assembly in New York, and Bill managed to inveigle himself and Frank onto their team. It meant that they would have press passes and would be there with everybody.

"What about all the events?" asked Bill when they were all discussing the arrangements.

"The best event for lobbying opportunities is the cocktail reception on the first day," said Christine. "Unfortunately, we've never been able to obtain an invitation – they are very restricted."

"Frank and I could probably attend as press, but I don't see how anyone else could obtain an invitation; you need to be very well connected."

"That gives me an idea," said Arnold, and he went off into a quiet corner to use his mobile.

After a few minutes he came back smiling broadly.

"I've managed to get two tickets to the opening cocktail reception at the UN General Assembly."

"How on earth did you manage that?" said Bill.

"I just spoke to our old friend Sam Schanks at Roanoke. When I mentioned the UN Assembly in New York, he told me that he was going to be there."

Arnold's voice then quietened into almost a whisper.

"This is only between us, right? Nothing in the *Post*, Bill."

Bill nodded in assent, and Arnold continued.

"Sam is trying to get his party's nomination for state governor, and he is meeting some of his party's grandees, who will be in New York for the UN Assembly. He'll be at the cocktail reception and he said he could wangle us a couple of invitations."

"That's fantastic," said Bill. "The old fox. But who's going to go, you only have two invitations?"

"No problem," said Amos. "Cocktail receptions are definitely not my scene. I would be only too pleased if Arnold and Dee went and not me. In fact, on the opening evening of the Assembly there is a meeting I would like to go to, given by the South American Native Peoples Alliance. It's one of Christine's project sheets that I'm interested in."

"I'll ring Sam back and tell him the invitations should be in Dee's and my name," said Arnold.

In addition to all the work to prepare for New York, Dee managed to finalise and upload their website. Their lobbying efforts relied upon having a global presence, and they would be handing out website details at the reception. The Earth Office had also had a constant stream of callers coming in person and telephoning, but most of them would have to wait until they returned from New York.

True to his word, a letter arrived from Sam Schanks with two invitations to the UN General Assembly Inaugural Cocktail Reception inside. In ornate gold lettering they 'requested the pleasure of the company of' Arnold and Dee.

§

Finally, the day arrived for their departure. Dee had arranged for them all to go by train.

"It's much easier than air, and we arrive right in the heart of Manhattan, at Penn Station," she said.

"I'll arrange for a minibus to take us to Union Station," offered Arnold. "Including Frank and Bill, there'll be seven of us plus luggage."

"Don't be silly, Arnold," said Dee, "We'll go by subway; Dupont Circle Station is only a minute's walk from here and then it's only five stops to Union Station on the Red Line."

Arnold wasn't used to lugging his rucksack around, but it was a beautiful day in Washington and everyone enjoyed the short walk to the Metro. The subway was particularly deep at Dupont Circle, and the group went down the long escalator to the platform in good spirits. They had been preparing for the trip for some while. Dee, in particular, had never visited New York and she was excited to see how the stories she had heard about the 'Big Apple' matched the reality.

Union Station was a wonderful piece of architecture – one of the great sights of Washington in its own right. They scanned the station as they searched for the Acela Express train platform heading to New York. The journey would take just under three hours and, without interruption from people dropping by or phoning in, they could settle down on the train and work out their strategy for the next few days.

Dee had managed get a special discount at the hotel by booking an extra room to use as a temporary office and place to meet people.

They had some free time before the Assembly started so that they could acclimatise themselves and also do some sightseeing if they wanted. The cocktail reception would start things off and the following day they would follow up with lobbying. Christine had managed to set up some appointments with people that were relevant to the various projects that they thought worthwhile pursuing.

Frank and Bill were in a nearby hotel arranged by the *Post*. Amos and Arnold had to share a room, as did Christine and Grace. Dee insisted on her own room, although nobody doubted that Frank would be there, rather than sharing with Bill.

The journey passed quickly and the train pulled into Penn Station.

"How far is it to the hotel?" bleated Arnold. "Do we need a cab?"

"It's only three stops form here," said Dee. "It's much easier to move around by subway than taxi. In fact, once the General Assembly starts, they close so many streets near the UN building, it's almost impossible to go anywhere by car."

The three stops involved a change of subway line, but they finally pulled into Grand Central Station. The station building was more like the Paris Opera House than a train terminus. Poor Arnold was still not happy dragging along his bag, but up and out of the station they finally made it to their hotel, just a block or two away.

There was something about walking along the streets of Manhattan, thought Dee. It seemed a cliché, but there really was a buzz which seemed to affect them. Even Arnold forgot about his backpack and drank in the atmosphere.

They dumped their bags at their hotel as quickly as possible and were quickly back out walking along the street. Their hotel was near Park Avenue, but they cut through 42nd Street to 5th Avenue. They walked northwards, soaking in the atmosphere, until they reached Central Park.

"I need a new dress for the cocktail party tomorrow," announced Dee.

She grabbed Frank's arm and they peeled off from the group and retraced their steps along 5th Avenue.

"They already act like an old married couple," Bill remarked.

Christine and Grace had been to New York many times and they took Amos, Arnold and Bill into the park. It was the best place to walk on such a lovely, hot New York day. There was something about the sight of water, even the small pond that they sat themselves around, that cooled and relaxed them in the heat.

They all met up later back at the hotel. It was a modest three-star hotel, clean, and usually occupied by business people rather than holidaymakers. For the group's purposes it was ideal, being only a stone's throw from the UN building.

§

The next day they were all free until the evening, except for Bill and Frank who had to report to the *Post*'s team at the UN. Christine and Grace wanted to finalise details for the group's lobby and were happy to enjoy the lull before the storm rather than sightsee. Arnold, Amos and Dee, on the other hand, were eager to take in a few sights.

"We have to do the Statue of Liberty," said Dee, excitedly. "I've always wanted to see it close up."

"We can do Ellis Island, as well," said Arnold.

"And on the way back we can visit Ground Zero at the World Trade Center site," Amos added.

Before they left Christine and Grace, they all went to a breakfast diner around the corner from their hotel.

"You can't be in New York without experiencing the 'New York Deli Breakfast,'" said Christine. "We always come to this diner."

After a huge breakfast, which would probably last them all day, Amos, Arnold and Dee made for the subway station. The three were just beginning to learn how to navigate the train system and, at Christine's suggestion, they bought week passes which enabled them to travel all over the network without having to buy tickets for each individual journey.

From Grand Central Station they took the number five train all the way to the tip of Manhattan, to a station with the unassuming name of Bowling Green. From there it was a short walk to Battery Park, from which they could take the ferry to the Statue of Liberty and Ellis Island. The ferry, conveniently, made a loop journey first to Liberty Island to view the statue, then to Ellis Island and finally back to Battery Park. These two sights, more than any other, summed up New York and New Yorkers more than any picture could. The 'liberty' that the statue embodied was the liberty from tyrannical government, and Ellis Island was the gateway to this freedom for the whole world to enjoy.

There was quite a queue for the ferry terminal; the glorious sunshine had drawn a crowd of people wanting to use the ferry. After extensive security checks they finally made it onto the boat. It wasn't a long trip to Liberty Island. As the craft approached and the statue loomed large in their field of view, they could appreciate the power and majesty of the structure.

"We can disembark, climb up the statue, and then catch the next boat on to Ellis Island," said Dee, scuttling toward the gangplank, which had just hit the ground.

"Is there a lift?" asked Arnold, hopefully.

"Don't be silly, Arnold," said Dee. "You have to climb the statue to get the full experience."

There were a lot of steps to reach the summit of the statue and Arnold could only make it to the pedestal.

"When we return to Washington, Arnold, you're going to join a gym and get fit," said Dee.

Arnold was not in a position to talk, let alone argue, as he was busy trying to catch his breath.

At the top of the statue, Amos and Dee could survey the whole of the New York skyline. There was something about looking down on the city that put things into a little more perspective for the two of them. Everything appeared so permanent when they saw it from the ground, but from above, it was the fragility of life which impinged on their senses. For a brief moment, standing there, they encompassed the whole city within their consciousness: the people; their lives; the structures; everything, in one thought.

For Amos, in particular, it brought home the magnitude of the mission the Earth Office had undertaken and his sense of purpose. There was a glimmer of fear, but only for a fleeting moment, before the calm of the city's consciousness overcame him.

Dee and Amos caught up with Arnold on the way down, whose breathing had returned to normal.

"You're quite right, Dee," Arnold said. "I definitely need more exercise. I will join your gym."

"We'll see," said Dee, in a matron-like tone.

They jumped aboard the next ferry and continued on the second leg of their journey to Ellis Island. The crowds had thinned out a little and they could sit down on the boat while it navigated towards the island. The view, as they approached, was quite different from their approach to Liberty Island. The main building was only a few stories high and there was a dome-topped tower at each of its four corners. In front of the building was a tall flagpole flying the stars and stripes.

They alighted on to the jetty and went inside what had become the Ellis Island Museum. Arnold began felt quite emotional standing in the great hall.

"I've no idea who or where they are, but I remember my father saying that some of his family had come to America. They would have come through here."

The three wandered round the exhibition. The hallowed silence of the Great Hall could not have been more of a contrast to the images and testimonies on display of the masses of people who had taken this path in the past. It focused their minds on the human side of the struggle for everyday life. Things that they now took for granted could not be taken for granted either in the past or at present in other parts of the world; simple things like food, water and shelter.

The three spent more time than they realised looking at the different parts of the exhibition. Here would be the testimony of a child, there an image of a sad but hopeful immigrant; a million stories pervading the walls of the building with their individual tears. On the way back to Battery Park the three sat quietly on the ferry.

The day was still bright and sunny. They decided to walk through Battery Park and up Wall Street to the Ground Zero site. Walking up Wall Street was quite fun, especially for Dee. Outside the Stock Exchange, she persuaded a passer-by to take a picture of the three of them next to the Charging Bull statue.

"You have to admire people who know when not to take themselves too seriously," she said as she put her arms around the neck of the statue.

"If the Statue of Liberty and Ellis Island represent life and hope, then the Ground Zero memorial represents death," said Amos, as they reached the site of the World Trade Center. "But it's not as simple as that, because the memorial also represents life and hope."

"To know New York is to know humanity," mused Dee. "We had to come here to see these sights, not just to understand the people of New York City, but to understand what life is all about, and life's relationship with the Earth."

"It underlies everything we're trying to do," said Arnold. "Where shall we go now?"

"Lunch, I'm starving," said Dee.

"I'm usually the one that says that," Arnold protested.

They stopped at a nearby deli.

"Life is also about food," said Dee, as she ploughed her way through a triple-decker sandwich.

"I have to say that as good as those huckleberry doughnuts were, they have a serious rival in this strawberry cheesecake," said Arnold, through forkfuls.

Amos ate his Waldorf salad in quiet amusement as he watched Arnold and Dee trying to out-eat each other.

After lunch they took the subway back to their hotel, boarding a number six train to take them via Grand Central Station.

"Did you ever see the film *The Taking of Pelham 123*?" asked Amos. "There were two films made."

"Brilliant film. I saw the version with Denzel Washington and John Travolta. Wait. It's not this train, is it, that was hijacked?" said Dee.

"Well, the train that was captured by terrorists was the number six line, but going south out of Grand Central, rather than north."

"I've had my fill of terrorists," said Arnold.

The rest of the group was at the hotel when Amos, Arnold and Dee arrived back. The hotel lobby was full of people checking in. Being so close to the UN, the hotel was always popular during the General Assembly.

Arnold and Dee went to their rooms in order to change their clothes for the evening's cocktail reception. Amos went to the bar, where Bill and Frank were talking with a couple of journalists. Bill introduced Amos to them; they were both covering the UN Assembly for different news organisations. They discussed the different delegations and the political undercurrents to the whole proceedings.

Amos was not interested in that kind of global politics. He was much more interested in one of Christine's projects that concerned indigenous people living in shanty towns in South America, particularly the *pueblos jóvenes* of Peru's capital, Lima. As with most places along the Pacific coast of both North and South America, there was always the threat of earthquakes. What prompted his interest in Lima was an article on preparing for an earthquake that Christine had culled from a magazine. Instead of giving the standard advice of standing in a doorway, or some other area of strength in the building's structure, the article claimed that the best strategy was to keep a pair of shoes handy by the front door. The reasoning being that the majority of buildings in shanty towns are so badly built that if an earthquake were to hit, the only way to avoid being buried alive was to run outside as fast possible. Wearing shoes would, the article proclaimed, prevent cuts from broken glass that would litter the streets. The group that he had arranged to meet that evening were trying to remedy the situation by lobbying for better building codes and proper enforcement across the board; lethargy and corruption seemed to be the main stumbling blocks to such progress.

Amos also felt a rapport with the South American Native Peoples Alliance. Being Native American himself – north or south, it didn't make much difference to him – Amos had a natural affinity with groups that supported indigenous peoples, who tended to be the poorest in any country.

The Alliance was meeting in a small restaurant that evening and, as an 'interested party,' Amos had been invited to join them when he had earlier telephoned his interest. He had spoken to the secretary of the organisation, Debora Majin, and had explained about the Earth Office, as well as his interest in Christine's Lima project. Debora knew about the problems of earthquake preparation in Peru, as she was from that country and had experienced earthquakes first-hand. The Alliance needed all the help it could muster; there were so many issues to raise among UN delegates and they just did not have enough people to do the job.

Before he left for his meeting, Amos checked in to the temporary office Dee had created out of the spare room. The whole group were there discussing tactics. Most of the countries that Christine's projects targeted were in Africa or Asia, but the earthquake project in Peru was also on the focus list. Any delegates from any of these countries would be approached. The important thing, Christine stressed, was to make contact, either with someone who could help or someone who could put them in touch with someone who could help.

"Following up contacts is just as important as making them in the first place," she said. "The idea is that if we can set up a dialogue with an individual, then over time we can hopefully make some headway on a particular problem we have identified."

"It's a long-haul job," said Arnold.

"A lot of schmoozing," added Amos.

"There is, of course, an element of social chitchat," said Grace. "But look at it from their point of view. Delegates and senior civil servants have important jobs in their countries. The problems that they have to face are mountainous and immediate. Some are corrupt and don't give a damn about anyone, except for themselves, but many are just trying to make the best of a bad job. We come along and try to prod them into doing something that will help their people, but in the future. However sensible and important our projects may be in the long term, there are often people dying in their countries right now. If these countries are using all available means to stop or reduce immediate problems, how many resources are available to mitigate future problems? Our job is to try to influence hearts and minds to change priorities in countries which are, at best, in a desperate situation and, at worst, chaotic."

"It's not a rosy picture you paint, Grace," murmured Dee.

"It's not all bad," said Christine. "We do sometimes make headway. Often the resources necessary to alleviate a problem are minimal and all we need is to create the will to do something; a change in law or something like that."

"Well, I'm off to my meeting for the evening," Amos said, turning to leave. "I'll let you know what progress I make."

"The rest of us need to make final preparations for tonight. We'll meet in the hotel foyer at six. What about transport to the UN, Dee?" asked Arnold.

"We're only a few blocks from the UN building! A taxi wouldn't even make it through the roadblocks. We'll walk."

"Frank and I will see you at the reception," said Bill. "We have to go earlier and meet up with the rest of the *Post*'s team."

§

It was a fifteen-minute walk for Amos to the restaurant. It was a beautiful summer evening and Amos enjoyed taking in the sights and sounds of the metropolis. The restaurant was down a side street in a fashionable part of town on the Upper East Side. He had looked it up on the internet, and found it to be a Peruvian restaurant, pricey, but the food was reportedly good. It had good music and the general consensus from reviewers was that it had a lively atmosphere – he would decide for himself.

It was, in fact, located in a semi-basement. A red awning proclaimed its presence and Amos had to negotiate a dozen steps down to the entrance. It was dark inside and Amos' eyes took a few moments adjust to the light level. There weren't many people in the restaurant, so Amos went over to the bar where a few people were milling about.

One of them approached Amos.

"Amos, is it you?"

The speaker was tall, dark-haired, and had her hair tightly tied back.

"Yes," said Amos.

"I'm Debora Majin. Thank you for coming."

She led him over to the other people she was with and introduced Amos to the group. He forgot each of their names almost as soon as they were introduced; he wasn't good at socialising.

"Would you like a drink?"

Debora offered him a Pisco Sour, informing him that it was Peru's national drink.

The group was quite varied. Some of them were clearly political, some not, but all showed a commitment to the welfare of native peoples in South America.

"I've asked a friend from the Peruvian Consulate to join us," said Debora. "He might be able to help you with the earthquake project you were telling me about on the telephone."

The restaurant manager came over and greeted Debora.

"I have a table for your party, my dear," he said. "Special price – ten dollars a head."

She thanked him and they all crowded around a large table in the corner of the restaurant, next to the toilets. It might not have been the best table in the restaurant, but at ten dollars a head nobody was complaining.

The group was interested in Amos' background. Many of them had never met a Native North American and none had heard of the Naskapi Indians. Dreams were important to many native cultures in South America, Amos learnt, and they would usually involve a Shaman or Medicine Man, who would induce a dream state by imbibing a narcotic brew.

"In my tradition," said Amos, "dreams are not induced in that way. Everybody has dreams, but for some there are special shared dreams which show future events."

The food had just started to be served when a man joined the group.

"Amos, let me introduce you to Guillermo Olivares from the Peruvian Consulate," said Debora.

"Please call me Gill. Debora has told me about you."

"Nice to meet you," said Amos.

Gill sat down next to Amos. He was short and thickset with a well-kept moustache. He had an affable nature and spoke freely, but whenever the conversation steered towards the political, he was able to deflect it to a less provocative path. He was a consummate politician, but then, as a diplomat, he needed to be.

Amos talked about earthquakes and how the poorer sections of society always bore the brunt of disasters. Gill was sympathetic, but it was difficult in the restaurant with the food, wine and conversation flowing in all directions, to have a detailed discussion.

After a while Gill stood up and apologised to everyone that he had to leave for another appointment.

"We didn't have a chance to talk properly," he said to Amos, giving him a card. "Why don't you come over to the consulate and we can have a proper discussion? Just telephone first to make sure I'm there."

After Gill left, Debora sat next to Amos.

"Gill is an important rising star in the Consulate. He will be ambassador one day, of that I'm sure" she said.

§

After dressing for the cocktail reception, Arnold waited for Dee in the hotel bar. It was busy and the bar staff were scurrying round serving cocktails and passing round crisps and nuts. Arnold had worn a suit and tie every day he worked as a lawyer, but his present garb felt uncomfortable. He didn't have to wear a tuxedo, which was a relief, but the dress code was jacket and tie. It could have been his shoes causing the problem; they were brand new and not as yet worn-in. He ordered a gin and tonic and sat down on a bar stool at the counter, playing with some peanuts in a bowl in front of him.

"Arnold, my old friend!" boomed a voice out of the crowd.

Arnold was taken by surprise as Sam Schanks strolled up to greet him.

"Hello Sam, how are you?"

"Great," said Sam. "I thought I'd walk with you to the cocktail party. Your office told me where you were."

"Drink?" said Arnold.

"I'll just have some tonic water in a cocktail glass with a cherry, please."

Sam laughed and tapped his nose.

"I never drink alcohol when I'm working, but anyone seeing my drink will think it's a gin and tonic."

Arnold wondered how many fake gin and tonics were being drunk in the bar.

"You did great in Boise," said Sam. "My pal in the Veterans Association in DC couldn't praise you and Amos enough. He said you really sorted out a nasty problem, which would have caused great damage to the Boise office if it had gone on any longer."

"Thanks," said Arnold. "And how are you progressing on the political front?"

"It's why I'm here," replied Sam. "But keep your voice down."

Sam looked around at the people near him, who appeared not to have noticed anything and said in a quiet voice, "Walls have ears."

Grace and Christine came in to the bar and swept through the throng to where Arnold and Sam were standing. Arnold did the introductions.

"So you two lovely ladies are helping Amos, Arnold and Dee?" said Sam. "I'm sorry I couldn't obtain invitations for all of you tonight. By the way, Arnold, where is Amos?"

"He's meeting with a group from South America. It's one of his projects, to help indigenous peoples."

At that moment Dee entered the room and came over to the group.

"Wow! You look fantastic," said Sam.

"Thank you, and thanks for the invitations for tonight," replied Dee.

"Now are you both ready?" asked Christine. "Arnold, you know what you have to do?"

"Absolutely..." said Arnold. "What do I have to do again? Only joking. Engage with as many people as possible, give out cards and try to follow up on good contacts."

"But most of all?" queried Grace.

"We write up everything afterwards," Dee told her. "That way everything is properly on file and we can maximise the effectiveness of the lobby."

"You all seem well organised," said Sam. "May I add one more thing? Enjoy yourselves! It's exciting. If you've never been to a UN General Assembly before it's a wonderful experience."

"Okay, we all have our UN passes, Arnold and Dee have their invitations – let's go," said Christine.

"And don't forget, if you need us, Christine and I will be in the basement in the Vienna Café," Grace added.

The group trooped out of the hotel. It was only a few blocks to the UN building but the streets were crowded and at the UN there was a queue at the entrance closest to 46th street, at the north end of the building. They were able to use the 'NGO' door, instead of the public entrance, but it was still a hassle to enter the building. After the security checks they found themselves in the main public lobby.

"I have to meet some people," said Sam. "I'll see you at the reception." He strode off.

"It's a bit daunting, at first," said Grace. "The General Assembly Hall is above us on the second, third and fourth floors. Below us there are five conference rooms and the Vienna Café. The ground floor is a public area with shops, a cafeteria, and other facilities. At the south end, towards 42nd Street, is the Dag Hammarskjold library. The cocktail reception is being held there in the library auditorium. In the library basement is the NGO Resource Centre, which you can use. There are lots of other parts, but it will only confuse you if I list them all."

"It's a lot to take in," said Arnold. "Let's have a wander round, we have plenty of time."

In spite of the throng of people, there was a calm atmosphere created by a clever combination of architecture and soft lighting. They wandered round the main lobby, taking in the Chagall stained glass window, and ended up in the bookshop. The crowds started to thin out and they made their way over to the library. A sign pointed the way to the cocktail reception. There was more security there, and they had to wait to show their invitations and 'brown passes' to the doorman. At last, drinks in hand, they were in.

Having never been to a function of this sort, they did not know what to expect. Maybe it was because it was still early, but there were hardly any people in the room.

"Give it time," said Arnold. "Let's just enjoy the drinks and canapés."

The room did start to fill up. A black woman in a blazingly yellow and red dress came up to where they were standing. She introduced herself as a delegate from Nigeria – they didn't catch her name. She was interested in nursery school education and proceeded to explain in detail the problems they had in Nigeria persuading mothers in rural areas to send their children to government nursery schools. Arnold managed to extricate himself and left Dee with the woman.

Arnold approached two men who were talking in the middle of the room. They were both from a medical charity. Arnold introduced himself and gave them a couple of cards. It turned out that the men worked in central Africa.

"I'm interested in Mozambique," said Arnold – it was one of the projects on Christine's list. "Is there anyone here I should speak to?"

The men looked around the room and pointed out a couple of people on the other side.

"I think they're from Mozambique. Try them," they suggested.

Arnold walked over to the couple the men had indicated. Both wore red badges, which signified the representation of their country, though not of ambassador rank. Arnold introduced himself and handed out his card. The man and woman were indeed from Mozambique; the woman was an attaché at the embassy in DC, and the man was a civil servant from the interior ministry.

Arnold started to explain why he was interested in their country.

"The population face a huge risk from flooding, which particularly affects the poor."

"The whole country is poor," said the woman. "I wish the government had more funds available to improve disaster preparation strategies."

"We have tried hard," said the man. "We have managed, with help from the US, to instigate an early warning flood risk system. This measure saves lives."

"What my organisation is pushing for is a change of mindset," said Arnold. "People should be encouraged to move to higher ground."

"If only it were that simple," said the woman.

Arnold continued to debate with them for a while. They weren't averse to some of his ideas, but it became clear that overcoming apathy amongst their compatriots was the main obstacle to progress. The woman gave Arnold her card and agreed to talk further if he wanted to see her in DC.

He looked around the room for Dee and spotted her talking to a Chinese woman. By the time he walked across to Dee, the woman had left.

"Any luck?" said Arnold.

"Yes, the woman I was just talking to was from the Chinese embassy in DC. She was interested in our work. I talked to her about storm and flood problems in China. She was quite knowledgeable and welcomed ideas."

"The impression I have is that everyone is well-meaning but ineffectual," said Arnold.

"We just have to keep on trying," urged Dee.

Arnold went off in the direction of a Latin American group and Dee ambled over to the bar.

When she reached the bar she looked across to a man standing a few feet from her and her entire body froze.

She couldn't say for absolutely certainty, but she was a little more than ninety-nine per cent sure it was him. It was his height and the way he was standing. She composed herself and walked over to stand just behind him; he didn't see her approach.

"Have we met somewhere before?" she asked him.

He swung round and she caught a moment – just a fleeting moment – of surprise in his face.

"I don't think so," he said in an even tone.

"I'm Dee Patel from the Earth Office. And you are?"

"Mustafa Al-Falah, I'm an attaché at the Syrian embassy in Washington."

The tone of his voice – even though he was speaking English – was unmistakeable to Dee. He was the third man, the one who had visited her abductors while she was being held hostage.

"I'm sorry, I must have been mistaken," she said, and turning her back on him, she walked away.

She sped out of the room into a quiet corridor. She had Helen Chandler's number on her mobile and she punched in the name.

Luckily, Helen answered straight away.

"Helen, it's me, Dee. I've just met the third man."

She explained to Helen the circumstances and her certainty about the man's identity, but as Helen explained, Dee had never actually seen the face of the man who had visited her abductors.

"Leave it to me," said Helen. "I'll check out this Mustafa Al-Falah and come back to you."

Dee scanned the cocktail party on her return, but Al-Falah was nowhere to be seen. Frank caught sight of Dee and walked over to her.

"I've just taken a photo of the Secretary General for tomorrow's *Post*," he said, beaming.

Dee didn't say anything.

"Are you all right?" he said.

"I've just seen the man who visited my abductors," Dee said, without emotion.

"Who? Where is he?" Frank asked, franticly signalling to Bill and Arnold to come over.

"He's already left the room," replied Dee. "His name is Mustafa Al-Falah."

At that moment Sam Schanks appeared.

"Now don't make a fuss," said Dee. "I'm fine, I've already spoken to Helen Chandler and she's on the case."

"She'll get that son of a bitch," said Sam, when he was told what had happened.

He suddenly grabbed Dee's arm and led her, with Arnold following, to a group surrounding a tall man in a suit.

"Let me introduce you to the UN Secretary General," he said, and, in typical 'Sam Schanks' style, bellowed across the group, "Mr Secretary General, may I present Dee Patel and Arnold from the Earth Office."

Arnold and Dee shook hands with the Secretary General while Frank took photos and Sam extolled the accomplishments of the Earth Office in suitably embellished terms.

The Secretary General was polite – he had never heard of the Earth Office – and after a brief exchange of pleasantries moved on.

Arnold and Dee continued to 'work the room.' They were

becoming more adept at the skill as the evening wore on. There was a continual flow of people joining and leaving the party, but Dee didn't see Al-Falah again and none of them found anyone from the Syrian mission.

When the reception ended – after a short speech from the Secretary General – the group met up with Christine and Grace in the Vienna Café. The café was packed, and they found Christine and Grace ensconced at a corner table. Many people in the room were smoking and there were ashtrays on all the tables.

"I thought smoking in public places in the US was illegal," said Arnold.

"It is, but we're not in the US, we're in the UN building," grinned Bill.

Christine and Grace were delighted with the number of contacts they had made at the cocktail party. Frank showed everyone the photograph of Arnold and Dee meeting the Secretary General. Needless to say, Sam's smiling face was also in the picture.

"You'll have to put that picture up on your office wall," said Christine.

Arnold's mobile rang: it was Amos.

§

Amos hadn't been keeping count of how many Pisco Sours he imbibed but by now it was quite a few. Debora had left the restaurant and others had joined his table. There were half a dozen people there, mostly from the Alliance, but two, a man and a woman, were only loosely connected to the rest.

They were both Columbian and were trying to persuade Amos and the others to join their anti-US movement. Amos should have realised the intentions of these two, but his guard was down after so many Pisco Sours his guard was down. He also made the mistake of trying to debate with them.

"I'm not interested in politics," he told them.

The two were part of a revolutionary group that had terrorised a large area of Columbia and Ecuador, before being routed by government forces.

Amos tried to stand up to leave the restaurant, but his legs were leaden from the effects of alcohol, and he had to hold on to the table in order to stop himself falling over.

It was at that point that the FBI raided the restaurant.

The two politicos tried to escape, but were quickly arrested, along with Amos and the rest of the table. His protestations were ignored and his inebriated state only made matters worse. Soon he found himself unceremoniously carted off to FBI headquarters in Downtown Manhattan.

Amos was put in a holding cell with a bunk. He wasn't particularly bothered and was content to lie down and sleep off the effects of the alcohol. The truth was that this was not the first time he had been in this position.

After a while he was woken up and led in to an interview room. He had sobered up and was fascinated to see how things worked from the other side of the law, as it were. The officer introduced himself.

"I'm Special Agent Steven Trainor. Why were you consorting with terrorists?"

He looked the officer straight in the eye.

"If you ask me 'When did you start beating your wife?'-type leading questions, I'm going to become annoyed," he said. "I'm happy to tell you what I was doing in the restaurant and any other information that I can give you. I can also give you the names of important people who will vouch for me. If you're after the two scumbags that sat down at my table, then I'm pleased you arrested them – but it's nothing to do with me."

He sat back in his chair and folded his arms.

"Okay, I'm sorry, let's start again," said the agent.

Amos gave a full account, answering questions for more than half an hour. After the questioning had finished the agent left the room, saying, "I just have to make a few telephone calls."

He came back into the room quite animated. "I just spoke with Special Agent Helen Chandler in Washington, DC. I didn't realise you had such powerful friends. Please accept our apologies."

"That's all right," said Amos. "I was a bit stupid not leaving the restaurant as soon as that couple sat down at my table. May I make a telephone call?"

§

"You're where?!" said Arnold.

He cupped his hand over the mobile and whispered to the group, "Amos has been arrested."

When Arnold arrived at FBI headquarters, Amos was sitting in the public lobby waiting for him. They took a cab back to the hotel. Amos looked terrible.

"I'm sorry Arnold, I've been really stupid," he said as they sat down in the back of the taxi.

"Nobody's perfect. What happened?" asked Arnold.

Amos told him about his meeting in the restaurant. It had all been going well, but he had evidently drunk more than he should and didn't spot the danger when the two miscreants joined his table.

"You weren't to know they were wanted by the FBI," said Arnold.

"I don't know if I'm cut out for our mission. I let you and Dee down," said Amos.

"Listen Amos, even the prophet Moses had his faults. Why do you think there are three of us? Why not two, or one? It's because we're there for each other. On Lake Pend Oreille, when that madman Harlan Tyler was shooting at us, I thought we were going to die. But you stood up and faced him and you saved the lives of the sheriff and me. You were there for me. Dee and I need you Amos – warts and all."

Amos smiled.

"Thanks Arnold. It's the dream; sometimes I'm scared."

"We all are," said Arnold.

§

The next morning they were all up bright and early for the start of the General Assembly; all except Amos who, after his rigours the evening before, had a lie-in and said that he would join them later.

They assembled in the Vienna Café. Arnold explained to the company what had happened to Amos the previous evening.

"It was a combination of bad luck and too much to drink; we all need to be more careful," he warned them.

They all went up to view the start of the Assembly. On the way, Arnold spoke to Dee.

"Are you okay?" he said. "Seeing Al-Falah, I mean."

"I'm all right now Arnold. At first…"

Her voice trailed off, but then she regained her composure.

"I wasn't so much scared as angry. The idea that that man could look me in the eye after what he had been involved in – and probably initiated. I was so angry. If I could have made the ground swallow him up, I would have done."

"Perhaps you could have, but you didn't," said Arnold.

Dee smiled.

"No, I was restrained."

They all took their seats overlooking the huge Assembly Hall. It was difficult not to be impressed by the scale of the auditorium. Just short of two hundred countries were represented, each with a block of six seats, arrayed in a circular arc facing a rostrum. One country, chosen by ballot, occupied pole position in the front row and the rest followed on in strict alphabetical order, two countries to each table. Like schoolchildren in a new class, the straightjacket of alphabetic order created some strange effects. Iran and Iraq shared a desk, with Israel only separated from Iraq by Ireland and located directly in front of Lebanon. Eritrea and Ethiopia at loggerheads for decades were separated by Estonia. The class was also quite unruly. People drifted in and out all the time and many were chatting to each other, even when the main speakers were talking. Most wore headphones listening to simultaneous translations that were available in six official languages.

So this was it, the political heart of the world – or was it the head? Or the stomach? Arnold couldn't help but wonder. Were they listening to the wind belched up by a bilious cadre of mostly tin pot tyrants, or was there really hope for the peoples of a planet coming together? Perhaps a bit of both. Either way, this was the only forum of its kind, whether they liked it or not.

The session started off with an address by the Secretary General, Ban Ki-moon. It was very headmasterly, instructing everyone to be good, to obey the rules, and pointing out one or two naughty children who must try harder. The proceedings then consisted of various leaders, starting with the US president, addressing the throng. Half way through the morning, Amos joined the group watching. The meeting then broke up for lunch and they all made a dash for the Vienna Café.

"I feel as though I've been in there for twenty-four hours, rather than four," said Arnold.

"It does sometimes seem just like a talking shop," said Grace. "But it's also what goes on behind the scenes that counts."

"It's also a light which shines on countries that would otherwise not be able to give an account of themselves to a watching world," added Christine.

Dee's mobile rang. She went to a quiet corner outside the cafeteria and took the call. It was from Helen Chandler.

"I followed up on what you told me about Al-Falah," she began. "I spoke to the team that deals with foreign embassies. On the day that you were abducted, there were half a dozen Syrian embassy officials that were unaccounted for. The team couldn't follow them all, but Al-Falah was definitely one of them, so he could have met your abductors. They told me – and this is in the strictest confidence – that they would step up their surveillance and target Al-Falah for a while to see what he does. They also told me something notable: Al-Falah was down as one of the delegates to the UN General Assembly – where you saw him. But, his name was removed last night and another name substituted – he's gone back to DC."

"That would explain why he wasn't with his delegation in the Assembly Hall this morning," said Dee.

"I'll keep you posted with further developments. By the way, I'm glad I was able to sort out Amos' difficulties last night. Poor Amos was in the wrong place at the wrong time."

When Dee returned to the cafeteria she told them all what Helen had said, although she didn't refer to the targeted surveillance of Al-Falah.

"We need to follow up on the contacts we have all made," said Christine. "I suggest Grace acts as anchor, here at the UN, and the rest of us split into two groups of two. What does everyone think?"

"I'd like to follow up with my contact at the Peruvian consulate," said Amos.

"I'll go with Amos," said Dee.

"I'm happy to go with Christine," said Arnold. "We've several contacts we can follow up."

§

Amos telephoned Gill Olivares and made an appointment to see him with Dee that afternoon. The Peruvian consulate was only a few blocks away from the UN building, down 49th Street in a quiet terrace of brick buildings, identified by a Peruvian flag jutting out from the first floor at an angle.

Amos and Dee climbed the small staircase to the front door, which was opened by Gill after they rang the bell.

"I'm here on my own today, all the staff are at the UN meeting," he said by way of greeting.

Amos introduced Dee and they were shepherded into a cramped office, dominated by a row of filing cabinets along one wall. Gill seemed flustered but was otherwise polite. There was some small talk, but Amos steered the conversation quickly round to the reason for their visit.

Amos launched into an impassioned monologue about the reasons why the poor suffer most when disaster hits a country. He concentrated on the earthquake risk for Lima and articulated a litany of problems which needed to be dealt with. It was a well-argued speech, but when he finished both he and Dee were surprised by Gill's response or lack of response: he just sat there in silence.

After a few moments he held up his hands in a gesture of resignation.

"I have heard what you said and in truth I must admit that everything you have said is perfectly true. But..."

He paused, as if searching for the right words.

"I don't mean to be rude, but it's like you are trying to sell double-glazing to someone whose house is on fire. We are going through some problems at the moment in my country. Economic problems – that goes without saying – but we are also in political turmoil, mostly because of rampant corruption. I don't know if the government will survive, even until the end of the week. And if the government falls, our diplomatic staff here, including me, may be recalled or even out of a job."

"I'm sorry," said Dee. "We had no idea. But you know that whatever problems there are in a country – even grave political problems – diplomacy carries on. And, however hard the fight, corruption has to be confronted and defeated."

"Of course, you're right," agreed Gill. "I do apologise. Sometimes the veneer of diplomacy wears away. I would like to help you but I don't know how. I would love to show you the problems we have in our country first hand. I wish you could come to Peru and see for yourself."

"Why not?" said Dee.

"Exactly," said Amos.

"You would come, really come?" said Gill. "I've some holiday time owing to me, and even for short breaks I am allowed to fly back home to visit my family. Could you come with me at the end of the UN meeting in two days' time?"

"I don't see why not," said Amos. "We'll have to check first with our colleagues, but I don't see them having any problem with the idea."

§

Christine and Arnold went back to the hotel office. They spent an hour telephoning all their contacts trying to set up appointments. It was a frustrating task. Most of their time was spent speaking to press attachés and assistants whose job was to palm them off with 'the minister is very busy, please phone again for an appointment' or worse with 'the minister's remit doesn't cover disaster preparedness, please refer to another ministry.' An hour of obfuscation and being passed from pillar to post was almost more than anyone could take.

"We have only had one success," said Christine. "I worked with the UNISDR – the UN International Strategy for Disaster Reduction – in the past. They run conferences, meetings and other events including an International Day for Disaster Reduction in October each year. One of their senior people has agreed to an informal meeting with us. She'll be in the Vienna Café later this afternoon. They are useful people to talk to; she'll give us a heads up on what's going on."

"I haven't had much success," Arnold said, despondently. "This can be a bit of a thankless task."

"We just have to keep on trying, Arnold," said Christine, trying to cheer him up.

After a little while Amos and Dee arrived back at the hotel office.

"Gill wants us to go to Peru with him, to see for ourselves some of the problems they have," said Amos.

"That's brilliant," exclaimed Christine. "Arnold and I are seeing someone from the UN Disaster Reduction Office later this afternoon in the Vienna Café. You two should come too."

Bill and Frank wandered in.

"We've all the stories and pictures we need," said Bill. "The rest of the afternoon session is just one interminable speech after another; we need a break."

Dee told them about the proposed trip to Peru. Frank was concerned about Dee's safety.

"Peru can be a dangerous place," said Frank.

"Don't worry Frank," smiled Dee, clasping his arm in hers and giving him a peck on the cheek. "Amos will be there and I can look after myself. Besides, I'll only be away for a couple of days."

"I'm still worried," he murmured.

"I handled my abductors quite easily, I'm sure I can handle anything. There are lots of church bells in Peru."

Frank smiled.

"I'll see you later," he said, as he and Bill went back into the Assembly Hall.

"It is very important to actually witness what is going on in the world," said Christine. "Here, with the best will, we can only theorise and talk to people in comfortable rooms. We don't engage directly with people who are suffering or see for ourselves how people are forced to live by circumstances. It's important to go and see and feel."

The group strode into the Vienna Café looking for the person they had arranged to meet. They saw Grace, who had just finished watching the meeting, sitting with a coffee.

"Did we miss anything?" asked Arnold.

"Only huge amounts of hot air, delivered ponderously by a raft of heads of state who love the sound of their own voices."

"I'm sorry that you had to sit and listen to all that, Grace" said Christine.

"There were a few high points," smiled Grace. "One of the speakers tripped and nearly fell over as he approached the podium and Ahmadinejad of Iran spoke for such a long time that we could all go out and have a coffee break without missing anything."

Christine spotted Margareta Pansieri and waved to her to come over to their table.

"She's a director of the secretariat of the ISDR based in Geneva." Christine whispered, before turning to greet her. "Hello Margareta, may I present Arnold, Amos and Dee of the Earth Office, the organisation working with us. Grace you already know."

They all greeted Margareta, who sat down at the table, placing a pile of papers in front of her.

"It is always so hectic for me at these General Assemblies," she said. "So many people to see and so little time."

Christine explained to Margareta how her organisation and the Earth Office were working together during the UN Assembly.

"We need all the help we can muster," said Margareta. "It is difficult at the moment, particularly in Africa; my area of focus. If anything, the situation has actually deteriorated since last year. In many countries corruption has become entrenched, and widespread indolence and incompetence of local and national governments mean that natural disasters, when they do occur, have a devastating effect on the population. Sometimes, I could just weep."

"Amos and I are going to Lima, Peru in a couple of days to see for ourselves," said Dee.

"In addition to all its problems, Peru is also in a period of political uncertainty at the moment. However bad the government may be, if it falls there will be even more chaos," warned Margareta.

She picked up her papers.

"Unfortunately I have another meeting to attend to, sorry I could not be of more help and good luck in Lima – I remember it as a city of contrasts."

"She seemed quite sad," said Arnold, after Margareta had left.

"You see that sometimes in diplomats or officials," Christine told him. "It's a malaise that goes with the job. They become so frustrated by the fact that they can achieve so little that they just become depressed and give up. Poor Margareta needs to change her job otherwise she will become ill."

"This won't happen to us," said Dee. "We've all got each other to keep us going."

The next day Arnold and Christine had more luck. They managed to catch up with some of the early contacts that they had made and were able to discuss, promote and cajole their targets. Arnold was not fully convinced that this represented a real achievement, but he was happy to go along with things.

Amos and Dee were more concerned with the arrangements for their trip. Gill was good to his word and arranged the necessary visas and paperwork. Their flight to Lima was direct from New York, but the eight hour length of the flight surprised Dee – she hadn't realised just how far Peru was from New York. The flight did not leave until early in the afternoon, so they would arrive late in the evening, but Gill told them that his brother would pick them all up from the airport and insisted that they stay with his family during their visit.

"Peru is a safe place, but you do have to be sensible," he said. "Particularly in light of the political situation at the moment, you are much safer staying with my family."

Amos and Dee asked Arnold if he wanted to join them on the trip; he was happy to decline.

"I need a few days rest to recover from all this diplomacy," he joked. "Seriously, I would like to do some research on Mount Rainier. I'm quite content to man the office for a few days."

The last day of the General Assembly saw an increase in the group's activities. Arnold and Christine, with Grace in tow, were in the swing of meetings, both formal and informal. Some of the delegations were hosting parties and they had to attend a number of these events one after the other. Arnold had had a brief conversation with Sam Schanks, who was scurrying around the diplomatic and political carousel; he was eagerly waiting and hoping for the official announcement of his party's adoption of him as candidate for governor.

They all said their goodbyes at breakfast in the Vienna Café. Frank was still not comfortable about Dee travelling to Peru but reluctantly accepted the situation.

§

Amos and Dee were picked up from their hotel on the way to Newark, New Jersey Airport courtesy of the Peruvian embassy. Gill was already in the car.

"It shouldn't take more than about forty minutes to the airport," he said.

Gill seemed much more at ease than the last time they had met him.

"I feel much better today, I am always more relaxed when I am on holiday. A diplomat's job can be stressful, but thankfully the political situation in my country has settled down a little; it does tend to change from week to week."

"It must be difficult coping with that kind of pressure," said Amos.

"You have no idea," Gill shook his head wistfully.

The car exited a tunnel from Manhattan into New Jersey and passed into an industrial landscape. Dee wondered what it would be like in Lima.

On the flight, both Dee and Amos managed to sleep for a few hours, but Gill stayed wide awake, unable to sleep in any mode of transport. It was dark as they came into land, and was close to midnight before they had managed to navigate through customs and immigration.

The terminal could have been anywhere in the world; it looked fairly new but consisted of the usual glass and concrete monument to air travel. Gill scanned the mass of people waiting at the Arrivals gate for his brother. The crowd was a mixture of limousine drivers in smart uniforms holding up placards, taxi touts, and assorted friends and relatives of incoming travellers. Some passengers were met by whole families, including small children, and must have been waiting for some time. It was an emotionally charged atmosphere, and Gill embraced his brother, Luis, as soon as they caught sight of each other.

Gill introduced Luis, who was much taller than Gill but sported a similar moustache. The ride to the family home was only about twenty minutes, and consisted of a bland, dual-carriageway style airport road – far from the vibrant sights and sounds Dee was expecting to see. Gill explained that they would skirt round the southeast of Lima to where the house was, and would miss the main part of the city.

After a few minutes of heading south out of the airport they came to a main intersection and turned left down a wide boulevard. They passed a huge Japanese car showroom, followed by another car showroom and then a third.

"They wouldn't be here if there weren't people to buy the cars," noted Amos.

"We are approaching a wealthier part of the city," said Luis.

They passed a casino and then a few blocks further on another casino, with a sign sporting 'Hello Hollywood' in enormous lettering. At the next intersection there was a magnificent two-storey glass and concrete building: it was an American burger chain restaurant. Both Dee and Amos were disappointed with what they had so far seen.

Further on, the roads changed. They became wide, tree-lined streets.

"This is San Isidro," said Gill. "There is a golf club a few blocks south of us. Miraflores, to the south of us, and San Isidro are the two premier suburbs of Lima."

They pulled up at a corner building that was surrounded by six-foot-high railings. It was white and modern in style, with a two-storey high portico supported by white columns at its entrance.

Luis helped them in with their bags and the brothers' mother came to greet them.

"I am Manuela, welcome to my home," she said, in perfect English. "Carmen will show you to your rooms."

She waved her hand and Carmen appeared and escorted them up a curved staircase that started in the middle of a marbled hallway.

"My late father was the Peruvian ambassador to London," Gill told them. "He and my mother lived there for ten years."

"It really is good of you to put us up," said Dee.

"It's my pleasure," replied Gill. "In the morning I will show you

Lima, both what the tourist usually sees, and the real city."

§

Amos and Dee awoke the next morning to the smell of cooking.

"Where are you taking your guests today, Guillermo?" asked Manuela over breakfast.

"Well, naturally we will go to the main square at the heart of the city, the Plaza de Armas. But before that I need to go to the foreign ministry."

Gill turned to Amos and Dee.

"The ministry is housed in a spectacular seventeenth-century building called the Palacio de Torre Tagle."

"We also want to visit the poorer areas of Lima," said Amos.

"After our tour of the historic city centre, we will go to one of the *pueblos jóvenes* – shanty towns – that ring the capital," said Gill.

"Please be careful in those places," warned Manuela. "They are full of *padrones*."

"*Padrones*?" queried Dee.

"Criminal gang members," Gill told her. "Don't worry, Mother, I will look after our guests."

Luis was waiting outside the house in the car. The sky was overcast and the temperature was in the mid-sixties Fahrenheit; not unpleasant, but there was a chill in the air.

"Do you think it will rain today, Gill?" asked Dee.

"It's possible, but unlikely. We have very little rain here in Lima. There was a sea mist – a *garúa* – early this morning, but that has cleared," said Gill.

They drove towards the town centre and the old part of the city.

"We Peruvians are proud of our ancient Inca past. The Inca Empire began nearly three and a half thousand years ago. But today, there is much poverty. In Lima's population of close to ten million people, less than a quarter are what you would call upper or even middle class."

"You paint a sad picture, Gill," said Amos.

"I don't mean to, it's just the way things are."

"In spite of its problems, Lima is a vibrant city, and we are proud to be its inhabitants – *Limeños*," said Luis.

They arrived at the foreign ministry and, while Luis went to park the car, Gill, Amos and Dee walked towards the building.

"Because of earthquakes most buildings in Lima have been rebuilt several times. This palace is an exception. It was built in the early eighteenth century as a colonial mansion and it survives intact to this day," said Gill.

"I love the carved wooden balconies, they're exquisite," Dee exclaimed.

Inside the building was just as beautiful. The Arabic-style arch and column first-floor cloister formed a rectangle enclosing a small garden. Amos and Dee were happy to wander round while Gill did whatever he had to inside.

After a few minutes Gill appeared with another man.

"These are the people I was telling you about, minister. Amos and Dee are based in Washington and have come to visit Lima to see some of the problems we face," said Gill.

The man extended his hand to Amos and Dee.

"Welcome to Lima. I am Fernando Leon, the Minister for Foreign Affairs. I do hope Gill shows you some of the good things to see as well as the problem areas in our city."

The Minister greeted them warmly and then moved on.

"Thanks for introducing us, Gill," said Dee.

"He's a powerful and influential man in Peru. He was a friend of my father and has helped me a great deal. In spite of everything, his heart is in the right place; if he can, he wants to help the poor," replied Gill.

Outside the palace, Luis was nowhere to be seen.

"He's doing a few chores. We'll catch up with him later," said Gill. "We can walk from here to the main square; it's only a few blocks."

The Plaza de Armas, or Plaza Mayor, as it was commonly known, was the main square in Lima. A fountain graced its centre and on all sides were major buildings of the city: the cathedral, Archbishop's Palace and other grand palaces.

Amos, Dee and Gill wandered through the square and sat near the fountain on a stone bench opposite the Palacio de Gobierno.

"This is the part of Lima which all *Limeños* are proud of," said Gill. "When I am in the city I often come here just to sit and relax and think."

"Sitting here," began Amos, "it's hard to imagine that close to ten million people live within twenty miles of this point."

"Lima is a city of great contrast and paradox," said Gill. "Take the climate. So close to the equator and at sea level it should be like a furnace, but instead it is cool and temperate. The Humboldt Current from the Antarctic keeps the city cool. I shall take you shortly to see one of the many poverty-stricken areas of the city. People there live from hand to mouth, sixty per cent are unemployed, and in addition to all that, there are the earthquakes. Lima is situated in the Pacific Ring of Fire, an arc around the pacific in which ninety per cent of the world's earthquakes occur. What you see here today, in this square, is the result of building and rebuilding over the centuries caused by devastating earthquakes that have occurred in the past."

"And it'd be the poor that suffer the most when there is a natural disaster," said Dee.

Gill looked pained.

"Someone once said that a natural disaster is in fact a social disaster waiting to happen, that may be triggered by a particular natural force."

Just as they stood up to leave the square, the changing of the guard ceremony at the Palacio de Gobierno started. A line of soldiers, each carrying a flag and wearing a plumed hat, marched in high-kicking goosesteps across the front forecourt of the palace.

"It's just like your changing of the guard at Buckingham Palace," said Gill.

"Not exactly," Dee replied, smiling. "But colourful all the same."

They found Luis and the car and drove out of the centre of the city. Along the way there were shops and supermarkets of all types; even an electrical import store full of computers and mobile telephones. Further out they began to go past a hotchpotch of buildings as they went through a poorer area. Finally, Luis stopped the car.

"The hill you can see is San Cristobal, it has a large cross on the top," said Gill, as he got out of the car. "From here we must walk; there is no proper road to San Cristobal, or at least to the small shanty town which covers the side of the hill."

Luis unlocked the cubbyhole under the front dashboard of the car and took out a gun, which he wedged in his belt.

"No guns," said Dee.

"It's not safe in some of these places, it's just in case," said Luis.

Amos stood next to Dee and they both faced Luis.

"Luis will stay with the car," said Gill. He turned to Luis and continued, "We'll call for help if we need it. We'll be okay."

They walked toward the settlement of makeshift houses that covered the side of the hill. There did not seem to be any breaks between houses, just tier upon tier of boxes, none quite lined up with their neighbours.

What surprised Amos and Dee were the different colours. Some dwellings were blue, some cream, as well as many other assorted hues. As they came nearer, the ramshackle nature of the shacks became apparent. There were few bricks; most of the buildings were made of wood, plasterboard and corrugated sheets for roofs.

There were plenty of young children, and they were soon surrounded by an inquisitive crowd. They did not notice many men, but as they passed along the narrow paths between the dwellings, they saw a number of women.

"The men tend to leave early in the morning looking for work, with the women staying behind looking after the children and seeing to the daily needs of the family," said Gill.

"What about water and power?" asked Amos.

"Some of these shanty towns have public utilities, but many have none. The women have to carry water from a tanker or communal tap and very few have electricity."

"What about healthcare?" Dee asked.

"Malnutrition, drug-resistant Tuberculosis, AIDS... You name it, we have it," said Gill.

They approached a woman who was washing clothes. She looked to be in her forties, but was probably much younger. Dee asked Gill to translate for her.

"Hello, my name is Dee. How long have you been living here?"

The woman had a deep, strong voice but was wary of her visitors; she spoke without looking at Dee.

"Her name is Nina and she has been living here for more than ten years," said Gill.

"We are worried about earthquakes and we have come here to try to see if we can help people plan for emergencies," said Amos.

Gill's translation was followed by a stream of speech from the woman, and Gill did his best to translate.

"We have do-gooders that come here all the time. They sound good, they go away and we never see them again. We have no voice in this country. The government is not interested in us."

The woman then suddenly looked frightened and muttered something under her breath. Dee did not understand what she said but picked out the word *padrones*.

Two youths were approaching the group. They could not have been more than sixteen or seventeen years old, but they were brandishing knives.

They shouted something at Nina. Gill whispered to Dee and Amos.

"They asked who her friends were. I don't like this situation, I think we should go."

"It's okay Gill."

Dee turned and faced the youths. They were half-smiling as they swaggered towards her. Dee stamped her foot hard on the ground. As they heard the crunch of her heel on the gritty soil one of the youths suddenly tripped and fell flat on his face in the dirt.

"*Lárgate*!" Dee uttered this word in a deep visceral tone, injecting a basal fear in all who heard it.

The youth picked himself up off the ground and ran away with his partner.

Nina crossed herself and looked directly at Dee.

"She says that you have the gift of the voice," Gill translated.

"It's the only Spanish word I know, and it means clear off; I learnt it from watching Westerns on TV," said Dee.

Nina was now transformed and happily showed the three around her humble home. It transpired that she had four children; the eldest was a single mother and HIV positive. Dee was almost in tears to hear her plight.

"You have to multiply this story a million times to appreciate the scale of the problem we have in Peru," said Gill.

They were about to leave when Amos said to the woman, "We will come back Nina, and we will bring you a voice."

Gill translated, and even though she looked puzzled, Nina waved goodbye as the three walked back down the hillside to their waiting car.

"What did you mean by 'bringing her a voice,' Amos?" asked Gill.

Amos did not answer but just smiled and tapped his nose.

They drove back towards the centre of town.

"Do you remember the electrical warehouse we passed near the Plaza Mayor? Could we stop there please?" asked Amos.

"No problem," said Luis. "It's a well-known store; they have all the latest imports. Computers, mobiles, whatever you want. They also have a branch in Miraflores."

Inside the shop Luis, Gill and Dee looked at the laptops on display. Amos went straight over to the main counter and spoke to an assistant. He could not speak Spanish but instead wildly gesticulated with his arms. The assistant seemed to understand what Amos was trying to say and disappeared into a stockroom. After a couple of minutes he reappeared carrying a pile of small boxes, one of which he opened.

Dee, who was on the other side of the store, made a signal to Amos asking what he was purchasing.

"I'M BUYING A MEGAPHONE," said Amos through the loud hailer: it was turned up to full volume. The whole place rattled with the noise.

After leaving the store, they bought some sandwiches and sat down in the main square to have their lunch.

"So what's with the megaphone?" asked Gill.

"Let me explain," said Amos. "We saw the grinding poverty that Nina and millions of others have to put up with. However terrible it is, there really is not much we can do about it. This is a problem that the people and their government have to sort out, hopefully with help from other countries. But our task in the Earth Office is not to solve the problem of world poverty. Our task is to help engage people with the Earth and alleviate the effects of natural disasters. We are a conduit for an Earth that is striving for consciousness through our consciousness.

"What Nina wants is a voice. What her people in the shanty towns want is a warning of danger. If there is an earthquake or a mudslide or whatever, a simple system of warnings will save many lives. The electrical store had ten megaphones in stock. I bought the lot for half price. We'll give them out and if danger comes, people will hear the warnings."

"It's not a bad idea," said Gill.

"It's brilliant!" exclaimed Dee.

They drove back to San Cristobal and found Nina, who was surprised to see them.

"We've brought something for you, Nina," said Amos.

He opened a box that he was carrying and took out the megaphone.

"It's a voice for you," he said.

Gill translated but Nina did not seem to understand; she had never seen a megaphone before.

"*Lárgate*!" Amos' voice bellowed out of the loud hailer.

Nina started to laugh; she had probably never laughed so much in her life before. Tears of joy rolled down her face. People came from all around to see what was happening.

Amos gave Nina the megaphone. She gingerly took it and spoke into it.

"Hola."

She had barely whispered into the device, but her voice rang out across the rooftops of the settlement.

Amos showed her how to use the megaphone, including a switch that activated a siren. She cradled the megaphone in her arms as if she was holding a small baby.

"You must keep it safe," Amos told her. "And if danger comes, use it to warn everyone. You must arrange with your friends a prearranged signal. That way, if there is a mudslide or an earthquake, everyone will know what to do. You are now in charge of the voice."

"I don't think I'll ever forget the joy in Nina's face when you gave her the megaphone," said Dee as they were on their way back to Gill's house.

"I'm going to text Arnold to source a hundred megaphones at cost price," said Amos. "We'll send them to you, Gill, if you agree to distribute them on our behalf to communities which are under threat from natural disasters. We can't save everyone's life if disaster strikes but maybe, just maybe, we can save a few lives. At least we can give some people a voice that they never had before."

"Of course I will help you," said Gill. "Luis and I have a circle of friends and family that we can trust. We will distribute as many loud hailers as we can."

When they returned to the house, Dee arranged the flight back to Washington and Amos texted Arnold.

"I wonder what Arnold will make of a text asking him to purchase one hundred megaphones," said Amos, with a twinkle in his eye.

§

Arnold felt tired and was pleased to be returning to Washington. He enjoyed the rough and tumble of diplomacy and the rounds of meetings and parties, but after the adrenalin rush wore off, it left him fatigued. He slept on the train going back and promised himself that he would join Dee's gym.

He asked Christine and Grace to move permanently into the office at Dupont Circle. There would be a lot of follow-up work on the contacts they had made and the joint arrangement with their organisation seemed to work well.

Charlotte was pleased to see them when they arrived back. Things had been quiet while they were all away and she had missed the activity. She insisted on knowing every detail of what had happened in New York.

Arnold asked Charlotte for directions to Dee's gym and set off early the next morning – at least, early for Arnold. As he walked along the route he passed the spot where Dee had been abducted. He made a mental note to ask Helen Chandler if the FBI had made any progress on the information Dee had given them.

The gym was relaxing. You could do as much – or in Arnold's case, as little – as you wanted. After a swim and a half-hearted go on a few pieces of gym equipment, Arnold felt refreshed and together with the walk there and back, he was satisfied that he was on the right path to fitness.

He was keen to follow on from Dee's research on Mount Rainier. The pictures of the mountain he found on the internet evoked again the shared dream that had initiated the events leading up to the Earth Office's creation.

The mountain was an active volcano, potentially even more deadly than Mount St Helens which erupted in 1980. Both volcanoes were members of the Pacific Ring of Fire, which accounted for the majority of active volcanoes in the world.

There were two major problems that made Mount Rainier so frightening. One was that Seattle – with a metropolitan population of nearly three and a half million – which was only fifty-odd miles north of the volcano. The second problem was that the mountain, which was more than 14,000 feet high, was covered in glacial ice. Any eruption would, therefore, melt vast quantities of ice which would, in turn, inundate the surrounding region. The more data that Arnold uncovered about the mountain, the more unlikely it seemed that the Earth Office could do anything worthwhile to mitigate such a disaster.

While he was deep in thought pondering these matters, Bill turned up.

"I've come to see how you are, Arnold," said Bill. "I also had to get away from Frank. He's driving me mad moping around all the time because Dee's away. Young love, eh!"

"She'll be back soon," said Arnold, still feeling disconsolate.

"What are you working on?" asked Bill, and Arnold told him about Mount Rainer.

"I could ask our research team at the *Post* if they have anything on file. I wouldn't like to be living near the mountain if the volcano decided to explode. I'm not sure that the Earth Office could even do anything useful if it did, though."

"I'm not sure if it could either," agreed Arnold.

"Have you heard anything from the FBI on Al-Falah?" asked Bill.

"No, I think I might telephone Helen Chandler and see if I can find out anything," said Arnold.

He picked up the telephone and dialled her number. She told him that she could not say anything, as there was an ongoing operation on at the moment, and that she would ring when she had any news.

The telephone rang as soon as Arnold had placed the receiver back in its cradle.

"You can congratulate me, Arnold," said the voice. "I've just been nominated by my party for the forthcoming governorship election for West Virginia. The official announcement should be hitting the wires any moment."

"Well done, Sam," exclaimed Arnold. "Bill's here too, and he sends his congratulations."

"Thanks," said Sam. "I couldn't have done it without you and I wanted you to be the first to know."

"The election will be a shoehorn for him," Bill said after Arnold had put down the phone. "The old fox finally made it."

"He's been a lot of help to us," said Arnold. "His heart's in the right place."

Arnold's mobile bleeped.

"It's a text message from Amos and Dee. I wonder how they're doing in Lima."

He read the message and looked puzzled.

"What is it?" asked Bill.

"They want me to purchase one hundred megaphones. And they'll be back in Washington tomorrow."

"Clearly they want their voices to be heard and you know what Dee's like when she puts her foot down," Bill joked.

The next day Arnold rang around a few wholesalers in the Washington area and managed to source the loud hailers that Dee and Amos wanted.

"What do you think Dee and Amos will do with them?" asked Christine, who was in the office that morning.

"Your guess is as good as mine," replied Arnold.

He had managed a second visit earlier that morning to the gym, but had succumbed to the delights of the cake shop next door. Charlotte had just brought in coffee for everyone when Amos and Dee arrived. They looked tired – their flight had been an overnighter – but they were in good spirits.

When he heard from Dee that she and Amos were back, Frank came straight over to the office. An hour later Bill turned up and the whole crew were assembled.

"First, I want to know what you want the megaphones for," said Bill.

"It was my idea," said Amos. "In fact, it was Dee who gave me the idea."

He explained to everyone about the visit to the shanty town.

"You have no idea what it's like until you see it," Dee told them. "We all see pictures of abject poverty on TV, but you don't appreciate the scale: not just thousand, or even tens of thousands, but millions. And this is in a city where there are areas of great wealth!"

"So where do the megaphones come in?" asked Arnold.

Amos told them about the incident with the *padrones*.

"It matched what the woman, Nina, said, that the poor don't have a voice. It was obvious that we couldn't solve the poverty problem, so I thought if we can't make everyone wealthy, at least we can give them a voice when disaster strikes – and a loud voice at that. All of the studies on the effects of natural disasters on the poor identify lack of communication and preplanning as the main problems. So why not give megaphones to certain trustworthy people and encourage them to set up networks where, if there is a mudslide or an earthquake, they can warn and organise their people? It might save a few lives."

"I think it's the best idea I've heard all year," beamed Christine.

"I agree," said Arnold. "But you have to make sure you give out the megaphones to the right people."

"This is where Gill and his brother come into the picture," Dee began. "They have agreed to distribute the megaphones on our behalf. That way, we know they will go to people who will use them and not just sell them for a few dollars."

"We can use Lima as a pilot," said Grace. "We'll follow up on what happens and if it is successful, we'll suggest expanding the scheme to other countries."

"You can call it Megaphones for Mothers," offered Bill. "I know it sounds a bit corny, but if it works, it will save lives. I might even be able to publish a paragraph in the *Post*."

The next day Dee managed to persuade Amos to join Arnold and her at the gym. There was a small cafeteria in the gym and they arranged to have breakfast there after they had finished exercising.

Amos was very fit and took the exercises easily in his stride.

"Don't forget," he said, seeing that Dee and Arnold were impressed with his fitness. "I worked in the mines not long ago, and you really have to be fit for that."

At breakfast they discussed strategies for the future, and in particular what they were going to do about Mount Rainier. Arnold described the additional research he had done, and combined with Dee's research, they had a good picture of the mountain, its environs and the potential problems.

"I don't think that any of us are in any doubt that there is going to be some sort of disaster there," said Arnold.

"I agree," said Dee. "Although I don't feel that it is absolutely imminent – we do have time. The problem is that even if we are correct, what can we possibly do?"

"What do you think, Amos?" asked Arnold.

Amos had not said anything and was content to let the others discuss the subject. But at Arnold's question, he put into words what he was thinking.

"You are both right: there is going to be a disaster and I think that we do have some time."

He paused, took a couple of sips from his orange juice, and then continued.

"We have all had a common dream, but each of our dreams is slightly different: we are each privy to different aspects of the same phenomena. In fact, our strength is in the way we complement each other. In the case of Mount Rainier, there are certain things that I will have to face, and I will face them. As to what we can do, I don't know. But in our enterprise have we ever really known what's around the corner? I think that we should go to Mount Rainier and leave what we can actually do about the whole situation open and unfixed for now."

Both Arnold and Dee thought about what Amos had said.

"I agree we should go," said Arnold after a pause.

"So do I," added Dee.

"What about the others?" asked Arnold.

"I'm happy to let Christine and Grace run the office while we're away," said Dee.

"What about Bill and Frank? They've become part of the crew, albeit part-time."

"They're welcome to join us for all or part of the time, if they want," said Amos.

The next few days were filled with preparations for the trip to Seattle. They did not know how long they would be away, but Christine and Grace were happy to run the office until they returned. Amos liaised with Gill in Peru about the transportation of the megaphones, while Bill and Frank were told that they were also able to visit Seattle for some of the time if they wanted to. They did have other assignments to follow, but the *Post* agreed to allow them some leave. Of course, it wouldn't hurt if they came back with a story.

Dee received one piece of excellent news from Helen Chandler. The surveillance that the FBI had put on Al-Falah had paid off, and he had been caught red-handed supplying weapons to a terrorist group. They had arrested the whole group as the weapons were being handed over. The Syrian government claimed diplomatic immunity for Al-Falah, who was unceremoniously expelled back to Syria. The Syrian ambassador was hauled up at the State Department and had to guarantee that there would be no repeat of such behaviour. The FBI did not know what would happened to Al-Falah after his expulsion, but breaking the 11th commandment – don't get caught – certainly did not go down well in that country.

Neither Arnold nor Dee spoke about Amos' suggestion that he would have an unknown task to face on their arrival at Mount Rainier.

"I've arranged the flights," said Dee, when they were back in the office. "What should I do about accommodation?"

"Don't do anything," said Amos vehemently. "We'll sort it out when we arrive."

Both Arnold and Dee thought it strange to leave their lodgings unplanned, but did not question Amos further.

CHAPTER 5

Considering that he was approaching his mid-seventies, Leo was in good shape. He had always been active; he remembered going hunting and on fishing trips with his father and other tribal elders. Even when he was chief – or Chairman of the Yakama Nation, to give him his official title – he would oversee the river management and logging facilities, not to mention frequent climbing expeditions up Mount Rainier.

He tried to encourage his son, Harry, to keep up tribal traditions and be close to the land. He appreciated that it was difficult, with the world as it was now, the world of commerce and balance sheets not being conducive to climbing, hunting and fishing. Harry was now chairman of the tribal council. His job involved managing casinos and factories, as well as the more traditional areas of forestry and river management.

Leo had spent his whole life fighting for tribal rights and he was proud of his record. The government had treated Native Americans badly in the past; the present was different. The Yakama Nation was wealthy, but there was a price and Leo was not comfortable with that.

Today was a happy day: his granddaughter Jackie was coming over to see him. She would be going back to college in a month but for the moment she was on vacation – she could enjoy the hot and lazy days of summer. It was going to be a scorcher, he thought. Despite the cool nights, the clear blue sky of the day could reach the high eighties.

He heard her station wagon draw up outside his house. Jackie was wearing jeans and a t-shirt, with a baseball cap to shade her from the sun. The cap had a picture of a bear holding a baseball bat in its mouth, the insignia of the Yakima Bears, whom she supported.

"Hi Gramps, had any more dreams lately?" she asked.

Leo's Indian name was *Iwákt tk'I*, which was Sahaptin (the language of the Yakama) for dream vision.

In common with the spiritual tradition – the *washat* – of the Yakama people, Leo was a Dreamer Prophet. Dreams were woven ties between the Yakama and Nature. His granddaughter continued the *washat* heritage and was also a dreamer, although neither of them had had visionary dreams for a long time. But that didn't stop her from asking, even light-heartedly, if he had had a vision.

"Hello Jackie, I haven't had any visions recently," said Leo. "But I have been thinking a lot about the Yakama Nation's place in the world. I have the feeling that we are approaching an important stage in our history."

"What do you mean, Gramps?" asked his granddaughter.

Leo hesitated as if he was trying to find the right words.

"I mean respect." he said, "We have, as a nation, battled for our rights. We have achieved an enormous amount for our people. We have financial clout; we have political clout. These are laudable ends that I have spent my whole life fighting for. But, the question is, do we have respect from all of the people in these lands? Do our fellow Americans respect us? I don't think we have achieved this last ideal – and it bothers me."

"Respect, Gramps, is important, but you only gain that from what you do and how you behave," said Jackie.

Leo smiled.

"You have such a wise head on your young shoulders. What are we going to do today?"

"Dad suggested I bring you to see the resort they're building at Naches. The hotel is almost finished and the casino area and other buildings are well under way," said Jackie.

"It's the grandest project the tribal council have undertaken," said Leo. "I would be interested to see how far they've advanced."

The journey from Toppenish took about an hour. They travelled through the broad streets of the town that Leo knew so well, onto Highway 12 going north, through Yakima and then on to Naches. The towns were like most small towns in America, with wide boulevards and flat scenery surrounded by fields and rocks and dust. In many respects it was a harsh environment, reluctant soil. Yet, over time, the people had integrated their lives into their natural surroundings and prospered. But Leo still kept thinking that if the price of prosperity was loss of respect, then that was unacceptable.

They stopped for a break at a diner in Yakima on the way. It was one of a large chain of restaurants across the US. Leo did not care for it much, but it was conveniently sited. He saw some people he knew – Leo seemed to know everyone – and introduced them to Jackie. They were interested in the new casino resort that he and Jackie were going to visit; it would mean a lot of new jobs for the area.

After Yakima, the road swung north-west towards Mount Rainier and the small settlements of Gleed and then Naches. On the way they passed vineyards, which were part of the Yakama's business interests. The climate was conducive to wine production as the grapes were prevented from overheating with the high daytime temperatures through the cooling effect of the cold nights. The small amount of rain that fell allowed the grapes to retain their sweetness. In many respects the climate was similar to the great Californian wine producing areas.

After Naches they turned left towards Tieton and, just as the road seemed to run out, they came upon a sign that read 'Mount Rainier Casino Resort.' In the distance they could see a circular building, and as they approached a huge domed building loomed out from behind it.

"What do you think, Pa?" said Harry as he came out to greet them. "Hi Jackie. Impressive, isn't it?"

Leo and Jackie were stunned at the sight. Few buildings in the region, outside of Seattle, were more than two stories high, and the scale of what they were witnessing was unsettling.

"We call it 'The Tower,'" said Harry. "Seventeen floors, two hundred rooms and a magnificent restaurant on the top."

"It is amazing," said Leo.

The Tower was a perfect cylinder of glass and concrete, with a capped dome on the top. Behind the tower the dome shape was repeated, but on a much grander scale, in a building which was two or three stories high.

"The views of Mount Rainier and the surrounding area from the top are incredible. Come and see," said Harry.

He led them into the Tower and they walked inside. The central core of the cylinder was an atrium, all the way to the domed roof, which was glass. Builders were still working and there was no furniture, so the reception area was just one vast expanse.

"The rooms are nearly finished and they will be testing the air-conditioning system soon," said Harry.

They went up in one of the bank of elevators and exited at the top floor restaurant. Harry was right about the view; it was a sensation. The restaurant, itself, was in the shape of an arc along the side facing the mountain, and although there were no tables or chairs yet, they could easily imagine what it would be like when it was fully operational.

"How do the people get here?" asked Jackie.

"The airfield is only fifteen minutes away," said Harry. "We're aiming to run an air shuttle service to Seattle airport. We'll also have coaches connecting us to all the towns between here and Seattle, as well as services to Tacoma. But it's not just us."

"What do you mean?" asked Leo.

"This is just the beginning," said Harry. "If we are up and running and successful, we can lease land to other hotel groups, who will build here. The aim is to be a mini Las Vegas out here in Washington State. People will flock here from all over the world. Let me show you The Dome."

They went down in the elevator to the ground floor and then walked through the atrium to the rear of the hotel. There was a wide tunnel that led to a domed building. The structure of the building had been completed but, like the Tower, the inside was empty.

"This will be the casino, theatre and cinema complex," said Harry. "It's only a shell at the moment, but as soon as they finish the Tower, they will work to finish the Dome."

Inside was like being in an aircraft hangar for jumbo jets.

"Outside, there will be two pools and we will also have a spa, indoor pool and gym in separate buildings next to the hotel," said Harry.

"It's an immense achievement, Harry," said Leo. "It will be a legacy for the Yakama people. I don't want to detract from what you and the tribal council have accomplished, but I have been concerned about how outsiders view us. I'm not sure that we have as much respect from them as I would hope."

"Listen Pa, you of all people know how much our people have suffered. It has been an uphill struggle for us to assert tribal rights and force the government to treat us fairly. Thanks to you, and other tribal chiefs, we are in a much better position. But, as you know, there is resentment against us and overcoming that does not always engender respect."

"I know, son, I know. You are quite right. But it is still something that I think we should bear in mind," said Leo.

"What do you think, Jackie?" asked Harry.

"I think this resort, when it opens, will radically change the lives of our people. It will bring wealth and jobs to the whole region. As far as Grandpa's point about respect is concerned, I'm not sure what extra we can do to improve that. Our people have gone through a long period of learning just to feel respect for themselves. Hopefully, outsiders will respect us more in time."

"They have just filled one of the pools, would you like to go for a swim?" Harry asked.

"I'd love that," said Jackie.

"I'll catch up with you in a few minutes," said Leo. "I want to have another look at the restaurant."

Jackie and her father strode out of the Dome to the pool area. There were spare costumes and towels available and after a few minutes they were both splashing around in the pool like children. The area around the pool was empty, but they could easily imagine what it would be like filled with sun-lounges, parasols and all the usual accoutrements of a poolside idyll.

Leo went back into the hotel and shot straight up to the top floor restaurant. Because of the foothills to the mountain and the low plains of the area, it was only possible to see the peak of the mountain from certain vantage points. Seventeen floors up was one of them and he gazed out towards the mountain in the far distance. The ice-covered peak was nearly three miles above sea level, and even from this distance he was still as awestruck by the mountain as he had always been. In his youth he had climbed to the top on several occasions. No matter how much familiarity he had with the mountain, he never failed to feel the majesty and the terror of the peak. He had always felt that his life was somehow entwined with the mountain. Not just in the general sense that it dominated the whole region, but in an intensely personal way. The mountain seemed to call out to him, and it was a fearful message whose meaning he could not quite translate.

He walked around the viewing area towards the rear and could see the whole plain below towards Yakima and Toppenish in the distance. He spotted Harry and Jackie in the pool below. It reminded him of the times he had taken Harry swimming as a child and it brought a smile to his face.

"Come on in, Gramps," said Jackie.

"The water's fine," Harry added.

He changed and dived into the pool. Even at his age he was still a strong swimmer. He then floated on his back with his arms outstretched and closed his eyes. With the sun beating down and the gurgle of water in his submerged ears shutting out the shrieks and laughter of his son and granddaughter, he had a vision.

It seemed to last several minutes, although he knew that only a few seconds had elapsed. It was the clearest and most terrifying vision he had ever experienced. He quickly pulled himself out of the pool and sat on the edge, his head in his hands, with tears streaming down his face.

Harry was the first to notice.

"What is it, Pa? Is everything okay?"

"The Earth is coming. The Earth is coming," repeated Leo.

Jackie put a towel around Leo's shoulders and knelt down beside him.

"What is it, Gramps? Tell me," she urged.

Leo began to regain his composure.

"I've had a vision," he told them. "A terrifying nightmare. The Earth is coming."

Even though Harry had never had a vision or prophetic dream, he had been brought up to respect the phenomenon when it occurred in others. It was part of his tribal consciousness. Leo had always spoken of dream visions and even Jackie and other family members had some connection to special dreams. He had, though, never seen his father affected so badly.

"What was the vision, Pa?" he asked. "What did you see?"

Jackie fetched Leo a glass of water. After he had taken a few sips, he tried to explain to them what his vision had revealed.

"It was a confusing mass of images, some of people, some of the mountain. I could see the white icecap of Mount Rainier. I was gripped by an incredible fear."

"What did you mean by the phrase, 'The Earth is coming'?" said Jackie.

"I don't know," said Leo, shaking his head. "I'm feeling tired now, Jackie. Could you please take me home?"

Leo hardly said a word on the journey back to Toppenish. Jackie had never seen him like this before. She knew that his vision was of immense importance, but the confusing imagery that he had seen made interpretation almost impossible. She decided she would talk to him at length in the morning. After a good night's rest and in a more relaxed frame of mind, she might be able to tease out the meaning of his dream.

"I think I'll stay with you tonight, Gramps," said Jackie when they arrived back at Leo's house.

He tried to dissuade her, but she appeared in no mood to argue.

Jackie thought about Leo's description of his vision as she settled down to sleep. The house was quiet and she could hear Leo snoring lightly in the distance. She soon fell asleep.

§

Jackie was woken early in the morning by the sound of a scream. Leo rushed into her room and she realised at once that it was her scream that had woken them both up.

"I had your dream, Gramps," she announced. "Or at least some of your dream. The sounds, the images, it was confusing and frightening. But I know what you mean when you say that the Earth is coming. It's not an object that's coming, it's a person – or to be more precise, three people – and they're coming today!"

"Yes, of course, you're right," exclaimed Leo. "I don't know why I didn't realise that yesterday. It is the representatives of the Earth that are coming."

"We'll go to Seattle airport and wait for them," said Jackie. "How will we know who they are?"

"I'll know them when I see them," insisted Leo.

§

It was another glorious, late summer's day in Washington, DC. Bill and Frank came over to Dupont Circle to see Amos, Arnold and Dee before they left for Seattle. Dee had booked them on an early flight the next day. Frank had wanted to fly out with them, but he and Bill were working on a story for the *Post* that would keep them occupied for the next few days.

Christine and Grace were well settled in at the office. The Megaphones for Mothers project – as it was now dubbed – was beginning to take on a life of its own. They had sent off the first batch of megaphones to Lima. Christine, through her diplomatic contacts, had promoted the project, and enquiries were starting to come in from all over the world. The key to a successful project was the involvement of local charities and NGOs on the ground, so the megaphones had to be allocated to responsible people who would use them correctly in an emergency situation.

Bill brought a folder full of information on Mount Rainier. An intern at the *Post* had put together an impressive collection of press cuttings and other information that they had on the mountain. He had also identified a reporter for one of the local Seattle TV stations who had made a special study of the mountain. Bill had contacted him and the reporter had agreed to meet the three in Seattle.

Arnold was not happy with the early morning start the next day, but he had begun to get used to them on travel days. It was a six-hour flight, and with the time change they expected to arrive in Seattle around eleven a.m. – at least they would have most of the day to organise accommodation, as Amos was still adamant that they should not make any prior arrangements.

The flight was uneventful, although they had deliberately requested seats on the left side of the aircraft so that they would have an aerial view of the mountain as they approached Seattle airport. Dee had yet to see Mount Rainier and sat in awestruck silence as the panorama unfolded outside the aircraft porthole.

"It's exactly as I remember it in the dream," she said.

Amos and Arnold made no comment.

They arrived in the baggage hall and retrieved their bags. Before they exited into the airport concourse, Amos stopped, laid his case on the ground, and started to unzip the bag.

"What are you doing, Amos?" asked Dee.

"There's something I have to do," he said in an even tone.

He pulled out of his bag his grandfather's multi-coloured leather coat which his mother had presented to him when he and Arnold were in Idaho. He carefully put it on and then led Arnold and Dee out into the airport arrival terminal. Somehow putting on the coat had transformed Amos. He became the embodiment, not just of the Earth, which they all felt, but also of his Native American heritage. He had quite literally assumed the mantle of his forbears. This was the sight that greeted Leo and Jackie, who had been waiting since early morning.

"We've been expecting you," said Leo, as he moved forward to greet Amos. "I am Leo Aleck, *Iwákt tk'I*, and this is my granddaughter, Jackie. Welcome to Seattle."

Amos responded formally.

"I am Amos Talbot, *Puwaamuun*, and these are my friends Arnold and Dee."

"How did you know we were coming?" said Dee, breaking the formality and taking Jackie's hand.

"My grandfather had a vision and then I also had a dream. We saw your arrival here," Jackie replied.

"Before we go any further, I must take a picture," said Dee.

She rummaged in her bag and took out a camera. She took pictures of everyone.

"I have to have one of Amos in his caribou skin coat," she added.

She asked a passer-by to take a picture of all of them. "They're to go on the office wall by my desk."

"It was a shared dream that brought Dee, Amos and I together," Arnold told the others, adding, "By the way, where are you taking us?"

"You are our honoured guests," said Leo, still retaining an air of formality. "Our community is located in Toppenish, which is a couple of hours from here by car. If it is agreeable to you, we would like you to stay with us."

"We would be delighted to stay with you and meet your community," said Amos.

"I don't know about anyone else," said Arnold, "but I'm starving, could we stop somewhere for lunch?"

Everyone laughed.

"I know a good place to stop for lunch," said Jackie. "It's in a fun part of downtown Seattle."

It only took about twenty minutes from the airport before Jackie turned off the main highway and drove through the city.

"We're going to a coffee shop. A well-known international coffee shop," said Jackie. "They opened their first ever coffee house here in Seattle in the early '70s. I often used to come here."

She parked the station wagon and they walked along a busy street. The ocean was on one side and on the other were small shops, boutiques and cafés.

"This area is called Pike Place Market," said Jackie as they reached their destination.

"There's one of these on a corner near my old office in England," observed Arnold. "I didn't know that this was their first one."

"There are a lot of things Seattle is famous for," Leo added. "The city is named after a tribal leader called Chief Seattle. There is an important historical link between the city and tribal population."

They ordered lunch, much to Arnold's relief, and spoke about the Earth Office. Arnold explained what had happened to him since the dream and how Dee and Amos had joined forces with him to set up the office in Washington, DC.

"And you've come to Seattle...?" Leo looked inquisitively between the three.

"Because of Mount Rainier," answered Amos.

"When Amos and I saw it from the air, we realised immediately that it was going to be central to our mission," said Arnold.

"We understand," Jackie assured him. "But what do you think will happen? Do you think there will be an eruption? Even if there is, what can we do?"

"Forgive my granddaughter," grinned Leo, "She is full of questions."

"It's natural. We ourselves are full of questions," said Dee.

"The short answer is that we don't know," began Amos. "To be more explicit, we believe that something terrible is going to happen and that it involves the mountain. We don't think it is imminent, but it is coming in the not too distant future. As to what can be done... We share the feeling that we can do very little. But we have learnt that things often turn out quite different from what we expect or imagine, and so we just have to be optimistic."

Back on the road, the highway curved in a semi-circular arc round the northern and eastern sides of Mount Rainier.

"There are lots of trees and hills blocking the view, but if you look out of the right-hand window, every now and again you'll see a great view of the mountain," said Leo.

"What tribe are you from?" asked Dee.

"We are part of the confederated tribes of the Yakama Nation," replied Leo. "I used to be head of the tribal council until I retired, and my son Harry is the current head. What about you, Amos?"

"My people are the Naskapi Indians from the Labrador Peninsula in Canada," said Amos. "Although I grew up in the Lake Pend Oreille area of Idaho."

"I visited Lake Pend Oreille once," Leo mused. "I remember that the fishing was wonderful."

"I caught a Kamloops trout," beamed Arnold. "It was my first fish."

"You always remember the first fish you catch. How big was it?" asked Leo.

"Almost ten pounds!"

"I recall, Arnold, that it was nearer to seven pounds," said Amos.

"Well it felt like ten pounds," murmured Arnold, much to the amusement of the others.

"What does your Indian name mean?" asked Leo.

"*Puwaamuum* is Naskapi for Dreamer. Dreams are important to my people," Amos explained. "My grandfather was a dreamer and a prophet; I'm wearing his special coat, which was handed down to me."

"I think we both have the same name," said Leo. "*Iwákt tk'i* is Sahaptin – our native language – and means dream or vision."

"What links us all," Amos added, "is not just our names, but a common purpose, which we share with all of humanity."

"We pass Naches on the way to Toppenish," said Jackie. "Do you think our guests would like to see the Casino Resort, Gramps?"

"It's my son's latest project as tribal council leader," Leo told the others.

"Definitely," replied Arnold. "It sounds like an interesting project."

Amos and Dee agreed, and they soon turned off the road onto a construction site. As soon as they caught sight of the hotel tower in the distance, a change came over Amos, Arnold and Dee. Leo noticed the sudden hush that had fallen upon the three.

"Is everything okay?" he asked.

"This place is important," Amos replied, slowly. "We've seen this tower before: it is part of our dream."

"There's a tremendous view of Mount Rainier from the top of the tower," said Jackie.

Harry was not there, but the works foreman recognised Leo and escorted the group to the top of the tower.

"I've seen the mountain all my life," Jackie told them as she looked out at the landscape, "but you never cease to marvel every time you see it. I'm not sure I understand why this place should be so important in your dream about the mountain. We're nearly fifty miles from Mount Rainier and anything that happens there would be too far away to put us in any danger here."

"Maybe that's the point," said Arnold.

"Your people have carved out a successful economic situation here," explained Amos. "It is important that funds generated at the casino are reinvested back into the community."

"You're right," agreed Leo. "But I've come to realise over the years that economic success, though welcome, is not enough."

"What do you mean?" asked Arnold.

"It's something I've been putting a lot of thought into and talking about in recent times. I'm concerned that our community is not respected in the wider world. In our drive for rights and wealth we've lost some of our humanity and, as a result, lost respect."

"You make a very telling point," said Amos. "It's one more thing to think about."

The final leg of the journey to Toppenish was spent in silence. Amos, Arnold and Dee were exhausted after the long journey from Washington, and Leo and Jackie had been waiting in anticipation at the airport since early morning. The entire group was exhausted. Amos had a window seat on the right-hand side of the car and caught glimpses of Mount Rainier as it popped in and out of view.

As they made the final approach to Toppenish, Leo explained that they could stay at a small hostel just around the corner from his house. The hostel was owned and run by the tribe, and was used for out-of-town visitors on tribal business.

Arnold replied that they were quite happy to stay in a hotel, but Leo was adamant: they were honoured guests and it was part of ancient tribal custom to look after guests.

"What do you want to do tomorrow?" asked Jackie.

"I think the first thing we need to do," said Amos, "Is see exactly what we are dealing with. We need to visit Mount Rainier."

"I'll come and pick you up tomorrow morning," offered Jackie. "We can go on the Muir Snowfield, which starts at Paradise."

"How early?" asked Arnold, hesitantly.

"Not too early," Jackie said with a wry smile. "I'll come at six-thirty a.m."

Arnold's face dropped.

Jackie laughed, "And don't forget to bring extra waterproof clothing, wear good climbing boots, and sport a warm hat and sunglasses."

§

Jackie was at their hostel bright and early the next morning.

"I've arranged to meet my cousin Oscar at Paradise. He's an official guide and will take us up to Camp Muir," said Jackie.

She took out a large rucksack and emptied out the contents onto a table.

"Each one of you needs a map of the mountain, a compass, flashlight, waterproof matches, first-aid kit, pocket knife and a fire starter."

She handed out the items to Amos, Arnold and Dee.

"It's going to be a really hot day today, do we need all this extra clothing?" asked Arnold.

"It may be hot down here, but on the glacier at 10,000 feet it can be pretty cold. The weather conditions often change suddenly and you have to be prepared for every eventuality."

Jackie thoroughly checked what everyone was wearing. "I've brought food for everyone," she said. "But it's always a good idea to carry extra food; we can purchase some more at Paradise. Do you all feel fit for the climb?"

"Fit and raring to go," replied Arnold. "We went to the gym every day before we came here."

"I'm glad to hear it," Jackie smiled. "Mount Rainier can be very unforgiving and it's an arduous climb. I've brought hiking sticks for everyone – you'll need them on the snowfield."

The drive to Paradise took them along the south side of the mountain to Longmire.

"It's important to arrive early to beat the crowds," Jackie told them as they navigated the mountain road, "The car parking at Sunrise is limited and we need to give ourselves plenty of time for the climb. My grandfather would have loved to come with us, but his climbing days are over. He used to be a mountain guide in his youth, you know."

At Longmire they followed the signs to Paradise. They were climbing all the time and it took about half an hour before they reached the car park.

"We're meeting my cousin in the Paradise Inn. There's also a visitor centre and ranger station on the site," said Jackie.

"How high up are we here?" asked Dee.

"We're about one mile above sea level," Jackie told her. "Camp Muir is nearly two miles up and the summit is three miles above sea level."

As they collected their kit from the boot, a figure waved at them. He was dark, with piercing eyes and an engaging smile.

"How are you doing, Jackie?" he said as he embraced his cousin.

He turned to greet the others. "Hi! I'm Oscar Washines," he said as he shook hands with Amos, Arnold and Dee.

"Oscar is my cousin," said Jackie. "Have you obtained the climbing permits, Oscar?"

"No problem. It's a great day for climbing. The weather reports so far are benign, but you know Mount Rainier – you never can tell. Let's hope we don't meet any black bears or mountain lions," Oscar grinned playfully.

"We've dealt with worse than bears and lions," boasted Dee.

They went into the Paradise Inn and bought extra water and food for the ascent.

"I think we're ready now," said Amos. "Where do we start?"

"This is where the skyline trail starts," said Oscar, as he led the group out of the car park and past the ranger's station.

The views of the mountain were breathtaking. Even though it was still summer there was a considerable amount of snow on the ground. The trail was paved at first and climbed at a comfortable pace past alpine meadows full of wildflowers. Ahead they could see a glacier and behind, in the distance, views of Mount Adams, Mount Hood and Mount St Helens.

"How long have you been a guide, Oscar?" asked Dee.

"It's a family tradition," said Oscar. "My father was a guide as well as Leo. Mount Rainier has always dominated tribal life."

Arnold was not as fast as the others, but he just about managed to keep up the pace, lagging behind only a little. Amos fell back and accompanied Arnold.

"You know, Arnold, up until now I felt a great dread of this mountain, bound up with the images in my dream. But now that I'm actually here, it feels quite different."

"But we know that something dramatic and terrible is going to happen here," said Arnold.

"Yes, but it can't be avoided; it's part of nature," Amos told him. "We're here to mitigate the effects, and to save lives, if we are able to. We, too, are part of nature."

Oscar, Jackie and Dee had stopped ahead, which gave Amos and Arnold a chance to catch up.

"We'll take a rest here," said Oscar. "We have to cross Pebble Creek next. We've travelled about 1600 feet up from Paradise."

"Are you ever concerned about the volcano, Oscar?" asked Dee. "Even though it's dormant, it could become active at any time."

"Sure. I've been up here hundreds of times – I've felt a tremor or two," said Oscar. "The biggest danger on this mountain is of a lahar."

"What's that?" asked Arnold.

"Basically it's a mudflow," explained Oscar. "The heat from the volcano melts the ice and there's a huge amount of ice to be melted from the glaciers around Mount Rainier. We often have scientists up here; they will be able to tell you much more. Two in particular – Ethan Malone and Vittorio De Angelis – are friends of mine. They are from the University of Washington, which has a department that studies volcanoes like Mount Rainier."

After their break, the group gingerly crossed the creek on steppingstones which jutted out from the swirling waters.

"There's no marked trail from here," Oscar told them. "We have to cross the snowfield to Camp Muir."

They all grabbed their hiking sticks and set off slowly across the snow.

"There's the Nisqually glacier on our left," said Oscar. "Keep away from rocky outcrops – they may have crevasses near them. And stay together; the ascent becomes steeper from here."

They were all in reasonable shape and, although he was puffing quite a bit, Arnold managed to keep up. Oscar regularly checked his altimeter.

"We're at 8,500 feet," he said. "We'll take a five-minute rest break. We need to climb another 2,000 feet to Camp Muir. This last bit of the ascent is the hardest; you'll find it more difficult to breathe."

The air was cold and there was a biting side wind. Oscar pointed ahead as they cleared a hill.

"That's Camp Muir," he told them. "Take it slowly. It looks nearby, but it will be forty minutes before we arrive."

He was true to his word. They finally staggered into the hut, pleased to be out of the icy wind. The extra food was welcome and after a few minutes they could take in the scenery.

"So, who wants to go to the summit?" asked Oscar.

Arnold blanched to a shade that was whiter than the snowfield they had just climbed.

"I would like to go to the top," Amos replied. "This mountain no longer holds any fear for me. I feel as if it is my home."

Amos's statement surprised the others, although they made no comment.

"I'm happy to go back," Dee announced.

Arnold just nodded in assent. He had not yet recovered the breath necessary to speak.

"I'll go back with Dee and Arnold," said Jackie. "I've reached the summit several times before."

They made arrangements to return to pick up the pair from Paradise the next day, and Jackie, Dee and Arnold set off back down the mountain. Amos and Oscar decided to rest at Camp Muir until eleven p.m. or midnight, and then resume their climb to the top. This allowed them sufficient time to finish their climb without having to spend more than one night on the mountain.

Amos and Oscar spent time outside the hut surveying the panorama in all directions. Amos had done some rock-climbing as a teenager and so was au fait with using ropes. They checked all their gear and decided to catch a few hours' sleep before the final part of the climb.

Amos slept easily and was woken by Oscar just before midnight.

"I've checked the weather reports and everything seems to be okay," said Oscar. "We'll take the Disappointment Cleaver route."

Amos could almost feel the mountain as part of himself as they started to climb across the Cowlitz glacier towards the summit. In spite of the piercing cold and the steepness of the ascent, Amos was unaffected and strode along as though he was out for a casual walk. The higher he climbed, the more in tune with the mountain he felt.

Disappointment Cleaver was an area of rocky debris and snow, and it was difficult finding a safe path through. Oscar was particularly worried about further rock falls, but Amos appeared unconcerned and trudged through without difficulty. Oscar wondered who was the novice and who was the guide.

Once through this area it was glacier-climbing all the way to Columbia Crater and the peak. The lack of oxygen made breathing more difficult and their pace slowed down. It was just as well, as they needed to tread carefully to avoid crevasses.

The summit was the other side of the crater. They picked their way round the rim and finally reached the summit. As he stepped up to Mount Rainier's highest point, Amos stretched out his arms and stood with his eyes closed. He had finally reached his goal. There were tears in his eyes.

"I'm part of this mountain and this mountain is part of me," he said. "There is no fear and only joy; there are no goodbyes, only hellos."

"Are you okay, Amos?" asked Oscar.

"Great, I feel great!" exclaimed Amos. "Let's go."

And with that Amos started back down the mountain. Oscar couldn't understand what had happened, but he put Amos's behaviour down to lack of oxygen and followed on behind him.

The views were stunning as they climbed back down the slopes. Every now and then Amos would stop to admire a view or point to something in the distance. As they reached lower altitudes the temperature rose and the wind became less severe. The meadows of alpine flowers were ablaze with colour and Amos thought he caught a glimpse of a bear in the distance; Oscar was not so sure.

Amos removed his outer clothes and marched into the Paradise ranger station wearing his caribou coat in all its glory. It was the strangest climb Oscar had ever experienced and he was pleased to be back.

Jackie was waiting for them.

"How did the climb go?" she asked.

"It was a wonderful experience," Amos replied.

While Amos was busy reading the notices on the noticeboard, Oscar took Jackie aside, out of earshot.

"That was the weirdest climb I've ever done," he said. "Amos never paused for breath. He acted as if it was his mountain. He never missed a footing. I felt like an amateur climber in the presence of an experienced professional – but he's never climbed before."

Jackie squeezed Oscar's arm and whispered in his ear. "It may very well be his mountain."

"The two seismologists you mentioned, Oscar. Could you please give me their details? I'd like to talk to them," Amos said, as the two returned to the noticeboard.

When they arrived back at Toppenish, Amos was still excited from the climb and did not seem at all fatigued. He strode over to Arnold and Dee and told them, "Oscar gave me the telephone numbers of the two volcano experts he mentioned. I think we should have a meeting with them."

"You seem different, Amos," Dee said, eyeing him intently. "What happened on the mountain?"

"I found peace. I realised that the future is not to be feared. My destiny is tied to the mountain. It scared me at first, but on the glacier and then reaching the summit, I lost all fear. It was like a heavy weight had been lifted from me – it was exhilarating."

"We've been following your lead, Amos," said Arnold. "What do you think our strategy should be?"

"We've come through a lot together since Roanoke," began Amos, his face set. "This is going to be our severest test."

Arnold put his hands on Amos and Dee. "We're in this together. We believe in our mission, and we'll do whatever it takes."

"We'll take it one step at a time," said Amos. "We've seen Mount Rainier and felt it underfoot. Next we'll talk to the scientists. We need to know exactly what we're dealing with. After that, I don't know, but hopefully things will fall into place – they always seem to."

"One thing's for sure, we can't do this on our own. We'll need help from Leo, Jackie, their people, and others we haven't even met yet," added Arnold.

"I hope Bill and Frank are able to come out here soon – we are going to need them," said Dee.

Dee telephoned the two seismologists that Oscar had told them about. They seemed keen to meet the group and asked lots of questions about the Earth Office and why they were interested in Mount Rainier. They gave Dee directions to where the university campus was located and the best place to park.

Jackie was happy to let them borrow her car.

"You should take the opportunity to look round the city while you are here," she said.

They set off the next morning. The campus of the University of Washington was located south of the city centre. Dee and Arnold collated the research they'd gained on the mountain and took a thick folder with them. Amos was still wearing his grandfather's coat, which was fast becoming his trademark.

They parked on the south side of the campus and emerged from the car park into an exquisitely laid out formal park.

"This must be one of the most elegant university campuses I've ever seen," Dee commented.

In the distance was an ornamental fountain in a large pond. The Department of Atmospheric Sciences and Geophysics was on the other side of the fountain according to the information they had been given and they strolled towards it, taking in the glorious show of trees and shrubbery.

As Arnold stopped to buy an ice cream from a street vendor, he turned and looked back in the direction they had come.

"Wow! Look at that view," he said.

Amos and Dee swung round to see what Arnold was referring to and were faced with the towering vision of Mount Rainier dominating the horizon.

"Great view isn't it?" said the street vendor, as he handed Arnold an ice cream cone. "This road is called Rainier Vista. It was designed and built to give a view of the volcano all the way down its length from here to the Frosh Pond."

"The Frosh Pond?" asked Dee.

"The pond where the Drumheller Fountain is situated. It's always been called the Frosh Pond because they used to throw all the freshman students into it," grinned the street vendor.

Just beyond the fountain they entered an ivy-clad building and managed to find the office number Dee had been given. The door was ajar and a sprightly, white-haired man in his late fifties came bounding out when he saw the three standing there.

"Hi, I'm Ethan Malone. You must be the Earth Office?" he said.

"I'm Dee, and this is Arnold and Amos," Dee replied. "We call ourselves the Earth Office."

"I'm really impressed with your organisation," Ethan told them as he ushered them in. "I've been looking it up on the internet. A smart website, and you've got quite a following."

He picked up a telephone and told the voice at the other end to come in.

"I've asked Vittorio to join us. What he doesn't know about Mount Rainier isn't worth knowing," said Ethan.

Arnold came straight to the point.

"We believe that at some time in the near future, Mount Rainier is going to erupt," he announced.

Before Ethan could comment, the door opened and Vittorio

ambled in. He was tall and athletic in build and appeared to be in his late twenties.

"What are the chances Mount Rainier will blow soon, Vittorio?" asked Ethan.

"Stone certainty. It's not a question of if, but when," Vittorio responded.

"Vittorio is a postdoc. He was my student and did his thesis on Mount Rainier," said Ethan.

"Well can you tell us what the situation is with the mountain at the moment, and what you think will be the effects when it erupts?" asked Arnold.

"These are the big questions," said Ethan. "It's what we spend our whole professional lives trying to answer. We never forget that a lot of lives are at stake. Let us show you around the department. You'll get a better idea of what we do here."

He led them out along the corridor to a large room which was dominated by a huge map of North Washington State that covered a wall.

"Mount Rainier is the highest peak in the cascade mountains," Ethan told them. "This department is a hub for the Pacific Northwest Seismic Network. We have seismic monitoring stations all over the Cascade Mountains, including Mount Rainier."

There were banks of monitors along one side of the room.

"If you come over here," offered Ethan, pointing at one of the screens, "you can see a live feed from a seismometer on Mount Rainier. It's quiet at the moment, but we can spot immediately any activity, day or night."

"What happens if you see something happening?" asked Dee.

"The federal government department that covers volcano hazards is the US Geological Survey. Mount Rainier is in Pierce County and together with the state authorities they devised a Volcanic Hazards Response Plan. Our group provides the continuous data monitoring of the mountain. If something happens then the Response Plan is activated and all the different government agencies work together to warn the population and organise evacuations."

"It sounds good in theory," acknowledged Arnold. "Will it work in practice?"

"Up to a point, it will work and probably work well," said Ethan. "The trouble is that even though Mount Rainier doesn't erupt as often as other volcanoes, it is by far the most dangerous to life and property. This is because there will be very little warning of an eruption and something like 80,000 people live in at-risk areas."

"What are the chances of an eruption?" asked Dee.

"Vittorio is the one to answer that question," replied Ethan. "He has gone through the history of past eruptions of the mountain."

"Minor rumblings are common," said Vittorio. "Big eruptions, on the other hand, occur on average once every five hundred to a thousand years. The last one was in 1894 or '95. The problem is that eruptions are irregular and without warning."

"What would happen if an eruption occurred?" asked Arnold.

"Follow me and I'll explain," said Ethan.

They all trooped out of the department building into the glorious sunshine outside. There was a park bench in front of the Frosh Pond. The group sat down in front of the fountain jet, with the Mount Rainier looming large in the distance.

"It's best to describe what would happen after an eruption whilst facing the mountain," explained Ethan. "The volcano is quiet at the moment. Don't let that lull you into a false sense of security, though. It's just dormant, waiting to blow at any time. In an eruption, the first thing we would notice is smoke billowing out from the crater at the top and all our seismometers would be off the scale. For those living near to the mountain, they would hear a roar and the ground would shake. Rocks and boulders – some quite big – would be fired into the air. Hot gases would escape, accompanying the flying debris, and rivers of molten lava would run. These are the things you would normally expect from an active volcano, but, surprisingly, these are not the biggest dangers. The mountain is host to glacial ice. Some 25 different glaciers sit on top of the mountain."

"We crossed two yesterday when Oscar Washines and I climbed to the summit from Paradise," said Amos.

"It is the glacial ice which is the real danger and this will affect people living much further away from the volcano," Ethan told them. "The heat from the eruption and from the molten lava melts the ice. The resulting mudflow – or lahar – is like a moving wall of concrete, and the wall moves fast – at between forty and fifty miles per hour. It destroys and buries everything in its path. We know where these lahars will occur from our observations and records of previous mudflows."

"What specific areas would be affected by these lahars?" asked Dee.

"A large mudflow would completely destroy Enumclaw, Orting, Kent, Auburn, Renton, parts of downtown Seattle, and would reach Puget Sound and Lake Washington," Ethan announced.

There was a stunned silence as they took in the enormity of what Ethan was describing.

"What about the eastern side of the volcano? All the areas you mention are north and west," said Amos.

"If you look at the mountain," Ethan pointed at the distant sight beyond the fountain, "On this side it's like a huge overhang of ice, that's why we'll get the worst of the lahars on this side. The eastern side will get the ash cloud because that's the direction the wind usually blows in."

"It's so beautiful, yet so deadly," murmured Dee.

"How dangerous would the ash cloud be?" Arnold asked.

"Ash clouds are not life threatening in themselves," Vittorio explained. "Although asthma sufferers could be badly affected if they are not wearing dust masks. The main effects are to disrupt transport and make life generally unpleasant."

"You've given us a lot to think about," said Dee. "Thank you for your help."

"Our mission is to help save lives," Amos told them. "We have an advantage because we have a special empathy with nature. We must use that to achieve our aim."

"I don't know anything about a special empathy with nature," Ethan said, "But what I do know is that any help you can give would be most welcome. No matter how many contingency plans we have, when Mount Rainier explodes it will be a disaster for the whole region. One other person you might want to talk to is Fred Farley. He's a reporter at *King TV*, channel 5, and he does special studies of Mount Rainier every now and then."

"He's the same person our friend Bill mentioned. We'll definitely be contacting him," Arnold told him.

As they walked along Rainier Vista on the way back to where the car was parked, they could not take their eyes off Mount Rainier in the distance. Dee took Amos' and Arnold's hands in hers.

"What are we going to do?" she asked.

"I have an idea," Amos replied. "We need to talk to Leo and the tribal council."

Amos would not be drawn further on his idea. They drove straight back to Toppenish, none of them feeling like sightseeing in the city. They arrived around midday and decided to have something to eat in the diner around the corner from their hostel.

"I don't think we have all that long before the eruption occurs," Amos announced. "We need to prepare and set up enough emergency help for the people who will be affected. The authorities, with the best will in the world, will be so swamped and ill-prepared they will be of minimal help – at least in the first few days."

"This much we know," agreed Arnold. "But how are we to put together an alternative emergency structure?"

"I will ask the Yakama Nation and surrounding tribes to help," said Amos.

"That's a big ask."

"I know, but it will be their ultimate spiritual mission."

After their meal Amos, Arnold and Dee went round to Leo's house and found Jackie there already.

"Thanks for the loan of your car," Dee said to her. "We had an interesting and informative meeting with the volcano scientists."

Leo's home was simply furnished. On the wall of the living room were family pictures and scattered around the room were native artefacts.

Leo offered them coffee.

"You have something you want to ask me?" he asked, as if reading Amos' mind.

"I want to address your tribal council," Amos replied.

Leo smiled and looked at the three of them in turn.

"I had my vision and Jackie had her dream," Leo began, "You want my people to help you. What you are asking is a great deal, but I want you to know that Jackie and I are one hundred per cent behind you. Your mission is our mission. It will be our nation's salvation. I will ask my son, Harry, the council president, to convene a special council meeting. Now, tell me what Mount Rainier was like, it's been many years since I climbed to the summit."

"Oh, you should have seen the flowers," exclaimed Dee. "The alpine meadows were a delightful carpet of colour. I would love to have picked a few plants, but that's strictly forbidden on the mountain."

"Did you see any bears or mountain lions?" asked Leo.

"I felt the presence of something as we climbed down," said Amos. "I thought it might have been a bear, but Oscar didn't see anything."

"How did you feel when you reached the summit?"

"I felt that I was part of the mountain. My fears completely left me," smiled Amos.

That evening Dee received a text message from Frank saying that he and Bill had managed to finish their assignment in DC and were on their way out to Seattle. They would be arriving around midday tomorrow. There was plenty of room in the hostel and Leo was happy to extend his hospitality to them.

"I'll be busy tomorrow arranging the council meeting and talking to tribal leaders, but Jackie will go with you to meet your friends at the airport," he said.

Dee managed to contact Fred Farley at *King TV*. He was interested in the Earth Office and the two had a long conversation about Mount Rainier. He thought it might be possible to do an interview on a nightly news feature show that the station broadcasts, and asked Dee and her colleagues to meet him the next day.

"I think it's going to be important to publicise what we want to do," said Amos after Dee had told him about Fred's idea. "Bill and Frank will be arriving at an opportune moment. Assuming that Leo persuades the tribal council to help us, we are going to need to reach out to native communities all over the region. An interview on an important TV show is just what we need."

Early the next morning Leo came round to the hostel. Jackie was due to take the three to the airport and he wanted to inform Amos that the council meeting was scheduled for that evening.

"I've spoken to all the tribal leaders," he explained. "Most are on board, but some are worried about the cost. It's unlikely that we'll receive any monies from the government, federal or state."

"I understand," said Amos. "Especially as we will be asking for an open-ended commitment. But I'll do my best to make a compelling case; all I want is for them to give us a fair hearing."

"I'll make sure of that," Leo reassured him.

Jackie arrived and they set off for the airport. Dee was excited at the prospect of seeing Frank, and they were all in good spirits. At last they had a strategy and, if everything went to plan, they could make an important contribution to saving lives if the mountain were to erupt.

The airport was busy that day and they were impatient as they stood at the arrival gate waiting for Frank and Bill. The plane from Washington, DC was listed as being on time, but Frank usually travelled with a lot of camera equipment, and it often took ages to come through baggage handling.

Finally, Dee screamed "Frank!" and rushed over, throwing her arms around him.

Bill was just behind him and seemed to be carrying most of the luggage.

They all greeted each other and Arnold introduced Jackie to Bill and Frank. Dee would not let go of Frank and they walked on ahead, in their own world.

"We had trouble finishing our assignment in Washington, otherwise we would have come out earlier," said Bill.

On the way back to the car park they brought Bill and Frank up to date on what had happened so far. The meeting with Fred Farley from *King TV* that afternoon and the tribal council meeting that evening proved that events were moving at a fast pace.

"When do you think the mountain will erupt?" asked Bill.

There was an awkward silence before Amos spoke up.

"It will be soon but it is not yet imminent. We really don't know when it will happen. We're not even sure how much notice we will have."

"I'm hungry," exclaimed Arnold. "Let's all go and eat. I'm sure Bill and Frank are starving, they've only eaten airline food for the last few hours."

Jackie drove them to a diner near the TV station. On the way they passed several points that gave good views of Mount Rainier in the distance. Amos, Arnold and Dee were used to seeing the mountain suddenly appear through the trees or at the end of a road as they drove around, but to Frank and Bill it was fresh and unusual.

"It's an amazing sight," Frank remarked. "We caught a glimpse of the peak out of the aeroplane window just before we landed. Down here on the ground it dominates everything."

"So what's the plan?" asked Bill.

As an experienced newspaper hack, he liked to come straight to the point.

"We need to prepare for the eruption and try to put into place as much help as we can for the people who will be affected," Arnold told him.

"We can't do it on our own. That's why we have asked Leo and his people too help us," said Dee.

"Even if they agree to help us we will, in fact, need much more help. We need to appeal for help from all the tribal nations in the surrounding region, and for that matter any volunteers who would be willing to help and support us," Amos added.

"That's where Fred Farley and *King TV* come into the picture," Bill looked between the three of them. "We have to persuade him to give us air time on his programme."

The TV station was located just outside the business district of Seattle. It was housed in a large but extremely bland office building with the words 'King Broadcasting Company' in discreet lettering next to the entrance.

Inside the building was a different story. TV screens were scattered all over the place, each showing the latest offering on channel 5. It was a hive of activity, but in common with most organisations of its type, it was organised chaos. Out of the *mêlée* an assistant showed them in to an office and bade them wait for Mr Farley to join them.

After several minutes, an urbane man in his late forties put his head round the door.

"Hi folks, I'm Fred Farley," he said.

Bill took the lead and introduced everyone.

"We know that you have a special interest in Mount Rainier, Fred, and that's why we've come to see you," Bill told him.

"Well, you have my attention. We often do stories on the mountain. Last year we had one on the exact height of the summit. All the maps show 14,410 feet, but when the mountain was surveyed using the latest GPS technology, it turned out to be closer to 14,411 feet," grinned Fred.

"We believe that the mountain is going to erupt in the next few weeks," announced Arnold.

"We've had lots of false alarms," said Fred. "Recently, we had a story on swarms of ice quakes. I interviewed Ethan Malone from the university. These quakes come in batches minutes apart, each less than magnitude 1. They can't be felt but they show up on the seismometers. According to Ethan they are just noise coming from glaciers grinding against the rocks underneath."

"We spoke to Ethan Malone, and he mentioned your name," Dee added.

"Why do you think an eruption is close?" asked Fred.

"We have all had a collective dream," said Amos. "And part of that vision includes a major eruption of Mount Rainier."

"Well that's fascinating, but I'm not sure if my viewers will go along with it."

"I can understand that," admitted Bill. "I'm a hard-bitten journalist like you and when I first heard about their dream I was sceptical – I still am. But I've seen a lot of things since then that I don't understand. There's also a Native American angle to the story."

"What do you mean?" asked Fred.

"Amos here is a Naskapi Indian and Jackie is from the Yakama Nation. There's going to be a vote tonight of the Yakama Tribal Council in Toppenish. They're going to decide if they will be backing Amos, Arnold and Dee on preparations for the catastrophe heralded by their vision."

"Well that certainly turns the story into something we would want to cover," said Fred. "We mustn't panic people, but a legitimate concern of the Native Indian population can't be ignored. If the council decides to back you, then we would do an interview tomorrow night after the early evening news. Contact my office as soon as you know the result of the vote. I have to prepare for tonight's show now, but I'll arrange for one of my assistants to show you round the studio."

With a flurry, he was out of the room and the assistant who had greeted them before came back in.

"Fred's asked me to show you round," she said. "Have any of you been in a TV studio before?"

"I think I'm the only one," Frank answered.

She led the group through a door and in a loud whisper indicated that they should not make any noise. There was a group of easy chairs in the centre of the room, facing several cameras. The room was gloomy, except for bright lights that were directed towards the chairs and a backdrop picture of Seattle at night. Fred was sitting on one of the chairs in animated discussion with a man wearing a microphone and headphones.

The assistant directed them through a door at the back into a room overlooking the studio – the control room. They could talk freely in there and they realised that Fred was, in fact, in a three-way conversation with the technician and the producer who was in the control room.

"If you're on tomorrow evening, this is the studio where Fred will carry out the interview," the assistant told them.

"It's helpful to familiarise ourselves with the surroundings here so that we'll be more relaxed tomorrow," noted Arnold.

They did not have much time to ready themselves for the council meeting that evening, so they made a hasty departure for Toppenish.

Council meetings were held at the Yakama Nation headquarters in Toppenish. They were usually restricted to council members only, but occasionally they allowed observers, who were not allowed to speak. Harry had managed to obtain permission from the council members to allow Leo to be present. Even though he could not take part, at least he could report to the others the details of the council's deliberations.

The Yakama Nation headquarters was a single-storey building on the edge of town. Leo was waiting for them in the car park as they pulled up.

"It should be okay," he told them. "We've got a few waverers; they're mainly worried about the cost. The council have allowed one of you to address them. You'll get five minutes, no more. They'll then discuss the matter and vote."

"How many of them are there?" asked Arnold.

"Including Harry, fourteen," replied Leo. "Each represents one of the tribes that make up the Federated Tribes. Which one of you is going to address the meeting?"

"I know Arnold is the lawyer amongst us," said Amos. "But as a Native American, I think it's down to me. This is about honour and respect and I think they will respect us more if I address them – if that's okay with everyone?"

They all agreed, especially Arnold, who was quite relieved. He could not forget that the last time he addressed a meeting there had been an earthquake – he did not want that to happen again!

§

The tribal council members started to arrive. Leo led Amos and his group into an anteroom of the council chamber. Harry came in and greeted everyone.

"I think the vote will go in our favour, Pa," he told Leo.

He turned to Amos and the others.

"When the council is ready they'll call you in, Amos. Remember that you've only got five minutes, followed by questions. Some of the members have misgivings about the cost; I'm sure you'll be able to convince them to vote in our favour."

He gave a thumbs-up sign and disappeared into the conference room.

It seemed like an eternity before Leo emerged and ushered Amos into the meeting. Harry was sitting at the far end of a large rectangular conference table with Leo and the thirteen other tribal leaders seated on each side.

Harry made some introductory remarks to those present on the work of the Earth Office and then invited Amos to address the gathering. A silence fell upon the room, broken only by the gentle hum of the air-conditioning. The fifteen faces looked at Amos with expectation. He stood facing everyone, his grandfather's coat adding to his form which seemed to dominate the room.

His voice began in a quiet, almost hushed, tone. In his preamble he thanked them all for the opportunity to address them with his proposal and then he launched into his oration.

"I address you as a Naskapi Indian. As Native Americans we have all suffered over the last few hundred years. We have endured a long struggle to gain our rights and a reasonable life for our people. During that time we never lost sight of the close relationship that we have with the Earth. We have always been, and will always be, part of nature."

Amos paused and took a few sips of water from a glass on the table in front of him before resuming.

"A few months ago the three of us who make up the Earth Office shared a vision. This dream instigated a series of events which brought the three of us together and has led us up to this point. The dream, like that shared here by Leo and his granddaughter Jackie, was complex, and each of us witnessed slightly different revelations. One common image, though, that we all saw, was the eruption of Mount Rainier. Our mission, which we see as the result of the Earth's struggle for consciousness, is to save life. We cannot stop Mount Rainier erupting – nature will take its course – but we can mitigate the worst effects."

Amos paused again, drew himself up and from deep within his body he spoke. His voice filled the room – some of the council members would say afterwards that his voice seemed to fill their whole being.

"The time has come for us to stand up as human beings and regain the respect that all human beings should have for life and for each other. I propose that the Yakama Nation, together with all those who want to help us, prepare to accommodate, without any charge whatsoever, however many people will be affected by the coming catastrophe. I propose that all this effort be centred on the Rainier Casino Resort at Naches, which is nearing completion. It will cost a great deal of money, but how much does respect cost? It cannot be measured."

The room was silent when Amos finished speaking. There were no questions so Amos returned to the anteroom.

"It was a great speech, Amos," said Dee. "We could hear you through the wall."

Amos had hardly left the meeting before the door flew open and Leo came bursting out.

"It's unanimous!" he cried.

Harry and all the other tribal leaders followed Leo out of the meeting room.

"They all want to know how their people can help," said Harry. "We'll have to set up a command post at the Naches Resort. I'll tell them to send over people to help run things."

"I'm glad it was unanimous, Leo," exclaimed Arnold. "It would have made things more difficult if some had voted against."

Leo smiled.

"I told the waverers that it was worth the money just for the free publicity we would get for the new resort when it opens."

"We're on our way at last, then" said Amos.

"I'll telephone Fred Farley's office right away and set up the arrangements for tomorrow's broadcast on *King 5*," Dee offered.

They all piled into Jackie's car and together with Harry and Leo set off in convoy to Naches.

There were still some building workers at the site when they arrived.

"Fortunately, we've got power, water, telephone and computer cables all installed," said Harry. "There's a large main office room on the ground floor of the tower. We can use that as the control room."

"It's getting late now and we're all going to need our sleep tonight," Arnold announced. "We may not be getting much sleep over the next few weeks. I know we're all hyped up, but we should all go to bed. We can start our work in earnest in the morning."

Harry arranged rooms for everyone and they all went their separate ways. After depositing his bags in his room, Amos decided to go to the top floor of the tower. He wanted to gaze out at the view of Mount Rainier before he went to sleep. Arnold and Dee were already there staring out of the window at the mountain.

"We couldn't keep away," Arnold explained as Amos sat next to them.

"It's like it's sitting there waiting for us," said Dee. "So serene, so majestic, and yet so terrifying."

"Nothing that is part of nature is to be feared," Amos told her. "But we can help take the fear out of the population that will be affected by the volcano when it becomes active."

They all met together early the next morning in the control room.

"We need to start to put together a plan of action," Harry began. "When the catastrophe occurs we have to be ready. The first thing we should do is apportion areas that each one of us will be responsible for – but before I do that, we need to know what to expect."

"We don't know exactly how many people will need our help," said Arnold. "But I think we should plan on having to cater for 20,000 people here at Naches. The number of people made homeless will be much greater than that number, but many should be temporarily housed in Seattle, Tacoma and other areas by the state authorities. There are basically three areas of problem we have to address: transport, accommodation and care. Transport will cover moving those affected to Naches. I'm happy to be responsible for this area.

"Accommodation will involve setting up a temporary camp for 20,000 people. Are you and Amos happy to arrange that?"

Amos and Harry nodded in agreement.

"Finally, care will involve a wide variety of areas. I suggest Leo, Jackie and Dee divide up these responsibilities."

"I'll arrange everything medical," offered Dee.

"We're happy to do the rest," said Jackie, nodding towards Leo.

"We'll mark out the control room into different sections," Harry decided. "Each section will have telephones and computer terminals."

One of Harry's assistants came in to the control room.

"The tribal council have sent some helpers; they've just arrived."

"Just in time! Send them in," smiled Harry.

About two-dozen young men and women flocked into the room. The next hour saw frenetic activity in the control room as helpers were set about their various tasks.

Harry had spent some time in South America when he was a young man, and had experience with working in refugee camps.

"We'll divide up the camp into four blocks: north-east, south-east, north-west and south-west, with the tower in the centre. The area in front of the dome on the east side will be the reception area. That's where the coaches will arrive with people. We'll move them into the dome and then allocate everyone a place in one of the blocks. A team of helpers will register everyone arriving, so that we can keep a track of everything. There'll also be a medical team on standby, as some people will have injuries."

"We'll need an ambulance bay on the west side at the entrance to the tower," added Dee. "The tower should be used as a hospital and medical centre. The hospitals in Seattle, Tacoma and the surrounding areas will not be able to cope with all the medical emergencies – we'll have to take some of their patients."

"We must try to create as good an atmosphere as possible," said Arnold. "We should refer to the blocks as Seattle, Yakima, Tacoma and Toppenish. Then we can lay out the blocks as avenues and streets. The centre of each block should have an open space for communal facilities."

"I estimate that we will need around fifteen avenues and fifteen streets in each block," Harry told them. "That would accommodate about two hundred clusters. Each cluster can be run by a Native American family, who would have to look after around twenty-five men, women and children. It would be a tented city. Each cluster could have four tents: small ones could take up to five people and large tents up to eight."

Harry organised the building workers who were on site to dig trenches in order to lay extra water and sewerage pipes. They had a good water supply but extra tanks were needed. The original system was not designed for such a large number of people. They could supplement their water supply with deliveries by water tank trucks, as and when it became necessary. They could also use the water in the swimming pool in case there were any fires.

Harry's team arranged for road and walkways to be installed throughout the camp. Rain was rare at this time of year but just in case they did not want the site to become a quagmire.

Dee's team had the most difficult task; they needed doctors and nurses in order to set up medical facilities. They planned to start by calling for volunteers after the TV broadcast that evening, and so not much could be done until the next day.

One success for Dee's team was the provision of coffee. One of her helpers had worked in the headquarters of Seattle's famous coffee house. The helper had spoken to a senior executive whom she knew and he had offered to set up a tented coffee stall in the camp. The company would set the whole thing up and provide free coffee. The helper also contacted three other coffee companies and managed to repeat the arrangement with them – none of them wanted to be left out. Thus each of the four blocks of the camp had their own coffee establishment.

Amos, Arnold and Dee had to leave Naches for the TV studio that afternoon, and again borrowed Jackie's car for the trip. Fred Farley wanted to talk to them before they went on the air in order to prepare for what they wanted to say and what questions he would ask them. There was still a huge amount of work to do to prepare the camp, but the TV broadcast was vital.

"One thing I've learnt, even after one day, is the tremendous amount of work and planning that goes into setting up a refugee camp," said Arnold. "At least we have prior warning. In nearly all emergency situations when tens of thousands of people are suddenly refugees, I don't know how they manage – it's frightening."

"This camp will be different," announced Amos.

"One thing I've thought of is terminology," Dee told them.

"What do you mean?" asked Amos.

"We need to do more than call the different blocks of the camp by familiar names. The words 'camp,' 'refugee' or 'displaced person' sound so impersonal and harsh. Are there some other words we can use that will help people feel better about themselves and their situation?"

"You make a good point," said Amos.

"What about 'tented city' for camp and 'neighbour' for refugee?" offered Arnold.

"That would mean we're planning a tented city in Naches to accommodate up to 20,000 of our neighbours affected by the volcano eruption," said Dee, testing out the preferred language. "I think that sounds much better than 'We're setting up a refugee camp.'"

"It's not just a question of semantics," noted Arnold. "The people in our tented city will be our neighbours – and if a neighbour is in trouble, you help them. The words you use reflect the dignity of the situation and of the people. It's also important for the Native

Americans in the tented city to feel a strong bond with those they are looking after."

"And how do we refer to the Native Americans who will be looking after their neighbours?" asked Dee.

"They are also neighbours, but they are acting as hosts, so let's call them hosts," Arnold replied.

The TV station proved to be just as chaotic as it had been the day before, and they directed out of the hubbub of the studio and into a small office. Fred came in with an assistant in tow.

"Hi folks," he said. "I'm glad you got the Yakama Nation to back you. I spoke to one of the tribal leaders and they're really keen on setting up your refugee camp."

"We won't be referring to it as a refugee camp," Dee emphasised. "It will be called the tented city at Naches. Refugees will be called 'neighbours.' We want to create a strong sense of community."

"I like that," said Fred.

"How much air time will we have?" asked Arnold.

"Okay, down to business," grinned Fred. "Only five minutes I'm afraid, and that will include a ninety second report. But it will be on the *Evening Magazine* show at seven p.m. It's one of our most popular programmes. I've also invited Ethan Malone from the university, who will give us the scientific lowdown on Mount Rainier. You will have to decide which one of you is going to appear on the show – there's only room for one."

"We have met Ethan Malone," said Dee. "He was very helpful to us and most knowledgeable. Amos will be the front man for us."

Arnold nodded in agreement. He was pleased not to go in front of the cameras.

"I will need a couple of minutes at least to explain what we're about."

"This is television, Amos, you can't make speeches," Fred told him. "You'll get about forty-five seconds. The rest of the time will be questions and answers."

"Will you allow a telephone number to be broadcast? It'll be for people to volunteer and after the eruption it'll be a helpline," said Dee.

"No problem." Fred turned to his assistant, "You need to arrange for the contact number to be shown at the bottom of the screen."

"What happens now?" asked Arnold.

"Amos will go to our hairdresser and makeup artist and then wait in the green room. The two of you are welcome to stay with him. Ethan Malone will be here shortly. Don't discuss things too much with him – we want all discussions to be on air. See you later."

Fred bounced out of the room. The assistant led them to the hair and makeup department. Amos was not really into hair and makeup, but he accepted that the exigencies of appearing on television necessitated that he undergo some sort of grooming transformation. Dee was glad to proffer advice to the beauticians and Arnold was only too delighted to be out of the limelight.

Ethan Malone greeted the trio as he settled himself into the hairdressing chair next to Amos. Ethan was an old hand at appearing on camera; whenever there was a story on Mount Rainier, he was hauled in as the resident expert.

If not for the fact that the trio were eager to return to Naches to continue with preparations for the tented city, it would have been a pleasant afternoon. But the anticipation of the broadcast and the stress of not being able to talk about Mount Rainier with Ethan took its toll.

Amos was sanguine, but Dee, and to a certain extent Arnold, became quiet jittery.

"I have to get some air," said Dee impatiently. "I'm going for a walk."

"I'll join you," offered Arnold, as he hurried out of the studio in Dee's wake.

In spite of the air-conditioning, the atmosphere in the studio was oppressive.

"There's a lot of responsibility on our shoulders," Arnold said as he caught up with Dee. "It's not going to get any easier over the next few weeks."

"I know, Arnold. It just gets to me sometimes."

"That's what Amos and I are here for. We all help each other."

"Amos seems unduly calm. He's changed, especially after his climb up to the summit of the volcano," Dee noted.

"You're right," agreed Arnold. "I think he saw more in his dreams than we did, but he's not sharing it with us."

"There's not much we can do except keep an eye on him."

"Before we go back inside, you'd better check with Jackie that the phone lines are manned," said Arnold. "As soon as the broadcast finishes, the telephone calls will start to come in."

They both felt refreshed after their breath of air. Amos was having a brief forty-winks in the green room, so they did not disturb him. The early evening news was on and they could view it on any of the TV screens dotted around the studio offices. Fred Farley's assistant checked with Dee the telephone number they wanted to give out and confirmed that the number would appear onscreen at the end of the broadcast.

Fred came into the green room just as Amos was waking up. He addressed Amos and Ethan.

"Let me go over the final run through with both of you. A voiceover will announce me. I'll then go through the main thrust of the feature, which will include a ninety second prepared film on the volcano. We have archive film that we're using. Then I'll introduce Amos and Ethan. Amos will go first. You'll have forty-five seconds, then Ethan will have the same time. I'll then pitch questions to both of you and we'll see how it goes. Finally I'll thank you both and remind viewers who want to volunteer of the telephone number, which will appear onscreen. Don't forget to look at me and don't worry about where the cameras are."

Amos had never been on television before so it was all new to him.

"Just remember to look at Fred," he kept saying to himself.

The assistant put her head round the door.

"We'll be calling for you in a couple of minutes," she announced.

Arnold excused himself and went into the bathroom.

"It's easier once the broadcast starts," smiled Ethan.

The assistant came into the green room and walked with Amos and Ethan to the set. She indicated to Arnold and Dee that they could watch the whole thing from the control room.

Fred was nowhere to be seen, but various technicians and assistants checked sound levels, adjusted their seating positions, applied last-minute makeup and generally distracted the two interviewees.

Finally, Fred breezed in, sat on one of the armchairs and, with a touch of powder from one of the makeup specialists, gave a thumbs-up sign to the director in the control room.

Arnold and Dee had seated themselves at the rear of the control room behind the director and his entourage, where they could watch the whole proceedings. Amos looked resplendent in his caribou skin coat. The studio arc lights shimmered off its surface and gave him a majestic air.

Then a voice boomed over the loudspeaker.

"Tonight from West Seattle, it's *Evening Magazine* with your host, Fred Farley."

The cameras focused on Fred.

"How many times have we looked out over the south-east horizon from Seattle to the towering Mount Rainier and wondered: Is this the day it's going to erupt? Well, not today – thank goodness – but Amos Talbot, a Native American based in Washington, DC, is convinced that it's going to happen soon. So what do we know about the mountain?"

The programme switched to a film clip. It showed shots of Mount Rainier interlaced with pictures of the Mount St Helens eruption of 1980. A voiceover explained the history of volcanoes in the Washington State area and why Mount Rainier was so dangerous. The film clip finished and the camera switched back to Fred.

"Amos and his colleagues who run an organisation called the Earth Office shared a dream or vision of Mount Rainier's eruption. They have come here to Seattle and teamed up with the Yakama Nation in Toppenish to build a tented city in order to accommodate up to 20,000 Seattleites, who could be made homeless if the volcano goes active. I know some say that animals can sometimes predict earthquakes by changes in their behaviour prior to an event, but people dream about disasters all the time – Why should we believe you, Amos?"

The camera view swung to Amos. He did not immediately start speaking and when he did his voice was quiet.

"Turn up the sound volume," said the director to one of his technicians.

"Firstly, I would like to say that people should not be alarmed," Amos sipped some water in front of him. "Secondly, I don't ask or expect anyone to believe me when I say that Mount Rainier will erupt soon. What I am saying, and more importantly what my friends and I are doing, is freely providing help to our neighbours – the people of Seattle, Tacoma and the area around Mount Rainier, for the time when the mountain explodes. This event is not, I repeat not, imminent. When it is about to happen I will tell you, Fred."

At that point Amos leaned forward towards Fred and his voice became clearer and more voluble.

"I am here to call upon all Native Americans in this area, and others who would like to volunteer, to help us in this mission. The Yakama Nation is setting up a tented city in Naches, a safe area east of Mount Rainier. We ask you to telephone a number, which will appear on your screens, and come to Naches. We don't have much time, maybe a week or two – I don't know how long. This is a time for us to step forward and demonstrate to our neighbours what kind of people we really are."

"Well that's an amazing endeavour, Amos," said Fred. "But what's really happening deep within the mountain? We have tonight an old friend of *Evening Magazine*, Ethan Malone, a UW professor and expert on volcanoes. Could Mount Rainier explode, Ethan?"

"Nobody knows," Ethan answered. "We at the University of Washington, and scientists at universities all over the world, are trying to discover ways to predict these sorts of events. In spite of evidence that some dogs, for example, change their behaviour before a volcano or earthquake, it's hardly a systematic way of predicting these things, and it doesn't always work. As a scientist I have to say that there is, so far, insufficient evidence. The same applies to dreams and visions that people might have. I have met Amos, and I have a great respect for him, his organisation, and of course, the Yakama Nation. But I have to say that at the moment the seismic activity on Mount Rainier is at its usual level."

"But if there were to be an eruption, would you be able to tell that in advance from the seismic data?" asked Fred.

"We might get some warning a few hours beforehand, if we're lucky, but it could happen without any warning," said Ethan.

"If it does happen, what will you and your friends do, Amos?" asked Fred.

"We hope that we will have some indication of when an eruption becomes imminent," replied Amos. "We would, of course, warn people and request that the authorities close the park and mountain – we don't want any climbers or visitors to be in danger. We would then make sure that all our coaches and crews were at their pickup points, ready to bring people to our tented city at Naches."

"Why did you choose the site in Naches?" asked Fred.

"Firstly, the safest area after an eruption is on the east side of the mountain. Secondly, the Yakama Nation owns a large area of land in Naches. Finally, the site in question is where the Nation is building a hotel resort and casino. The buildings are virtually completed and we can use the hotel tower to house a temporary hospital and medical centre. These are the reasons why we consider the site to be ideal. We would be pleased Fred if you would bring a TV crew to Naches and show viewers what we're planning."

"We'd love to do that," said Fred. "Ethan, if the volcano goes active, what should people do? What do we have to worry about?"

"If it's a major eruption the big worry is that a lot of the glacial ice would be melted and form lahars. These are described as moving walls of concrete. They consist of melt water and debris and would destroy a lot of properties. We estimate several tens of thousands could be homeless. If you receive a warning of an approaching lahar, you must immediately move to higher ground."

"As Amos said, this is not something which is imminent," Fred smiled into the camera. "Also, the authorities have detailed plans of how to deal with emergencies of this kind. Thank you Amos and Ethan for coming on the show today. Here is the number to ring, at the bottom of your screens, if you want to volunteer to help Amos and the Yakama Nation build their tented city."

"Music and fade," said the director.

Arnold and Dee went down to the studio floor.

"Well that went very well," said Fred. "We'd certainly like to come out and see your tented city, Amos. Speak to my assistant and she'll work out the arrangements."

"I'd like to come as well," added Ethan.

"You'd be welcome any time," Arnold replied.

Amos, Arnold and Dee did not arrive back in Naches until late that evening. The telephones had started ringing as soon as the TV broadcast was on the air. Apart from a few crank callers, they were inundated with people who wanted to volunteer.

All the local tribes in Washington were sending people to see what help they could give. There were also a number of non-Native Americans who wanted to give their services – all were welcome.

Apart from the TV broadcast, all the helpers had been telephoning Native American groups over the whole country. Harry reckoned it would take at least a week for even a rudimentary camp – or tented city – to be set up. He did not think they would be properly ready for ten to fourteen days.

The building crews had, however, made good progress on laying the piping for water and sewerage. They would be finished the next day and Harry had arranged for temporary roadways and walkways to be laid as soon as possible after that.

Fortunately, Mount Rainier appeared supremely quiet at the present time and they hoped it would stay that way – at least for the next couple of weeks.

Over the next few days the tented city started to take shape. Dee managed to persuade a senior physician from a hospital in Seattle to come in and advise them on what they needed to do to set up a hospital quickly. Staffing was not a problem, there were a number of Native American doctors and nurses who volunteered to come in. A whole group came from some of the big reservations in Arizona and Oklahoma. Dee wanted to make sure that there were plenty of medical teams that could go out with the coaches to bring people in, many of whom might need first aid or more.

Arnold was in charge of transport. He calculated that they would need around one hundred buses or coaches and ten ambulances. The ambulances were not a problem; there were a number of small hospitals all over the Seattle region and he found he could cadge the odd ambulance here and there to make up the numbers. There were plenty of bus and coach hire companies, but it was expensive to hire that many and nobody was going to let them have them for nothing. He then had the brilliant idea of using school buses. It was the school summer break at the moment and all school buses were parked in garages doing nothing. He contacted various school districts and managed to beg and borrow quite a large number that they could use – at least until the end of the school holidays.

Jackie decided to take responsibility for entertainment. Apart from the everyday work of cleaning, cooking and living, what were

20,000 people going to do? Some would have their own televisions, but she felt that it was incumbent on her to provide communal entertainment for everyone – children as well as adults.

She contacted a Native American rodeo show. It was playing in North Dakota and had just come to the end of its run. They had a few weeks before the next series of shows and agreed to come to Naches. Not only would they come to Naches in the next few days but they would bring everything with them, including generator trucks. Harry was concerned that even though they had power from the local electrical grid that a volcanic eruption may cause it to fail. He had mentioned this to everyone and asked if they could find portable emergency power generators. The rodeo show was a great way of providing entertainment and having emergency power on tap if it was needed.

Leo knew some people in the entertainment industry in California. One of them was involved in a chain of drive-in cinemas. With a lot of arm-twisting he inveigled them in setting up an outdoor cinema in Naches on the outskirts of the tented city. It would take a few days for the whole thing to be set up but they could show films as well as TV sports games.

Children's entertainment was not a problem. As it was the school holidays, there were a lot of Native American teachers who stepped forward to help. Leo and Jackie arranged the teachers in small groups, with each group being responsible for around thirty children.

Jackie even had an approach from a library. They served small communities in outlying areas and had a library van. They volunteered to drive around the tented city, with anyone being able to borrow books just like a normal lending library.

Bill and Frank were in charge of the media. Fred had promised to send a film crew as soon as the tented city was ready. Realising that, as soon as the eruption actually occurred, there would be a media frenzy, they set aside a piece of land on the outskirts of the tented city, but not too far from the tower, as a press compound. There was enough room for TV crews to park their trailers and they set up a special tent for press conferences.

Harry, together with various tribal leaders, spent most of his time in meetings. Security and safety were important areas they had to deal with. The local police forces for the Naches and Tieton areas could not be expected to cope with an influx of 20,000 people. The police chief in Yakima had contacted his superiors and they were sending a number of officers from other areas of Washington to provide adequate cover. A temporary police station was going to be set up on the Naches site. Two FBI officers were to be included in the complement.

In addition, Harry agreed to provide up to one hundred security personnel. These would be carefully vetted by the police chief's staff and enrolled as temporary deputies. A lot of volunteers who were coming forward were ex-military and provided a ready pool of potential security marshals.

Storage and supplies were a major problem; feeding and supplying 24,000 people – 20,000 neighbours and 4,000 hosts, helpers and organisers – was a logistical nightmare. Storage tents had been set up in a secure area near the tower which would alleviate the pressure for supplies.

Harry managed to locate some cold storage trucks used to store meat and other perishable produce. Fruit and vegetables were no problem; one of the main business enterprises of the Yakama Nation was fruit and vegetable growing. Regular deliveries of fresh produce could come in each morning. They also had a winery, although they did not want to overdo the supply of alcohol.

Even though the temperature was in the eighties during the day, it was cold at night, so they needed plenty of blankets. Some people might only come in the clothes they were standing up in, thus it was necessary to have a plentiful supply of clothes available.

It was surprising how many small but important items had to be provided. Face-masks – to protect against an ash cloud – had to be ordered in the thousands. Similarly, spare dust filters for all the vehicles were a priority. Every bus, coach car or other type of vehicle had to have its dust filter changed once or even twice a day if there was an ash cloud. Even though they were safe from the direct effects of an eruption, they were in the front line for a dust cloud. Everyone had to carry certain items all the time: torches, face-masks, spare batteries, etc. All these items had to be ordered, delivered and stored.

Arnold tended to work in the control room most of the day. As such, he found himself in charge of administration. He was good at organising people and the others were only too pleased to pursue their own tasks rather than become embroiled in office organisation.

He arranged for a skeleton staff to work the night shift, midnight to eight a.m. It was not so necessary to have a night shift before all the people started arriving, but once the tented city started to fill up, the control room would be fully manned twenty-four hours a day.

The restaurant on the top floor was turned into a cafeteria and recreation lounge for all the helpers and medical staff. It was also an informal meeting place and an opportunity for everyone to touch base with each other.

§

It was early evening and Arnold was in the cafeteria. He liked to come in at that time, when he could watch the sun set over the mountain. He had a birds-eye view of the tented city and its environs. The others also tended to congregate at this time in the tower.

"Fred's coming tomorrow with a camera crew," Bill told him as he arrived. "Frank and I will show him around. They'll put together a feature item and broadcast it tomorrow evening."

"I think by tomorrow we'll be as ready as we can be," said Harry. "I'll come with you when you show Fred Farley around. It'll be a good opportunity to make a final inspection of the whole facility and try to spot any gaps that need filling."

The camera crew arrived early the next morning. They brought their own command post outside broadcast unit. They were able to edit and upload anything direct to the station in Seattle via a satellite link. Fred was due to arrive mid-morning, by which time everything should be set up.

A steady stream of volunteers was still arriving. Many had caravans and other vehicles but they also brought with them their portable hide tepees. These were not just for fun but an important link to their heritage – it was a matter of national pride.

It made the silhouette of the tented city a hotchpotch of different shapes: Motor-homes, tents, tepees and other assorted vehicles and awnings. It did not matter, so long as the people coming to the city, vulnerable as they would be, felt that they were guests in a welcoming home.

They met Fred at the reception area in front of the dome and took him and his crew through the procedures they would use when people arrived.

"We've worked out detailed plans for pickup points throughout the area that are most likely be affected by any eruption," said Harry. "We have more than one hundred buses and other vehicles. Anyone with injuries or needing medical attention will be taken first to the front of the tower hospital and then everyone else will be welcomed at the reception area."

They walked through the entrance to the dome from the reception area. On the left were serried ranks of dolls and teddy bears.

"A lot of children will be feeling scared and upset," Harry continued. "They'll pick up these negative emotions from their parents. Every child will be given a doll or toy bear to hold as a comforter."

In front of them were dozens of small cubicles, each with a computer screen and a helper.

"Everyone will be logged in here as they come in, and a host and tent place will be allocated. We'll also note any special needs. After registration everyone will be escorted to a tent. The buses, after they have deposited their occupants, will go to a garage area. We have teams of mechanics who will check over vehicles, change dust filters if necessary, fill them up with gas and ready them to go out for their next pickup."

Fred and his team were recording everything on camera.

"I'll need to do interviews," Fred told Harry. "Will that be okay?"

"No problem, you can talk to whoever you want."

They walked towards one of the four blocks of the tented city. A sign said 'Welcome to Yakima.' Fred strolled down one of the avenues that made up the block. A Native American woman was standing in front of a barbecue cooking some chicken wings.

"That smells delicious," said Fred.

The woman offered him a wing.

"Where are you from?" asked Fred, with his mouth full.

"My family are Cherokee from California," the woman told him. "My husband is a car mechanic and I am a bookkeeper. We brought our family here to help the Yakama."

"Is this your tent?" asked Fred, directing the camera on to a brown tepee made of animal skins.

"It's our most precious possession," replied the woman. "It's been in our family since my great-grandfather's time."

Fred led the camera crew to the centre of the Yakima block, which mainly consisted of an open space. A wooden structure was being erected.

"What's that going to be?" he asked.

"It's a café," said Harry. "Each of the four major coffee companies in Seattle has agreed to set up a branch in our tented city – one in each block."

"How much are they paying you?" asked Fred.

"No money changes hands," said Harry. "All the coffee will be free."

"Free?" queried Fred. He was not able to fully understand the concept. "Why are they doing it?"

"Because you help your neighbour when they are in need," replied Harry. "Everything in the tented city is free. It's what we're here for."

"But you must be getting money from the authorities," bleated Fred.

"Not a cent. What isn't given to us voluntarily, we pay for."

The enormity of what Harry had just said started to impinge on Fred's consciousness. He made no further comments.

Back at the tower Harry offered to show Fred their hospital. The senior physician whom Dee had brought in was still there. He had agreed to stay on and run the hospital, although at the moment there were no patients.

It was difficult to estimate how many hospital beds they would need. They decided to keep things flexible. Three floors of the tower were converted into hospital wards, including a small obstetric unit.

"How many babies are you expecting to be born here?" asked Fred.

"For 20,000 plus people you would have to expect, on average, one birth per day," said the hospital director. "We have a portable oxygen tent – just in case. We've also devoted a whole floor as a fracture clinic. We're expecting a lot of injuries to be broken bones."

"What will you do if you have more patients than you can handle?"

"We can use other floors of the tower as temporary wards for less serious cases. In extreme conditions we can convert the dome into a hospital annexe. It's air-conditioned and won't be used as a reception area once the site is full."

"What about surgery?"

The director and Dee, who had just arrived, led Fred and the camera crew along a corridor on the floor below the top floor restaurant.

"This is the part of the hospital we're most proud of. It's an operating theatre suite. It's been set up from scratch in just a few days. There are three operating theatres, plus auxiliary rooms" the director beamed.

"What about surgeons?" asked Fred.

"We have two general surgeons amongst our volunteers," said Dee. "If we need more specialists there are surgeons in local hospitals in Yakima and Toppenish who will come in and perform operations if they're needed."

"And everyone is offering their services for free?"

"Absolutely."

Fred approached an orderly who was stocking a shelf with bandages.

"Can you tell us who you are and where you're from?" he asked.

"My name is Donna. I'm from Montana and I'm a third year medical student at the UW Medical Centre," she responded.

"What made you volunteer?"

"I'm Native American, and when I saw the appeal on your programme, I wanted to help," said Donna.

"Did you have any problems from the university?" asked Fred.

"Not at all, I'm a member of the Snake River College and my mentor thought that it would be a good idea for me to come here."

"I have to tell you, Dee, I am impressed with what you have done here. Where shall we go next?"

"How about the best view in Naches?" said Dee.

They went up to the top floor restaurant.

"This is what it's all about," Dee told him, as she looked out of the windows at the panoramic view of Mount Rainier in the distance. "You can also see the whole tented city from up here."

They sat down and ordered coffees.

"What will you do if nothing happens?" asked Fred.

Dee smiled.

"As Amos explained to you, we don't ask anyone to believe us. For us, we know that Mount Rainier will erupt, because we have seen, felt and experienced it in our dream vision. As for you, you have to make up your own mind."

§

The next morning Amos awoke a little after six a.m. Dawn was just beginning to break over the landscape. It was only a fleeting moment, lasting no more than a second or two, but just as he woke – just at the point of waking – he knew. He knew that it was today that the mountain would explode.

He quickly dressed and went up to the top of the tower to get a glimpse of the mountain. The cafeteria was empty, apart from a couple of medical helpers having a coffee break, and a lone figure standing at the window gazing out at Mount Rainier. As he approached the figure, he realised that it was Leo. Without turning around Leo said:

"It's today, isn't it, Amos?"

"Yes," said Amos. "It looks so quiet and peaceful from here."

"It's going to be a busy day."

§

Ethan was woken by the sound of dogs barking in the distance. He had a second-floor flat with a balcony near the Geophysics department and liked to sleep with a window open. He shuffled out onto the balcony and was greeted by a cacophony of dogs howling and barking all over Seattle. He had never heard such a chorus before.

The telephone rang. It was Amos. There was no preamble.

"It's today."

"I'll call you back," said Ethan without hesitation.

He rushed over to Geophysics to the seismometer laboratory.

"I was considering calling you," the technician on duty told him. "There seems to be an unusual amount of activity on Mount Rainier."

He scanned the outputs; he had seen similar before. Mount Rainier often went through these periods of mini-quakes. This was slightly different though. He could not exactly put his finger on it, but the vibrations of the mountain seemed to be a bit more sustained than usual. Was he imagining that? And what was usual? He rang back to Amos.

"I have to admit, Amos, that there has been some activity on the mountain."

"We've contacted the Mount Rainier park authorities," Amos replied. "We're trying to get them to close the mountain. It's not easy to persuade them, they're expecting a lot of visitors."

"I'll see what I can do," said Ethan.

Dee tried to telephone Fred Farley. She only managed to contact the station switchboard, but she left a message for Fred to contact her urgently.

Harry called for a meeting of all the helpers, hosts and medical staff in the dome at eight-thirty a.m. Word had got around that the eruption was going to occur later that day. The atmosphere at the meeting was tense but upbeat. After all, this is what they had been planning for.

"First," said Harry addressing the throng. "I want to thank you all for the hard work you've put in these last few weeks, turning a building site in the middle of nowhere into a home for a huge number of our vulnerable neighbours who will be affected by the volcano's eruption. Second, after today, this site will not be in the middle of nowhere. It will be the tented city at Naches and it will be the centre of the universe for 20,000 Seattleites. We don't know the exact time the volcano will go active, but go to your stations, and good luck! Finally, I would ask all the bus drivers and their medical crews to please stay behind after everyone else has gone."

There was cheering and applause when Harry sat down as almost of them left. He was genuinely surprised and heartened by the outpouring of support.

Arnold stood up and addressed the bus crews.

"Everyone knows where their pickup points are. Make sure you have everything on board that you will need. We have set up a small fire department here in our city; we don't have many trained firemen and women, but some of the fire crews will be joining you. Our main task is to pick up people and bring them here safely. We don't expect you to be directly involved in rescue operations. However, keep in touch by radio, and if you need help from a rescue crew, we'll try to direct one to you. Please don't put yourselves in danger. We need you to be safe so that you can do your job."

It would take a couple of hours before all the crews would reach their stations. During that time everyone was preoccupied with checking that things were ready for the eruption. By mid-morning the bus crews had all reported in that they were waiting at their pickup points. Only one bus had broken down, and Arnold had sent out a repair crew to speedily put it right.

Amos, Arnold and Dee were up on the top floor Tower cafeteria. Harry, Leo and Jackie had also congregated there. Bill and Frank were already sipping coffees and looking out at the panoramic view.

"Here's to the whole gang," said Bill holding up a coffee cup. "Now comes the hard part: the waiting."

Ethan came into the room and walked over to the group.

"Hi everybody," he greeted them all. "I couldn't keep away – may I volunteer?"

"What's the seismic situation at the mountain?" asked Arnold.

"I receive updates from my department on my telephone," replied Ethan.

He showed Arnold the screen on his telephone. It was the live output from one of the seismometers on Mount Rainier.

"I can liaise between here, my department and the Director of Emergency Management for Pierce County," he said.

"What do the seismometer readings show at the moment?" queried Dee.

"Just low-level activity. What disturbs me most, and why I'm here with you guys, is that the activity is sustained – it's more than just a wobble."

"Come on Ethan," smiled Bill. "What's really changed your mind about us?"

Bill had a knack of coming right to the point. Ethan was clearly embarrassed.

"Okay, I left Ethan the scientist behind at the door. What really got me thinking about you and your prediction about the mountain were the dogs."

"What dogs?" asked Dee.

"Didn't you hear them early this morning? All over the town there was a chorus of barking and howling from the pet dog population. I've never heard anything like it before. Clearly they were picking up the seismic activity from the mountain. But we often get minor trembles like this. What bothered me was, why now? What is different this time round?"

Dee's telephone rang.

"Hi, it's Fred Farley here, what can I do for you, Dee?"

"It's today," said Dee.

"What's today?" asked Fred, not realising what Dee was talking about.

"You asked me to let you know when Mount Rainier is going to erupt," Dee told him. "It's going to happen sometime today."

"Wow! Thanks for letting me know."

Dee hung up the phone.

"I don't think he believes me," she said.

Morning turned to afternoon. The pickup crews were all waiting patiently at their stations and the tented city waited in anticipation.

"Bill was right," murmured Harry. "The waiting is the hardest part."

Ethan's telephone rang. The ringtone was Beethoven's fifth. The three short notes were followed by a long note that was Morse code for V for victory. It was a live feed from Ethan's department.

"I'm looking at the live seismometer feed on my screen," said Ethan. "It's increased in strength from this morning. In the past when this kind of pattern was followed, it reached a peak and then ebbed away."

Ethan was busily looking at his telephone screen whilst everyone else was looking out of the window at Mount Rainier.

"There's a puff of smoke!" shouted Amos. "I can see a puff of smoke!"

Ethan looked up.

"The seismometers have just gone off the scale," he exclaimed. "We should hear the explosion in around ten seconds."

Nobody spoke, they just all gazed out at the mountain. After an interminable time, which could have been no more than ten seconds, they heard a distant thunderclap. Even this far away, they could feel a slight vibration as the mountain shook.

They all rushed down to the main control room. Calls were coming in from everywhere. The pickup crews had all felt and seen the explosion. On the television screens the puff of smoke had turned into a column of billowing smoke and dust reaching up into the sky.

All the TV channels had cut into their programmes with the breaking news of the volcano. The local stations also gave out emergency bulletins.

"We still don't know how serious the eruption is," said Ethan. "We have a lahar detection and warning system in place, but we won't get much notice."

"What about molten lava flows? How dangerous are those?" asked Arnold.

"They're dangerous, but only if you are close to them," Ethan replied. "The good news is that they won't extend more than about ten miles from the volcano, which keeps them entirely within the Mount Rainier National Park area. No, as I've said before, it's the lahars that pose the greatest danger to people and property. In a major eruption the lahars could go all the way to Puget Sound and the Pacific."

The next hour saw the volcano increase in activity, culminating in the first lahar warning. Pickup crews were also radioing in that they were starting to pick up passengers; the first neighbours would be arriving shortly at the tented city.

An enterprising newspaper journalist managed to persuade a helicopter pilot to fly near the volcano. It was a foolhardy action because molten rock was being thrown hundreds of feet into the air, but it gave Ethan important information as to what the volcano was doing. It also gave amazing shots of the lava spewing out and bubbling up in the mouth of the crater. Soon afterwards, however, the aviation authorities banned all flights in the area. Ethan had seen enough footage, along with fixed cameras on the mountainside, to be convinced that this was a major eruption, although he could not be sure that the lahars would travel all the way to Puget Sound.

The plume of smoke from the volcano was the consummate picture that was flashed across the world. As expected, the wind was blowing from the west and dust and smoke from the plume were beginning to fill the air.

Harry was in the reception area waiting to greet the first people to arrive. As it happened, the first arrivals were in an ambulance and were taken straight to the tower hospital. There had been a gas explosion in a building near to where one of Arnold's ambulances was stationed. The explosion was nothing to do with Mount Rainier. The worst injuries were carted off to a local hospital, but the more minor injuries would have had to wait several hours for an ambulance. Arnold's crew volunteered to bring the remaining injured people to Naches. The injuries were mostly minor burns and some broken limbs but they did need attention.

The first bus to arrive at the reception area came from the Puyallup river area not far from Tacoma. It was a particularly high-risk area from lahars and mudslides, and as soon as the lahar warning had been broadcast, people had started to move to higher ground. The bus brought in several families, all wearing face-masks. Everyone was calm but there was an atmosphere of fear and uncertainty about what was happening, and relief that they were safe.

While the children were distracted with the choice of doll or teddy bear, the helpers were able to register them all on the system and to allocate accommodation. They had decided, as far as it was practical, to allocate places according to the areas people came from, the idea being that it was important to try to keep a sense of local community going.

People began to come in thick and fast, with a constant stream of buses winding their way in single file formation towards the tented city. One thing Harry and everyone else had forgotten about was the pets. It wasn't a great problem, as many of the hosts were quite used to dealing with dogs. So long as they were not a nuisance, it was decided, everyone could bring in their pets. In fact, Arnold turned the situation around and suggested they introduce dog training classes as a way of keeping both pets and their masters occupied.

Apart from being an annoyance, the ash in the atmosphere caused some health problems, particularly for children prone to asthma. The worst cases were transferred into the hospital tower. The air-conditioning filtered out the dust particles and medical staff was on hand if necessary.

Most of the people coming in were concerned about friends and relatives who were not with them. Harry set up, in the dome, a computer station dedicated to finding lost people. It was linked in with temporary accommodation sites run by local authorities all over the area. There was a queue of people all day long trying to locate lost friends and relatives.

§

After a few days the ash cloud abated and the sun could be seen through the dull gloom that had dominated the sky since the eruption. According to Ethan the seismic activity had considerably diminished and aircraft were once again allowed to fly in the area. It had been a major eruption, but the lahars had stopped just short of Puget Sound. Around 50,000 people had been made homeless, and rebuilding would go on for several years. The number of 'neighbours' in the tented city peaked at just over 17,500.

Bill and Frank were in the control room when Harry appeared in an excited state.

"I've just had the state governor on the telephone," he beamed. "You won't believe what he's just told me."

Harry was pacing up and down the room.

"What is it, Harry?" asked Bill.

"It's the president, he's coming to Seattle!" replied Harry.

"Well there's no surprise in that. As soon as aircraft were cleared to fly into Seattle, it would be odd if he didn't come," Frank reasoned.

"No, you don't understand," said Harry, who could hardly speak.

"He's heard about our camp – our tented city. He's going to come here. They're sending over some people from the Secret Service this afternoon. He's going to make a fifteen-minute flying visit by helicopter tomorrow."

"There'll be a press invasion," said Bill, looking across at the number of film crews already on site, "We have to extend the press compound and set up a podium for the president's speech. I'll get on to that right away."

"I think we should use the cinema arena," announced Frank. "The dome is too small."

The next few hours were frantic. The cinema screening scheduled for that evening had to be cancelled – fittingly, it had been *All the President's Men* starring Dustin Hoffman, Robert Redford and Jack Warden.

The plan was that Air Force One would land at Seattle early the next morning. After meetings with the state governor and emergency coordinators, the president would fly around the volcano site and land at the tented city around mid-morning. He would inspect the facility, make a short speech, and then fly back to Seattle.

Bill was right about the media invasion. Apart from an article that he had written for the *Post*, the national press had not picked up the story of the tented city.

It was different now. Not just the national press but the international press were represented in their droves, eagerly anticipating the presidential visit. Bill was under no illusions – they would all be gone after the president left – that was just the way the bandwagon rolled.

The helicopter landing field was next to the cinema area, which in turn was next to Yakima Block. The Secret Service did not want the president to have to move around too much, so the plan was just a quick tour round Yakima. It was a very tight schedule with a detailed minute-by-minute plan.

§

In the control room the next morning Harry was receiving updates on the president's movements. The helicopter ride from Seattle would only take a few minutes, so they did not have much notice as to his exact time of arrival. As soon as confirmation came that he was in the air, everyone went over to the helicopter field to greet him. Harry and the tribal council, together with Amos as representative of the Earth Office, were in the greeting line-up.

The helicopter touched down and the president stepped out onto the ground, followed by the first lady and the state governor. He waved and flashed a smile at the assembled press pack, which was strategically placed a few yards away. Other members of the entourage followed.

The president shook hands with Harry, all the tribal leaders and Amos. Amos and Harry were scheduled to show the president around Yakima block, and as they walked around the site the president stopped now and then to speak to families and hosts. After a while the president turned to Amos.

"I heard about your efforts here from our party's new governor of West Virginia, Sam Schanks. He couldn't sing your praises highly enough and said that if I was coming to Seattle I should visit your tented city."

Amos was so flabbergasted that he could only mumble a barely audible reply.

As they turned a corner they were confronted by a large-framed young man standing with his family and an elderly Native American couple.

"Where are you from?" the president asked.

The young man stepped forward.

"We're both from Enumclaw, Mr President. Before this disaster we had never met, but now we're going to go into business together."

"It's good that you're thinking of the future," said the president.

"We brought our pet dog here," the young man continued, "To be frank, he was uncontrollable and driving us all crazy. But my friend here had the magic touch and now our dog is well behaved."

"I'm pleased to hear it," the president laughed. "What business are you going to start up?"

"We're going to set up a dog training school," said the young man.

"Is that a library?" asked the first lady, looking towards the vehicle to their left.

"Yes, ma'am," Harry replied. "It's a mobile library, which goes round the whole tented city."

The president and first lady stepped into the vehicle. There was a librarian seated behind a small desk.

"Do you have many readers?" asked the president.

"Oh yes, Mr President" the librarian told him. "We have people who never normally read for pleasure sign up and borrow books. We have had such a high demand that we've had to order more books from our main library."

"That's wonderful," exclaimed the first lady.

As they made their way back to the cinema area the president spoke to Harry.

"You've created the most remarkable place here."

In front of the microphones on the podium the president addressed the audience. His speech was shown live by a number of TV stations, so those who could not squeeze into the arena could follow it on their own televisions.

His speech followed a fairly predictable course. A preamble on the volcano risk in the Seattle area was followed by a list of thanks to the various agencies involved in rescue work.

"I would like to acknowledge and thank the Earth Office, the Yakama Nation and other tribal nations for their help in this time of need. Our nation will never forget the debt that we owe the Native American population and the high esteem and respect that we hold them in."

His speech continued in the same vein.

Leo grabbed Harry's arm tightly.

"Did you hear that, son?" he said. "He used the word respect. It's the first time an American president has used that word in relation to Native Americans and meant it!"

"I know, Pa," Harry smiled at him. "I know how important that is to us."

At the end of his speech – and to great applause – the president bade farewell to everyone. Just as he was about to board his helicopter, he said a few private words to Harry. Harry looked quite shocked and just managed to blurt out a 'thank you' to the president for his visit.

After the helicopter had carried the president and his entourage away, Leo, Bill and the others asked Harry what the president had said to him. Harry's eyes welled up with tears.

"The president knew that we had done all this ourselves. He said he had instructed the secretary to the treasury to make an ex-gratia payment to us of two million dollars. As president, he could sanction such a payment in an emergency. He knew it would not cover what it had cost us, but said it was the least he could do – as one neighbour to another."

Over the next couple of days the volcano became more quiescent. There was no more lava coming out of the crater and things were now moving into post-eruption mode. The population of the tented city was rapidly reducing, with people deciding to either move back to their homes that were now safe or, if their homes were damaged or destroyed, make arrangements to stay with family or friends.

"We're not completely out of the woods," said Ethan. "But the mountain is definitely looking safer. I think I'm going to take a closer look."

"You are not going to climb to the summit, are you?" asked Dee.

"Not a chance, that would be much too dangerous to do at the moment," Ethan told her. "I'm thinking of driving up to Sunrise. At 6,400 feet, it's the highest point on the mountain accessible by car. It's an easy trip from here; I just go straight up Highway 410 and take the Sunrise/White River turnoff."

"What's actually there at Sunrise?" asked Arnold.

"There is a visitor centre and day lodge. I think they're intact. There should be a good view of the mountain from that location."

"We'll come with you," Arnold said, Dee nodding in agreement. "What about you, Amos?"

"Why not? I haven't seen the mountain from that side."

§

The next day was bright and sunny. The clear-up and rebuilding following the eruption was only just beginning, but there was a fresh positivity in the air. Seattleites had faced the worst disaster in living memory and had come through it stronger and more cohesive. The last few neighbours in the tented city were leaving and all the tents and remaining infrastructure were being dismantled. The Earth Office group were talking about going back to Washington, DC.

Jackie wanted to come and see the mountain and she offered to drive everyone in her car. Bill stayed to tie up any loose ends with the press corps, who were leaving, but Frank came along for the trip together with his camera. They set off for camp Sunrise at around ten a.m.

There was hardly any damage visible as they approached the mountain. Most of the lava streams and lahars were on the north side of the volcano, and their approach from the east was remarkable pleasant. Camp Sunrise had sustained some damage, but it was generally intact, although one flying boulder had smashed through the roof of the visitor centre.

Jackie parked the car and they walked around surveying the area, Frank busy taking photographs. They could easily see the summit of the crater from their position.

"The mountain has definitely lost some height," Ethan told them. "The height of the summit will have to be re-measured."

There were rocks strewn all over the place but the glaciers were all there, despite some having lost a considerable amount of ice. The silence of the landscape was broken by a sudden grinding, rumbling noise accompanied by a few bursts of hot gas. The group had not realised that Amos had become separated from them; he had wandered off and was looking at an unusually shaped rocky outcrop about eighty yards from the rest of the group. A crevasse had opened out in front of Amos, trapping him against the outcrop.

"Amos!" Arnold shouted.

"It's okay, Arnold," said Amos, turning to the group. His voice was calm, almost serene. "This is what I saw in my dream. It's what I've always known. I'm part of the mountain and the mountain is part of me. I'll see you in your dreams."

Amos stood tall against the rays of the sun, which lit up his face and sparkled on his coat.

"No!" Dee screamed as another crevasse opened up, this time behind Amos.

Amos appeared to be standing on an island platform of rock. It happened in an instant: one second he was standing there, and in the next he was gone. The ground shuddered and everyone staggered to keep upright. Then the crevasses closed up, as if nothing had happened.

A thick silence fell as the group stood in a deep state of shock, Dee sobbing in Frank's arms. They returned slowly to Naches and recounted what had happened to everyone. It was a rare, but not unheard-of, occurrence. The chances of recovering a body were virtually nil.

The Earth Office had arranged to return to DC the next day. Everyone was assembled in the Tower cafeteria.

"It's so sad," said Dee. "Amos achieved so much, only to be killed at the last moment by the very mountain whose volcano he was fighting against so successfully."

"You mustn't see it that way," Leo reassured her. "Amos was a prophet, a dreamer. He had already had a vision of what was to happen. He knew the time and manner of his own death. He had accepted that he was going to be part of the mountain – he was going to be part of the Earth. His spirit carries on as he, himself, said at the moment of his death; we'll see him in our dreams."

Arnold's mobile rang. He excused himself and answered it in a quiet corner of the room.

"Is that you, Arnold?" said the voice at the other end of the line.

"Yes, who is it?" asked Arnold.

"It's me, Cal – Sheriff Johnson from Clark Fork. I've been trying to locate you and Amos."

Arnold told him what had happened on the mountain and that he would have to pass the tragic news of Amos's death onto Monique.

"I'm so sorry to hear about Amos's death," said Cal. "But I can't pass on the news to Monique – I'm afraid she died this morning after a long illness. It seems they both faced death on the same day."

"I'm very sad to hear your news, Cal. She was a lovely woman," Arnold told him.

"Listen Arnold, as a friend and law officer, Monique made me an executor of her will. After you and Amos visited, she changed her will. She added a clause that if when she died Amos was not alive then you would be sole beneficiary. She trusted that you would not allow the Clark Fork River and Lake Pend Oreille to be polluted by gold extraction from her property. You don't have to do anything at the moment, but when you're ready, come to the lake and I'll sort out the legal paperwork – we can also go fishing."

"Thanks for letting me know, Cal. I'll be in touch," said Arnold.

He returned to the group and told them about Monique and the house in Clark Fork.

"Before you all go," Harry announced, "The tribal council and I have decided to create a small park in front of the tower. It will commemorate the events surrounding the volcano eruption and the creation of our tented city. We would like to name it the Amos Talbot Park – if that's okay with you all?"

They all thought that that would be a fitting memorial to Amos.

§

The messages of condolence poured in after they all arrived back in DC, including a personal letter from the president. Dee had the letter framed and put on the wall of her office next to a photograph of Amos. The photograph was the picture she had taken of Amos as they arrived at Seattle airport. It showed him full length wearing his grandfather's coat.

The Earth Office grew from strength to strength. Bill retired from the *Post* and worked three days a week in the office. Christine and Grace headed an international division of the office with a large staff under them. Dee and Frank married the following spring, with Arnold arranging for Dee's parents to come over to Washington for the nuptials. Dee's father was an amateur photographer and he and Frank hit it off straight away, talking all the time about lenses, f-numbers and a whole lot of stuff that Arnold did not understand. Arnold offered Monique's house to the happy couple for their honeymoon. It was an ideal location.

Arnold and Dee were jointly in charge of the Earth Office, but their decisions were always coloured by what they thought Amos would have done.

Sometimes things became a bit much for Arnold and he would go fishing at the lake for the weekend in order to relax. He would occasionally fish with Cal or even Will Ortega from the Veterans Office in Boise, but more often than not he would fish on his own. He had all the paraphernalia: boat, tackle, fishing rods and flies, but he would never catch anything because he would never put his rod and line in the water. He would just sit in his boat and stare at the deep, cold, pool of water that was the lake. Only then could he talk to his friend Amos, and in that state of being half in this world and half in the world of the waters of the lake, he would find peace.

Lightning Source UK Ltd.
Milton Keynes UK
UKOW041157180413

209411UK00001B/10/P